The Diplomatic Heir

Etherya's Earth, Book 7

By

REBECCA HEFNER

Contents

Cover Design: Starlight Cover Design, starlightcovers.com
Editor: Megan McKeever
Proofreader: Bryony Leah, www.bryonyleah.com

To you, amazing readers. For waiting so long for this book. For your nev-er-ending support. For loving these characters too and crying and laughing along with me. I adore you and thank you from the bottom of my heart.

PS—I threw in some extra scenes with Miranda and Sathan for YOU be-cause, let's be honest, we've missed them, right? Hope you enjoy the banter from the OGs as much as I did.

Love, Rebecca

PURGES OF METHESDA
THE PASSAGE
CAVE OF THE SACRED PROPHECY
Valeria
Naria
STROK MOUNTAINS
Astaria
PORTAL OF MITHOS
River Thayne
Lynia
Uteria
Takelia
DEAMON CAVES
Restia
HUMAN WORLD

The Fairy Tale of the Demise of the Elven Kingdom

The great flood wreaked havoc on the realm. In the history of humans and immortals, there were many tales of destruction. Yet nothing demolished an entire species like the flood that destroyed the Elven kingdom.

Kindhearted and simple, the Elves inhabited their tiny corner of Etherya's Earth long before the goddess created her beloved species. The mystery of their creation by the Universe lingered until it faded with time, as all things do. Eventually, the Elves stopped questioning their existence, choosing to worship their benevolent god who provided bountiful harvests and cool breezes on summer days. War was a nonexistent concept for those who had everything their heart desired, and they lived without conflict until the flood ravaged their lands.

The first wave crested without warning, flashing through the villages and submerging the thatch-roofed homes as most Elves slept peacefully in their beds. Those that survived the first wave perished in the swells that arrived shortly thereafter. None would survive the onslaught.

Or so everyone believed.

But some did survive, changing the history of the planet for eternity.

One would become the malevolent Deamon Crimeous, whose story stretched for eons before he was finally vanquished when the prophecy was fulfilled by his daughter, Evie.

Unbeknownst to most, there were others who survived. Elves who fled to the human world, through the ether, to blend in with the mortals who were barely learning to use fire and bronze. Humans' short lifespans and *penchant to believe in magic and omniscient gods ensured they would forget the Elves with each new generation, thus creating an opening for the immortal Elves to build a new society.*

Although the Elven population was small, they were determined.

One man emerged as leader, possessing a cunning mind and natural leadership abilities. Dakath, Elf of the Old Realm, became Dakath, King of the Elves and head of the Elven council. He gave many directives, but one was abundantly clear: Elves were not to procreate with humans or return to the immortal world. They had barely escaped destruction in the old realm, and he believed returning to it only tempted fate. Centuries later, when the Vampyres and Slayers broke into war, Dakath's belief the immortal world was cursed was only exacerbated.

King Dakath also developed an intrinsic belief that Elves should retain their pure bloodline. This would prove to the angry god who had destroyed their world that they revered him; that they didn't take their Elven lives or heritage for granted. If their loyalty and devotion could be proven, perhaps they would never suffer the agony of such terrible destruction again.

Centuries passed as Dakath helped the Elves acclimate to the human world, blending in with the inferior creatures as their new society evolved. They could work with the humans and learn from their advances and failures, but otherwise they were to remain separate. Since humans would always age and eventually die, this feat was rather easy in the scheme of time.

Any Elf who formed a romantic bond with a human would be sentenced to death. This order was given after the first Elven-human hybrid was conceived, only to be subsequently murdered by the council, along with the babe's Elven father who impregnated the human. Dakath would not chance igniting the wrath of their ancient god once again by allowing his people to procreate with a species that would denigrate the Elven race he endeavored to sustain.

The order was decreed to all the Elves, and it became common law shortly thereafter. And perhaps it would've endured had Dakath, King of the Elves, not impregnated a human woman several eons into his reign...

Chapter 1

Rausch Gap, Pennsylvania
Three months after Callie defeated Bakari and destroyed the ether

Esmerelda, daughter of Dakath and Dyana, was, quite simply, never meant to exist. In fact, her presence upon Etherya's Earth would be called a fluke by her dear mother and a travesty by her father. Or a pestilence. Wrinkling her nose as she stood under the thick canopy of leaves that offered protection from the sprinkling rain, she pondered. Yes, pestilence was more likely the word her father would use to describe her.

It only made sense considering his primary goal was to eradicate Elven-human hybrids.

Since Esme was the result of Dakath's dalliance with her human mother, it made her a rather interesting target indeed.

Sighing, Esme leaned against the rugged bark, supporting her back on the large trunk as she gazed to the sky. Gray clouds stared back through the trees crying soft tears of rain. Every so often, a drop would land on her face, cooling her skin as she stood in her moment of solace. Her team would need her soon, but for a few minutes, she reveled in her solitude.

She had been alone since her father murdered her mother centuries ago, and she would always choose to remain that way for a plethora of reasons. First and foremost, Esme was a runner. A solitary soul who lived in the shadows in an effort to stay off the radar of her powerful father. People who got close to her usually ended up dead, so she'd stopped forming any sort of meaningful connection centuries ago.

Just recently, Dakath had tried to poison an Elven-human hybrid child in the Arizona desert before Tatiana intervened and convinced Calinda to save him. It was one of many steps Callie had to take before fulfilling the prophecy and destroying the ether. Darkrip and Arderin's daughter had done her part, ushering in the next phase of the transition.

And that was where Esme took over. Her role as leader of the Immortals Transition Unit, or ITU, was key in the next phase of the immersion of immortals with humans.

Esme had assumed other roles in the past. Most of them consisted of surreptitiously protecting immortals and hybrids in the human world from her father and his Elven council. Others consisted of just helping immortals in general. Most in the immortal realm were realizing what Esme had known for ages: there were many immortals who lived in the human world. As the species began to amalgamate, she felt more would emerge looking for a safe haven. As someone who'd been alone her entire life, she certainly understood the sentiment of needing help in a world where she didn't belong.

There was something noble in protecting others, and Esme found it a fitting purpose. It gave her something to do in a life that was never supposed to be lived. She did her best to stay off her father's radar and had grown quite resourceful as a result. As long as she stayed on the move and didn't draw attention to herself, she could do some good in a world that sorely needed it.

Of course, her father's threats would always loom over her head, which meant it was easier to accomplish her goals alone. Allowing someone to care for her would be extremely selfish. It would force them on her same solitary journey of evasion and fear, and she would never choose that for someone she loved.

So, she'd erected walls. Walls that were quite thick and buffered by a layer of geniality and good-natured quips. She presented a brave face to the world, which made her quite proud because damn it, she *was* brave. She'd evaded her father for centuries and would continue to do so until he eventually wiped her off the map...or she just became too tired to run. For now, she had a renewed determination with the eradication of the ether. Succeeding in a transition between humans and immortals would create something meaningful on Etherya's Earth, and Esme was determined to ensure success.

Sometimes she wondered where the fire that burned within to help people originated. Although her father was now quite evil, there had been a time when he was revered by the Elves for his kindness and bravery. Perhaps she had inherited that from him before it became twisted in a mangled heap of hatred and viciousness.

Her beloved mother had also been altruistic and exceedingly beautiful inside and out. Those attributes were what first caught her father's eye all those centuries ago. Ultimately, they led to Dyana's death.

The old anger surged as her father's image formed in Esme's mind. Thick brown hair atop shrewd hazel eyes and pointed ears encased his angular features. Although Esme had inherited her mother's blond hair, she had Dakath's eyes. Each time she looked in the mirror, they were a stark reminder of the man who'd borne her but detested her very existence.

The hatred between them was a twisted game her father relished. For centuries, Esme had racked her brain wondering why he didn't just kill her. It seemed so much easier in his larger scheme. And yet, although he'd hurt many she'd befriended or cared for, he'd never harmed a hair on her head.

It baffled her until Esme realized the imminent truth: the joy her father experienced from torturing her greatly outweighed any bliss he would feel from her death. After all, one could only die once, but torture was unlimited in its scope.

And, sadly, her father was the ultimate expert at torture.

She often thought about the maniacal way he tormented her from afar. Every few decades he would back away and leave her alone. Decades when the humans broke out in war and it was easier for Dakath to remain inside his fortified home in the rural mountains of Romania. But then he would return, usually leaving a poisoned immortal body in her path, and she knew he was resuming his hunt. She was the mouse caught in his trap, only to be released when its neck was moments away from snapping. Every time she evaded the snare, she rebounded, only to be caught again.

Closing her eyes, she sank into the tree as she massaged the tense muscles where her shoulders met her neck. Goddess, she was tired. She was fully committed to initiating the transition plan with the humans. The initial stages would take several months as they began the first phase of implementing immortals into the US government. Once Phase I was complete, she wanted to escape somewhere remote and quiet where she could meditate and rest for a moment.

She would continue to help the ITU as they implemented Phase II and beyond, but she would hand the reigns to someone who could assume a more permanent leadership position. So far, her father had left the ITU alone, and she knew that grew less likely each day she remained with them. It was a constant battle balancing her desire to help immortals with her need to stay off her father's radar so no one got hurt.

Esme had become an expert at living a solitary life over the centuries. Every place she inhabited was small and nondescript. She'd learned to move in shadows and run when necessary. Squishing her eyes together, she tried to remember the last time she'd felt joy. When had she truly laughed? Hell, she hadn't even owned a damn puppy since the last one she'd adopted in the sixteenth century returned from a jaunt in the woods with a fatal gash on its neck.

Esme had cradled the dog on the front porch of her small home in remote Italy, crying into its soft fur as it died in her arms. Then she'd stood, searching the woods as she wondered if one of her father's henchmen had sliced the animal on Dakath's orders. The heartlessness of the deed provided strong evidence, and her suspicions also indicated imminent danger if her father knew her location.

After burying the puppy, she vowed never to care for another pet, knowing it would give her father an opportunity to torment her. She'd wiped her tears, packed up her belongings and fled, unable to take the chance her father knew her whereabouts.

It was one of the multitude of times she'd run.

Blowing out a breath, her lips fluttered together. Evading her father was just fucking *exhausting*.

"You found a nice hiding spot," a deep baritone chimed, causing her to shiver. Squeezing her lids, she reminded herself of her vow to never form connections. This meant connections of any kind, but she most certainly couldn't form romantic connections. Even with massive Slayer-Vampyres with glowing half-fanged smiles and genuine hearts. No matter how close she felt to him, she had to maintain her resolve. It was the only way to protect the man who seemed determined to worm his way into her fortified heart.

Opening her eyes, she pasted on a dazzling smile. "Yeah, just meditating under the trees. I'm pretty Zen, if you hadn't noticed."

"You are pretty Zen," was his genial reply, and her heart leaped at the emphasis he placed on the word "pretty." Staring up at Tordor, son of Queen Miranda and King Sathan, Esme inwardly commanded her lady parts to knock it off. Of course, they didn't listen, and she felt her pulse throb in the place between her legs that nice women didn't talk about in polite society. Goddess, why was he so...*big*? Hot? Kind? *Sexy*?

All of the above.

"All of what above?" he asked, dark eyebrows drawing together over those gorgeous olive-green eyes inherited from his mother. Silently kicking herself, Esme realized she'd said the words aloud.

"Nothing." Waving a dismissive hand, she straightened and pointed toward the camp. Their team of twelve immortals and hybrids had been camping at the Pennsylvania town of Rausch Gap as Esme made contact with her liaison inside the US government. The team had strategized that the United States was the first human government they would connect with and secretly infiltrate.

Rausch Gap was an abandoned town Esme had discovered years ago. Its rural location offered a fantastic place for her team to camp, but it was close enough to civilization that they could purchase supplies when needed. Its proximity to Washington, DC was an added bonus since they planned on approaching the US government first.

Their plan was to keep immortals hidden from humans while they implemented the first phases—which would be easy since humans were a vastly oblivious species. The ITU would continue to fortify the invisible wall that now stood where the immortal ether once had, separating the human and immortal realms. In the future, humans would eventually comingle with immortals and the wall would be rescinded. After all, that was what the prophecy intended when the ether was destroyed.

But for now, they needed to transition slowly and only inform those on a "need to know" basis. This included Esme's liaison at the US government, who also happened to be a Slayer.

"Ready to head to DC?" she asked, beginning the walk back to camp as Tordor fell into step beside her. "If things go wrong, I'll need some of that negotiation juju you have in spades."

His warm chuckle surrounded her, and she imagined leaning closer so she could feel that smooth laugh against her ear...and maybe hump his very chiseled leg while she curled into him. Leg humping was a thing, right?

Inwardly snickering, she recalled the last man she'd had sex with over a decade ago. A one-night stand who'd scratched an itch before she left him in a hotel room in California. Esme scratched that itch every so often, moving on before any connection could be formed. Men like

Tordor required connection...and commitment...and promises of futures yet to come.

Basically, all the things she couldn't offer. Nope. She'd have to keep her mental humping to herself, even if he was the personification of Henry Cavill with fangs.

"I've always had a knack for negotiation," he said, shrugging as they trailed over the wet grass. "I mean, my parents reconnected two species who were at war for a thousand years. It's probably in my DNA."

"In every single cell," she teased, giving his arm a few good-natured pokes as they strolled. "It will certainly come in handy when we approach Clayton today. He's a valuable ally and his connection with the high-ranking human general is fortuitous."

"I'm looking forward to meeting him." Halting, he faced her as his full lips formed a genuine smile. "Thank you for including me in your team. I feel like I finally have a purpose."

"You're welcome." The rasp in her voice must've come from her suddenly parched throat, and she circled her tongue in her mouth, wondering why it was so dry when other parts were definitely wet...

Those forest-green eyes flashed with admiration—and something more that she refused to acknowledge—before she broke eye contact and resumed walking.

"But don't go thinking I'm soft," she teased, lifting a finger. "I expect you to pull your weight around here, buddy. No special treatment since you're a royal set to inherit a realm one day."

"Yes, ma'am," he said with a salute. "I'm your loyal soldier and will follow every command."

She shot him a suspicious glance, wondering if he caught the slight double entendre that laced his words. His angular features remained impassive, so she chalked it up to the hormones raging through her frame and did her best to shut them down.

"You're royalty too, you know. Princess of the Elves."

Scoffing, she shook her head. "I'm not a princess and never will be. Dear ol' Dad would have seventeen heart attacks if he heard you say that. Hybrids like me are an abomination to him."

They reached the camp, the ITU recruits milling around their tents as they packed supplies for the day's mission.

"As a hybrid myself, I don't get the sentiment. My parents embrace all immortals."

A tiny droplet of rain landed on his cheek, resting above a slight freckle before it began to trail down his face. Esme imagined touching the tip of her tongue to the drop before licking it away. Her attraction to him was frightening, perhaps because it was the strongest attraction she'd felt to a man in...decades? Centuries? Hell, maybe forever.

Considering "forever" wasn't in her vocabulary, it was something she needed to squash immediately. Easier said than done when he was looking at her with those compassionate eyes as the heat from his broad frame enveloped her...

"Esme?" he called, his voice soft as he studied her.

"Sorry. Zoned out." Placing her fingers between her lips, she gave a loud whistle, summoning the recruits. "We roll out in twenty minutes, team! The drive will take a little less than three hours. Remember to remain alert and ready on the drive and once we arrive."

Several "*aye aye*"s reverberated across the camp before she grinned up at Tordor. "Ready to kick some ass?"

"Born ready." He shot her a quick wink, damn near making her knees buckle, and she puffed out a breath.

"Good stuff. I'm going to pack my supplies." With a quick salute, she pivoted and trailed to her tent.

His gaze burned her even though she wasn't facing him, and she wondered why she could feel it lingering on her back as she widened the distance between them. Their connection was palpable—almost like an invisible tether that zinged with the energy of unrealized promises and whispered caresses against her heated skin.

Since connection had no place in her world, Esme climbed into her tent and took a moment to breathe. Then she began to prepare her backpack for the mission, wishing she could suppress the longing she shouldn't feel for the man who had a bright future where she had none.

<h1 style="text-align:center">Chapter 2</h1>

T ordor, son of Miranda and Sathan, heir to the throne of the immortal world, observed Esme step into her tent, noting she seemed a bit distracted. It was rare for the leader of the ITU, who was usually a whirlwind of positive energy and strategic, calm commands, but he figured even strong leaders had their off moments.

She'd knocked the wind out of his lungs the second he'd seen her on the battlefield when his cousin Callie defeated Bakari and destroyed the ether. Esmerelda had confidently explained she was the leader of the Immortals Transition Unit, or ITU, which existed to help immortals navigate new situations, especially ones that involved the human world. The immortal realm had been separated from the human world since the dawn of time, but with the destruction of the ether came the dissolution of that barrier.

Esme and her team had offered their help, and Tordor had jumped at the opportunity. The immortals hadn't planned on ever approaching humans, so the fact he was presented with someone with experience and connections in the human world was beneficial.

The fact she was undoubtedly the cutest female he'd met in his life was just a bonus. A magnificently splendid bonus.

As the son of two royals elevated from war and destruction, Tordor had been raised to become heir. As his parents split their time between the austere compounds of Astaria and Uteria, he was groomed to inherit the kingdom one day. A Slayer-Vampyre hybrid prince who symbolized peace in their reunited world. It was an auspicious objective, and Tordor did his best to play his role and make his parents proud. He loved them immensely and understood how hard they'd fought to secure peace. His birth and future inheritance of the combined throne symbolized the future of the kingdom.

Unfortunately, there was one small problem: Tordor had absolutely no desire to take their place.

He'd realized it when he was quite young, and unfortunately, the feeling remained as he grew into adulthood. In those early years, he'd struggled with the knowledge, ashamed and afraid to let his parents down. But eventually, his parents had noticed and they'd sat him down when he was fifteen to have an important talk.

His mother, whom he loved with all his heart, had gazed at him with emotion-filled eyes the color of his own and told him she feared he wasn't happy.

"I'm happy, Mom," he'd said, squeezing her wrist as she sat beside him on the couch. "You and Dad give me everything, and I'm extremely lucky and privileged. I have nothing to be sad about."

"You've always been too serious like your dad," Miranda teased, wrinkling her nose at Sathan as he scowled.

Reaching over from the nearby chair, he cupped Tordor's shoulder. "Being serious is totally fine, son. We can't all be terrible comedians like your mom."

"Hey!" Miranda chimed.

"Guys," Tordor said, showing his palms as he chuckled. "I'm fine, seriously. There's just so much pressure to be heir and I want to make you both proud." Expelling a deep breath, he ran his fingers though his thick black hair, identical to his father's. "I know half the kids in the kingdom would kill to be in my shoes. I don't want to seem ungrateful..."

"But?" Miranda asked, lifting her eyebrows.

"But, I...I don't know if I want to rule." Making sure to look them both in the eye, he did his best to explain. "You're both such great royals and were born for the roles. Hell, you earned it through so many years of war and pain. I want to earn my place on Etherya's Earth too, whatever that will look like. Does that make sense?"

"It does," Sathan said with a nod. "There is honor in earning your place. We have no desire to make you do anything you don't want to do, son."

"Can you just do us a favor?" Miranda asked, love shining in her eyes as she smiled. "Can you continue to be honest with us? I didn't have that type of relationship with my father and I want so badly to have it with you. I don't care if you become a milkmaid. I'll be proud of you no matter what."

"Are there still such things as milkmaids?" Sathan murmured, squinting at the ceiling.

"Oh, hush!" Miranda scolded. "Anyway, you understand how much I love you, right, sweetie? I just want you to keep talking to your ol' mom."

"I understand," he said, slipping his hand into hers to offer comfort. "I love you both so much. I don't want to let you down."

"Never going to happen, Tor," Sathan said, patting him on the back. "And we certainly don't mind ruling until you decide you're ready, however long it takes. It will give your mom something to do besides driving me and Uncle Kenden crazy."

"Excuse me, I do no such thing," she said, defiant as she lifted her chin. "You two fuddie duddies won't spar with me as much as you used to because you're scared I'm going to beat you."

"Or it could be that we have other responsibilities and need to focus our time on defeating Bakari..." He rubbed his chin. "But that doesn't stop you from asking us fourteen times a day."

Miranda stuck her tongue out at him as he playfully scrunched his features. Tordor watched the interplay, immensely thankful he'd been born to parents who exhibited deep, true love. It created an innate need for him to find the same one day, and he knew he would never settle for less.

They'd ended that conversation with Tordor promising to continue to communicate his aspirations as he grew older. Eventually, he grew into his confidence, and as he entered his mid-twenties, he explained to his parents that he might never wish to rule. They had accepted it, although both had still urged him not to close the door completely. The opportunity to assume his role as heir and the one true king of the immortal world would always loom over his head.

For now, he would allow the possibility to remain, even though it was very faint in his mind. Instead, as the years passed, he found a new passion. One he immersed himself in that brought him great happiness and fulfilled his soul. As it turned out, Tordor happened to be a fantastic diplomat and negotiator.

As he'd stated earlier to Esme, it certainly wasn't a shock considering he was the product of two immortals who literally pieced a realm back together. If anyone should have peace-keeping diplomatic skills, it was Tordor. But more than that, it was immensely satisfying and brought him great joy. Helping two parties evolve from deep disagreement and mis-understanding to a place of agreement and resolution filled something deep in his soul. It was why he'd created the Office of Official Complaints several years ago to resolve issues throughout the kingdom. It freed up his parents to focus on ruling and allowed him to do something that fulfilled him.

When Esme had shown up with her cheeky grin, confident swagger and team of ragtag hybrids and immortals, Tordor had jumped at the chance to offer his negotiating skills. The ITU had erected a temporary barrier to keep the realm hidden so they had time to approach the humans. Tordor saw nothing more noble than creating peace and bridging the gap between two previously unconnected realms upon Etherya's Earth.

Spending time with the adorable human-Elf who'd taken up constant residence in his head didn't hurt either. There was something about Esmerelda, with her quippy zingers and vibrant personality, that kept him on his toes. And something deeper that curled in his gut when she stared at him with those limitless hazel eyes. They held swirls of green and brown laced with honey-yellow flecks, and on many occasions, he'd caught himself trying to count them all. Currently, the tally was eleven flecks in her right eye and nine in her left, but he certainly wouldn't mind getting closer so he could truly study them in earnest...

Shaking his head, he told himself to stop dreaming of pretty little Elves and focus on the task at hand. Today, they were entering Phase I of their plan, and Tordor needed to be on his game. Their plan was to approach Clayton Westfield, a Slayer who'd lived in the human world for centuries. Esme had met him somewhere in her travels, and Tordor did his best to squash the jealousy before it began.

As a human-Elven hybrid who exhibited Elven traits, Esme was immor-tal and had lived for centuries. Human-immortal hybrids whose immortal DNA was suppressed were mortal and only exhibited their human traits. Conversely, hybrids who expressed their immortal DNA were immortal. This led to many hybrids who passed as humans having to reinvent themselves every century and begin new lives. Esme had mentioned in passing she'd met Clayton almost two centuries ago. Had they been lovers during any of their encounters, or were they just friends who shared a common heritage?

Tordor hadn't gathered the courage to ask, but he was still curious. As a man in his late-twenties, there were so many things he'd yet to experience in his immortal life. One of them was being in love. After all, he was the child of two people who were destined soul mates, and Tordor wanted the same. Which led to something else he'd never experienced: he was still a virgin.

It was something he fully embraced and held no embarrassment about. He wanted nothing less than a great love and wanted to share those first intimate moments with someone he felt a true connection with...and possibly even loved. Although he'd dated sporadically, he'd just never met someone who made him yearn to share those deeply personal moments.

Until her.

The sentiment was true, and Tordor admitted he was extremely attracted to the leader of his newly adopted team. Every time he was within five feet of her, his body seemed to buzz with an incandescent energy he'd never felt. But more than that, he admired her and was deeply curious about her story. She was the child of an immortal king too, although her upbringing was quite different. How many similarities did they share? How many differences? He yearned to sit down with her and just talk...to ask her about her fears and her dreams and if she'd ever been in love...

Considering they had a huge task to accomplish, Tordor understood there wasn't going to be a lot of chitchat time. Still, he hoped to continue to earn her trust. He felt they were becoming friends and couldn't deny he hoped it would lead to more one day. Would she be the one he finally lowered his walls for? The one he made love to as he stared into those honey-flecked eyes?

Scowling as he trailed to his tent, he grabbed his pack and slung it on his back. Would someone as worldly as Esme even consider sleeping with a virgin? Tordor was a confident man, but being intimate with someone for the first time would be at least mildly intimidating for anyone, right? Deciding not to focus on the irksome thoughts—especially since he was about to meet a man she proclaimed to be a long-time friend—Tordor mentally reminded himself not to let the jealousy flare as it could very well be unwarranted. Assuming anything about Esme's past did him no favors, and it was imperative he remained focused on the task at hand.

The team finished gathering their supplies and formed a circle as Esme called for their attention.

"As discussed, once we park the cars, we'll head to the Lincoln Memorial. Everyone has their positions and assignments that we've already gone over in detail."

Several of the soldiers nodded. "Yes, ma'am."

"Tordor and I will meet Clayton on the bench by the north end of the reflecting pool at the Lincoln Memorial. We'll appear to be tourists who run into Clayton. I'll pretend to be his old college buddy and we'll sit and chat like old friends. No one will know we're discussing the future of immortals and humans." Her hands lifted as she grinned in wonder. "Nothing like strategizing the future of several species over a lazy chat, right, guys?"

Several team members smiled, and Tordor picked up where she left off. "We'll be in broad daylight and don't anticipate any threats, but you all will be on alert in your various positions around the park. Keep an eye out for anything suspicious."

"Aye aye," they responded, some saluting as others touched their belts, confirming the presence of the guns holstered there.

Turning, Esme trained those stunning eyes on him as her lips formed a brilliant smile. "Well, then, I guess we're ready."

"Ready and at your command, Captain Esme."

"Ew." Her button nose wrinkled and he held in his chuckle. "Just Esme is fine. We're going to work that serious formal streak out of you one day." Jerking her head, she urged them along. "Let's go."

Tordor digested her words, silently envisioning one way they could work out his serious streak. He was quite sure he'd relax if they were sweaty and naked while his lips trailed over every inch of her skin...

Telling himself not to be a creep, he climbed into the front seat of their rented Jeep as Esme slid behind the wheel. Once everyone was situated in the vehicles, they set out on their journey to approach the humans.

Chapter 3

The ITU made it to DC and parked their cars at the previously scouted garages. Once everyone had dispersed to their assigned posts, Esme held her hand to her forehead, shielding her eyes from the sun as she surveyed the reflecting pool. She spotted Clayton eating a sandwich on a far-off bench.

Fondness welled as she admired the thick hair that fell over his brow, remembering how she'd teased him for always needing a haircut. She'd met him on her first excursion to America in the mid-1800s. Esme was curious about the new country and interested to see how many immortals had migrated there.

Clayton first spotted her at an open-air market in Philadelphia. He'd sauntered over and leaned down to whisper to her as she examined some apples at the fruit stand.

"Didn't think I'd meet another immortal here."

Glancing up, her fingers tightened on the apple as she evaluated whether he was friend or foe.

"Nor did I," was her gruff response.

"Just noticed the tips of your ears," he said, showing his palms. "They're slight but evident to a fellow immortal."

Esme's eyes narrowed. "You're a Slayer."

"Always have been," he teased, leaning into a slightly dramatic bow.

Taken by his calm and playful demeanor, she'd dropped her defenses and embarked on a deep friendship. She visited him every time she traveled to America, and eventually, his pursuits became romantic. Esme held him off for years until finally capitulating when she visited him in the early 1920s.

He'd taken her dancing at one of the roaring clubs where jazz reverberated off the walls. They'd danced long into the night, and he'd walked her home, his fingers twined with hers as she contemplated taking a small respite from her solitude.

When they reached his front door, he pushed it open and faced her, gently urging her inside.

"I'm leaving in a few days, Clay," she said, her voice raspy.

"I know." Glancing down, he kicked the floor with his toe. "I won't push you, Esme. If you can only give me tonight, I'll cherish it. And if you can give me the rest of your time here, I promise I'll let you go when you're ready. But let's have some fun first." He waggled his eyebrows.

She'd followed him inside, allowing herself some rare days of happiness and companionship. And then she'd left him, sealing her goodbye with a kiss to his cheek and a promise to check in often.

True to his word, Clayton had let her go and they'd moved solidly back to the friend zone. He'd become a trusted confidant in her small circle, and she was thankful her father had never harmed him.

Returning to the present moment, Esme glanced at Tordor.

"There he is, just as we discussed. Well done, Clay."

Striding forward, Tordor fell into step beside her.

"Not too eager," he said softly, brushing her forearm with the backs of his fingers. "Remember, we're supposed to be lazy sightseers."

Realizing he was right, she slowed her pace, gingerly trailing beside him as they approached Clayton's bench. Straightening her shoulders, she prepared to lay on the act. When they were close, she gasped and broke into a huge grin.

"Clayton?" she asked, her mouth dropping open in fake surprise. "Clayton Westfield? I haven't seen you since college graduation."

"Well, I'll be damned," he said, setting the sandwich and wrapper on the bench before standing and wiping his hands. "Esmerelda Spalding. How the hell are you?"

They embraced before he gestured to the bench. "I was just on my lunch break. Sit down and tell me how you've been. Is this your husband?"

Grinning at Tordor, she shook her head. "Nah, I wouldn't do that to him. This is my friend Tordor and he's in town to see the sights. Figured the Lincoln Memorial reflecting pool is a must."

"Absolutely." Extending his hand to Tordor, Clayton said, "Nice to meet you."

"A pleasure," Tordor said, shaking his hand. Esme noticed the slight muscle that twitched in his firm jaw as he assessed her friend. Was he...jealous? Deciding to deliberate on that later, she refocused on the task at hand.

"I can sit for a few minutes," she said, lowering to the bench and swinging her legs back and forth as Clayton joined her. "Want to sit?" she asked Tordor, gesturing beside her.

"I'll stand," he said in that deep, serious tone, crossing his arms over his expansive chest. It was what they'd planned, after all, so Tordor could surreptitiously keep watch, but it reminded Esme how *large* he was. Beginning to speak, she continued to gesture with her hands good-naturedly to give the appearance of a genial conversation.

"So, what did the human general say?" she asked, lowering her voice to slip into the business talk. "Is he prepared to work with us in the transition?"

"Yes," Clayton said, lazily crossing his ankle over his knee. Esme noticed the slight bristle in his spine even though he aimed to appear laid-back and calm. "General Markson is one of the highest-ranking officials in the US government. He agrees it's best to keep politicians out of the loop for now. Politicians are concerned with power, and he is an honorable human who is concerned with keeping people safe."

"Immortals have no desire to hurt humans," Tordor said, "but we understand they might see us as a threat."

"Exactly," Clayton confirmed with a nod. "Humans have barely figured out how to tolerate *each other*. Throwing a smattering of immortal species in the mix isn't going to end well. General Markson has agreed to our immersion plan." Gesturing with his head toward her fanny pack, he reached over to tap it. "I'm assuming your phone is in here and the eighties called and said, 'Nice job on the rad accessory.'" Esme scrunched her features at him as he chuckled. "Markson has a private cell configured to securely take our calls. I just texted you his number."

"Awesome," Esme said, breathing a sigh of relief. "So, we'll begin to transition hybrids and immortals into human governments, passing as humans so they can earn the trust of the politicians and high-ranking officials."

"Yes," Clayton said, his foot bobbing atop his knee. "It will take several years, maybe decades, and we'll need to assign trustworthy immortals who are willing to create human lives. Once they have infiltrated the upper levels of government in all the industrialized countries, they will begin to reveal their true heritage. It's the only way the general and I can foresee not shocking the humans into something drastic like nuclear war. If they already trust the people who reveal themselves as non-human, they are more likely to listen and try to accept them."

"Only then can we have a true transition where the immortal world and human world coexist," Tordor said, gently kicking the ground with the toe of his boot.

"Precisely," Clayton said.

Inhaling deeply, Esme pondered. "And the general agreed to leaving the makeshift invisible wall we erected in place while we implement our plan?"

"Yes. I'm not sure he's thrilled about having a clandestine wall separating the worlds, but it's the only way to maintain separation for now." Lifting his finger, he said, "General Markson loves his wife, children and the grandchild he now has on the way. He understands that child might not see a future if we botch the transition. It has to happen thoughtfully so the world doesn't go into shock."

"Thank the gods," Esme breathed, throwing her arms around Clayton's neck and squeezing. "I knew you'd come through, Clay. Thank you for all your help. You know, if you weren't already a high-ranking official in the government, I'd recruit you for the mission."

Chuckling, Clayton smoothed a hand over her hair. "I enjoy working at the Pentagon. You remember when the world broke into war at the beginning of the twentieth century? It was a nightmare, and I felt a calling to help. I'd been living in the human world for centuries and didn't want to see it fall into disarray. I joined the American army and never looked back. When the war ended, I found other ways to help. I like humans, and life in their world is much better when they're not trying to kill each other."

"Hear, hear," Esme muttered.

"Esme says you two have been friends for quite some time," Tordor said.

"We have," Clayton said, smoothing his hand over her hair again as Esme smiled into his kind eyes. "I tried to keep her all to myself, but she's squirrely and never stays in one place long. Right, darling?"

Gently removing his hand, Esme squeezed it to soften the blow before resting it back on his thigh. "Hard to stay in one place when your dad's dead set on poisoning everyone."

Clayton opened his mouth to speak and she shook her head. "I have no desire to discuss him. We're here to talk about the transition plan, and you've done great work here, Clay. Thank you."

"You're welcome." His brown eyes glowed with sentiment as he continued. "The next step is to introduce you to General Markson. It's going to be difficult because he has tight security and is usually under surveillance by high-ranking spies of other countries. It's how all the human governments keep tabs on each other."

"Which means the US government is also spying on high-ranking officials of every other country," Tordor said, arching a brow.

"Every single one," Clayton confirmed with a nod. "Markson is going to arrange a meeting for us at a clandestine location with top-notch security."

"Good," Esme said, gnawing her lip as she strategized the weeks and months ahead. "Miranda and Sathan have already selected immortals they wish to participate in Phase I. I'm excited for General Markson to vet them."

Clayton's mouth opened as he began to form an answer and Esme heard the loud chirp of a bird in her ear. It was something she would've never registered except for the fact that it signaled something ominous in the far reaches of her mind.

As Clayton attempted to speak, his mouth froze, open and shocked as his expression fell...

Moments ticked by with such slow gravity she could feel the passing of each tick as it clicked in her brain.

Tick...tick...tick...

Color drained from Clayton's face as he gasped...lifting his hand to clutch his throat...his shoulders convulsing as his eyes grew wide and bulged from their sockets.

Red rivulets of blood began to trail over the fingers that gripped his throat, and adrenaline forced Esme to shake away the fog and jump into action. As her friend fell to the bench, she replaced his hand with her own, crying his name as she struggled to close the wound. A gaping hole now ravaged the spot where her friend's Adam's apple had once rested. His arms grew lax, falling to the ground on each side of the bench as he gasped his last breath.

Leaning over him, Esme clutched his face in her blood-soaked hands. "No...no...no... Clayton! Please...don't go..."

Several people began to rush over, and one man shouted, "I'm a doctor!" before crouching in front of Clayton and beginning CPR, although it was pointless. The immortal she'd known for years, and one of her oldest and most trusted friends in the lonely world she inhabited, was gone.

"We have to go," Tordor said, his tone gentle but firm. Grasping her wrist, he tugged her away from the crowd of people that were rapidly encircling Clayton. "We have our human IDs, but having the authorities run them is going to open a can of worms we can't close."

"We can't leave him," she cried. "The humans could discover he's a Slayer—"

"We'll have to call Markson and hope he can extricate the body before the humans examine it," Tordor said, tugging her away from the crowd. "I don't want to leave him either, but he wouldn't want to compromise the mission."

Racked with pain, Esme glanced once more at Clayton, sending him one last silent goodbye before placing her blood-soaked hand in Tordor's and hurrying away from the commotion. Almost deaf from the incessant ringing in her ears, she gained the wherewithal to lift her head and scan the horizon, knowing one thing for certain: her father had finally decided to interfere with her mission. She'd been lucky in the months since the ether was destroyed, but that luck had run out.

As she trudged away, allowing Tordor to lead her to a nearby park so they could be shrouded by the trees and shrubs, she defiantly lifted her chin and raised her arm, extending her middle finger toward the horizon. Giving the henchman who'd shot her friend a silent "fuck you," she closed her eyes, knowing deep in her bones her father had given the order to assassinate Clayton...and wondering the entire time why he continued to torture her and didn't just murder her instead.

Chapter 4

Once the team reconvened in a secluded wooded area several miles from the reflecting pool, Tordor leaped into action, taking charge to determine the next steps.

"We need to return to Rausch Gap immediately," he said, aware of the fury simmering in his veins as he observed the blood on Esme's hands. Seeing her flesh covered in remnants of violence rocked him to his core, causing something intense and protective to well deep within. "It's obvious Esme's father's men have found us, and they're not big fans of our mission."

"God damn it," Esme said, shaking her head as she gazed absently at the ground. "I should've known it was only a matter of time. Now that he's made a move, you can bet he's going to do his best to interfere with our transition plan."

"Judging by what just happened, he's jumping in at Threat Level 1," one of the soldiers, Brienne, said. She was a Slayer-Elven hybrid who'd lived in the human world since birth. Tall and strong with short, spiky blond hair and unwavering support for Esme, she was a valuable asset to their team. "We need to have a strategy session immediately."

"Agreed," Esme said dejectedly. "But once we're back at Rausch Gap. Not here."

Clearing his throat, the Slayer warrior Larkin asked, "If you're a target for him, why would he kill Clayton instead of you? I'm sorry to ask such a blunt question, but I think the time for pleasantries is over."

Clenching her blood-soaked fist, her nostrils flared as she spoke. "Because the bastard lives to torture me. I figured out ages ago he gets much more pleasure from tormenting me than killing me. I fucking hate him."

"Okay," Tordor said, gently cupping her shoulder. "This is important intel, but lingering here together isn't safe. First and foremost, Esme needs to make contact with General Markson. We have to ensure Clayton's body is removed from human custody."

"I'll lead the team back to Rausch Gap," Larkin said. "You two stay behind and work with Markson to recover Clayton's remains. In the morning, we'll have a strategy session."

"Combating my father is no easy task," Esme said. "He possesses powers similar to Crimeous and Tatiana. I'd love to ask Tatiana for help, but she disappeared after the ether was destroyed."

"Maybe we can find her," Tordor said. "I'll call Uncle Latimus and see if he can help us. He's excellent at navigating these situations."

"I know someone who might be able to help us," Larkin said. "I'll detail everyone in our strategy session tomorrow. In the meantime, let's roll out. Make sure you're not followed," he commanded to the team, and they saluted before retreating to their vehicles.

"We have your back, Esme," Larkin said, encircling her upper arm and giving a compassionate squeeze. "This is a tragic setback, but you're not alone." With one final nod to Tordor, he pivoted and walked away with Brienne.

Facing Esme, Tordor assessed her grief-stricken expression. "Let's head deeper into the park and find a secluded area for you to call Markson."

Esme's eyes fell to her hands, her chin quivering. "Fuck, I'm so pissed and I think I'm going into shock. I need to get this blood off."

"Follow me," he said, his tone reassuring and firm, hoping to help keep her steady. They briskly walked farther into the park, locating an area with thick green holly bushes. Glancing around to ensure they were alone, Tordor removed his backpack and located some tissues and water. Lowering to one knee, he wet the tissues and reached for her arm. Gently and methodically, he began to clean away the blood.

After he'd done all he could with the meager supplies, Tordor rose, stuffing the blood-laced tissues back in his bag. "Do you want me to call Markson?"

"No," she said, reaching for her phone. "Clayton gave him my name and it has to be me." Locating the number, she dialed and lifted the phone to her ear.

"General Markson, this is Esmerelda Spalding. I got your number from Clayton Westfield and needed to call you earlier than anticipated."

"I am aware of the situation," Markson's deep voice responded as Tordor listened in. "I'm sending four of my private security soldiers to take care of the body. They work for me and have no ties to the government. They will ensure the body is burned and any records destroyed."

"Thank you," she said, pain cresting her expression as she clenched the phone. "He didn't deserve to die today."

"Do you have a suspect in mind?"

Inhaling a deep breath, Esme began briefing General Markson about her father. Tordor's body hummed with the slight fear the new threat would compromise their chances of working with him.

"We'll do the best we can to deal with my father, and I believe it's best we don't involve you in the situation with him. All we need from you are the terms you originally discussed with Clayton. We still want to implement the plan if you're willing to help us."

Silence stretched before Markson replied, "I'm willing. It's the only path forward. I've postulated several different plans of action now that the ether is destroyed, and infiltrating governments from the inside and gaining humans' trust is the only one I can foresee having a chance of success."

"I appreciate your commitment to the cause, sir. Once Clayton is cremated, please let me know. I'd like to pick up his ashes and honor him by spreading them to send him off to the Passage. He didn't have any other family or close relatives and he deserves that."

"Will do. Once you're ready, please call me to discuss next steps. I'll need to personally vet each immortal you'll be placing in the government roles. I briefly discussed a timeline with Clayton, but I'd like Phase I completed before the end of the summer. This gives us over two months to get everyone vetted and implemented. Cold weather always brings heightened tensions with Russia since they control most of Europe's energy, and my time will be dedicated to maintaining peace there."

"I understand and will be in touch soon. Thank you, General."

The phone screen went dark and Esme lifted sad, sullen eyes to Tordor. "Can we find a hotel? I need to shower. I just..." She raised her arms, rotating them as she slowly shook her head. "I have to wash off the rest of the blood."

Slinging his pack over his shoulders, Tordor led her to the street before hailing a cab. He directed the driver to take them to a hotel located in a nearby industrial area they'd previously scouted. Esme was quiet beside him as he secured a room at the front desk using the credit card his Uncle Heden had prepared for him when they entered the human world a few months ago.

"Thank the gods for your rich human uncle," Esme murmured as they grabbed the plastic keys and trailed to the elevators. Stepping inside, he pressed the "2."

"His offer to fund our team was amazing, but that's Uncle Heden for you. He's loaded and always happy to help. He and Sofia have created so many profitable businesses and apps, and they have money to spare."

"It's very appreciated," she said, stepping into the hallway once the doors opened.

They stopped in front of Room 216 and Tordor handed her one of the plastic keys. "I'll go buy you some new clothes at the shopping center next door while you shower. Text me what sizes to get because I know nothing about female clothing."

His heart swelled when she gave a half-hearted smile. "I will. Just a T-shirt and some pants without blood on them will do." Sighing, she stepped inside. "See you in a bit."

"I'll hang the clothes on the doorknob and wait for you in the lobby. I'm also going to call Latimus and discuss today's events. If there's a way to immobilize your father, he'll find it."

"Thank you."

"Esme," he said before he could stop himself. "You don't have to mourn him alone. I'm here for you—"

"Thank you, but I always mourn alone," she interjected softly, still facing away as she gazed at the floor. Her shoulders sagged as she entered the room. "See you in a few."

Accepting her unwillingness to let him comfort her, Tordor backed out of the room, giving her the solace she craved. Heading downstairs, he used the lobby bathroom, washing his face and hands before cleaning out his bag. Fury swelled as he threw away the bloody tissues from earlier, and he vowed to keep Esme and their team safe.

Afterward, he headed to the strip mall next door, reading Esme's text and purchasing the clothing she suggested. After leaving the bag hanging on her door, he headed downstairs to the outside courtyard of the hotel. Pulling out his phone, he called Latimus.

They spoke for several minutes as Tordor brought him up to speed. Latimus indicated he felt it might be time to track down Tatiana and ask for her help against Dakath. Although the woman was wily, she had knowledge of many things, including the Elven council and its malicious ruler. They ended the call with Latimus promising to get back to Tordor once he'd formulated a plan.

Settling back on the outdoor couch, Tordor placed his hands behind his head as he waited for Esme. Resting his foot on the stone fire pit, his thoughts drifted to her as they quite often did.

Although he longed to comfort her, Esme was a lone wolf, and allowing someone in would require trust. Tordor hadn't quite fully earned it yet, but he was a determined man. Breaking through her thick walls would take time and patience, and thankfully, he had both in spades. One day, if he continued his efforts, he believed his strong, resilient Elf would finally open up to him.

Feeling his heart thunk in his chest, Tordor rubbed his pec above the beating organ, acknowledging that once he'd breached those walls, the likelihood of him allowing her to erect them again would be low.

For once he'd earned her trust and openness, Tordor wondered if he would possess the will to ever let her go.

Chapter 5

E sme slid off her clothes and made her way to the shower in a daze. As she stood under the spray, she allowed her tears to mingle with the rivulets of water, grieving for a friend whose only mistake in life had been caring for her.

She'd spent so much of her life in solitude trying to prevent the outcome she'd witnessed today. Memories flashed through her brain of all the meals she'd eaten in silence, cuddled next to warm fires since she wouldn't allow anything living to offer warmth.

She was usually able to push emotion aside. To remind herself there was a strength in paving her own way and the result of caring for someone was to make them a target.

But every once in a while, during the wretched lonely nights, she would bury her face in her hands and allow herself to cry. To rally at the unfairness of the world and let her human emotions surge.

Those times were rare, but they were cleansing. They allowed her to buck up and continue her path in the world.

Returning to the present moment, the warm water sluiced over her as she experienced one of those brief instances. Her tears offered both relief and strength. Inhaling a calming breath, she straightened her spine and turned off the water.

Stepping onto the mat, she grabbed the nearby towel and dried her skin. Approaching the foggy mirror, she wiped away the condensation and leaned toward her reflection. Hazel eyes with firm resolve and unfettered emotion stared back as she clenched the counter below.

"I *will* avenge you, Clay," she vowed through gritted teeth. "Your sacrifice will not be in vain. We won't let my father interfere, and we'll successfully transition the species to live together on Etherya's Earth. Mark my words."

Silence was her only response as she the seconds ticked away, reminding Esme of the slow and steady passage of time.

Exhausted, she trailed to the bed, tossing away the towel and climbing underneath the covers. Resting her cheek on the pillow, she grasped the other pillow tight, hugging it to her chest as she buried her face in the soft fabric and mourned the unbearable loss of her friend.

The Vampyre Compound of Lynia

Jaxon, son of Vampyre warrior Tyrell, ran his palms over his weathered jeans as he waited for Commander Latimus. Being a rather laid-back soul, Jaxon rarely experienced nervousness, but being summoned to meet with the highest-ranking Vampyre soldier could rattle anyone. Racking his brain as he sat in the office of the compound's military training facility, he tried to discern why Latimus wanted to meet with him.

In truth, Jaxon had been a pretty shitty soldier. A century ago, when he turned eighteen, he'd automatically enrolled in the immortal army. The War of the Species was still raging and his father had died on the wrong end of an eight-shooter, so Jaxon wanted to help the cause. Unfortunately, after a lackluster performance during his training and the realization he didn't respond all that well to authority, Jaxon knew he'd made a mistake. Army life was definitely not for him.

But he'd made a commitment and tried his best to perform his duties. Thankfully, Latimus had noticed his subpar performance and pulled him aside one night on the moonlit training field.

"Jaxon," Latimus had said, rubbing his forehead in frustration. "This can't continue. You've been late to training three times this month and completely blew the formation at the last Slayer raid. Your performance is compromising this battalion, and I won't stand for it."

Sighing, Jaxon kicked the ground, genuinely feeling contrite but knowing he needed to be honest. "I'm sorry, sir. Truly, I am. I support the cause and want to do my best to serve our kingdom. I just..." Lifting his hands, he struggled to find the words. "My father was a great soldier, but I fear I did not inherit his skills."

"You can say that again," Latimus muttered, running a hand over his slick black hair. "I can't continue to let you off with warnings. I revered your father, and he died honorably in battle. My deference for him is the only reason I haven't expelled you from the army."

"I understand." Rubbing the back of his neck, Jaxon searched for a solution. "My mother—the goddess bless her soul—was devastated by my father's death and took her own life to be with him in the Passage. I felt joining the army would avenge them in some way."

Latimus crossed his arms over his chest and tapped his boot on the ground. "My sister gossips at royal fundraisers that you're late because you're sneaking out of the beds of rich aristocrats who are no longer pleased by their husbands." Scraping a hand over his face, he arched a derisive eyebrow. "If only you could be so *attentive* to your duties as a soldier."

Jaxon pursed his lips, remaining silent since the commander's words were true.

Rubbing his chin, Latimus continued. "Since you have a knack for stealth, what would you say about becoming a spy?"

Jaxon's eyebrows lifted as he contemplated. "Would I spy on Slayers?"

"And Deamons," Latimus said with a nod. "I have a soldier currently posted on the outskirts of the Deamon caves, near the foothills of the Strok Mountains, but Darkrip can transport and has been spotted throughout the realm. I'd like to have a spy who can investigate those occurrences."

"Alrec, son of Jakar, is your outposted soldier," Jaxon said, hoping to showcase his surreptitiousness. "He rides in on his horse, meets with you for a few hours, and rides away, only to return in six months like clockwork."

Latimus's fangs flashed in the moonlight as he grinned. "Very perceptive. Alrec has a family at his outpost and does not wish to leave them any longer than he has to."

"Good for him," Jaxon said, genuinely happy for his fellow soldier. "Not sure I'd sign up for one lady for eternity, but if it floats his boat, that's all that matters."

"Your spy position would be more mobile than Alrec's since he is stationed to one region. I would send you throughout the realm, and in the interest of ending this infernal war, I might possibly send you to the human realm from time to time to study their weapons and gather information on new technology." Huffing, he placed his hands on his hips. "Humans are inferior beings who will most likely exterminate themselves in a few centuries, but I'll begrudgingly admit they know how to make some damn fine weapons."

Rolling his tongue on the roof of his mouth, Jaxon took one final moment to contemplate. Extending his hand, he straightened his spine, ready to take on the assignment. "Sir, if you'll have me, I would be honored to take this position. I think I can serve the kingdom much better as a spy than a soldier."

"Agreed," Latimus said, shaking his hand. "You'll report directly to me, and due to the nature of your assignment, it will need to remain between us."

"Absolutely. I'll report to you tomorrow at dusk."

"Be on time," Latimus said, lifting a finger. "I understand wanting time with the ladies, but this is a serious post, Jaxon."

Giving a firm salute, Jaxon uttered a resounding, "Yes, sir!"

Chuckling, Latimus patted him on the shoulder. "Good day, Jaxon. Go get some sleep."

The commander had shuffled across the training field, disappearing over the horizon, while Jaxon thanked his lucky stars he hadn't been fired. Instead, he'd been offered a job that—although he hadn't known it at the time—was an absolute perfect fit.

Now, decades later, the War of the Species was long over and the subsequent conflict with Bakari had also been resolved. Peace had come to the immortal realm, and Latimus had relieved Jaxon of his job as a spy, promising to continue paying his monthly stipend for eternity as payment for a job well done during the two conflicts.

Jaxon had enjoyed his job immensely, and now that he'd been "retired" for several months, he was starting to get quite bored. Perhaps Latimus had summoned him to discuss a new post. Possibly something in the human world now that the ether had been destroyed. Buzzing with curiosity, Jaxon stood when Latimus entered the room.

"Hey, Jaxon," Latimus said, shaking his hand before gesturing for him to sit again. Lowering into the chair, he observed Latimus sit behind the functional wooden desk he kept at the training center. Placing his forearms on the table, Latimus leaned forward and cocked a brow. "How's retirement?"

Chuckling, Jaxon placed his ankle over his knee, wagging his foot as he toyed with a stray thread that hung from the cuff of his jeans. "Honestly, sir, I was just thinking I'm kind of bored."

Latimus's lips curved as he threaded his fingers atop the desk. "Not going to lie, I was hoping you'd say that."

"Well, hot damn. Do you have a new assignment for me, sir?"

"First of all, let's cut the 'sir,'" Latimus said, slicing a finger over his throat. "It makes me feel old."

"Not to be a dick, but you are kind of old...sir."

Latimus shot him a droll glare. "You always were a pain in the ass, brother."

Laughing, Jaxon nodded. "One of my most consistent qualities."

Leaning back, Latimus steepled his fingers as he rested his elbows on the arms of the leather seat. "I received a secure call from Tordor a few hours ago. It seems Esme's father, Elf King Dakath, is more of a threat than I realized."

Intrigued, Jaxon's spine straightened. "Is Tordor okay?"

"He, Esme and their team are fine, but her father seems determined to meddle with the transition plans they've formulated for the humans. It's imperative this transition go smoothly, and it will likely take years. If we have an enemy threatening the mission, I need intel on him to fight him effectively."

"How much of an enemy?"

"Sadly, he murdered one of Esme's contacts in cold blood only hours ago," Latimus said, harshly swiping a hand over his face. "As soon as I think we're done with death and destruction, it seems to find us, no matter what."

"The more we mingle with humans, I fear the violence will only increase," Jaxon said softly.

"It's true that humans are destructive, but Arderin assures me there's an abundance of goodwill in their species too. She lived there for several years and has an affinity toward them. And Heden chose to become one, so I guess they're okay, even though he's a pain in my ass too."

Jaxon breathed a laugh. "Heden has been invaluable to the cause, from what I hear."

Sadness clouded Latimus's features. "He always has been," he said softly, swallowing thickly before he continued. "As he gets older, I'm reminded his time on this planet is limited. It's..." Clearing his throat, he shook his head. "Well, it's tough to contemplate, but I also remind myself none of our futures are set in stone, even if we're immortal, and that's where you come in."

Nodding, Jaxon planted his feet on the floor and rested his elbows on his thighs. Leaning closer, he asked, "What do you need me to do?"

"I need intel on King Dakath, and the one person who can give it to us disappeared after the ether was destroyed." Gathering some papers on the desk and stacking them, he handed them to Jaxon. "Here is what I've compiled on the Elf king so far, mostly from the soothsayer manuals Miranda and Kenden discovered several years ago. There's not much there, but it's a start. Apparently, he's quite powerful and has powers similar to Crimeous."

"You want me to track down Tatiana," Jaxon said, leafing through the disjointed notes, "so I can ask her how to combat someone with his powers. Do we know where she is in the human world?"

"No idea, but I'd start with the family Callie helped in the Arizona desert. They share a connection with her and can likely start you on the path."

"And once I find her?" he asked, running his hand through his thick brown hair. "I can't very well force her to give me the intel."

Sitting back, Latimus's jaw ticked as he contemplated. "Tatiana was extremely helpful in the battle against Bakari. I'm hoping she still has some goodwill left. I trust you can gain her alliance so she can give us intel on something that can maim or weaken Dakath. That will go a long way toward easing the path for Tordor and Esme as they begin the transition with the humans."

Jaxon's brow furrowed as he studied the notes. "What about Dakath? Do you want me to investigate him too?"

"According to Esme, he lives in a fortified castle in a remote area of the Carpathian Mountains of Romania. I'm not sure approaching him on his turf is warranted yet since it could escalate things further, but we'll discern as things progress."

"Got it."

"This isn't an order, Jaxon. I offered you full paid retirement and you earned it. It's a request, and you're more than welcome to say no."

Lifting his gaze, Jaxon grinned into his commander's ice-blue eyes. They'd evolved from commander and subordinate over the years to friends, and for that, Jaxon was extremely thankful. He knew no other man more honorable than Latimus, nor no other man as completely besotted by his bonded mate. "That pretty Vampyre aristocrat hasn't made you soft, has she?" he teased. "Not so long ago, you'd give me an order and bark at me to make sure I was on time."

Smirking, Latimus lifted a finger. "I'm just a man who wants to honor my word...and if you call my bonded pretty again, I'm likely to relieve you of your voice box. No one's allowed to call her that but me."

Tossing back his head, Jaxon broke into joyful laughter. "Man, you're whipped. I love it."

"She literally owns my balls, brother," Latimus said, playfully rolling his eyes. "It's pathetic. And what about you? Still sneaking into beds you shouldn't be?"

Forming a slight frown, Jaxon tried to recall ever wanting to settle down with one woman...or ever feeling the yearning to build something with someone else. For whatever reason, his life had been a string of one-night stands that he found rather enjoyable. When they were over, he moved on, never regretting the fact he didn't want more.

"I don't know," he said. "I think some of us just aren't wired that way. I like having a good time and floating through life untethered."

"Hey, to each his own," Latimus said, showing his palms. "We all manifest happiness in different ways. And I'm getting the vibe that leaving retirement might make you pretty happy."

"It would. I miss doing surveillance and helping our people. I'm happy to find Tatiana and take the Elf king down a notch. He sounds like a bad dude who could use a little comeuppance."

"Then it's settled," Latimus said, rising and extending his hand.

Jaxon stood and shook it, anticipation coursing through him at the prospect of returning to the field. "When should I report for duty?"

"I'll have Heden create an ID for you and prepare a credit card and cash. He, Sofia and the twins arrive tomorrow for Adelyn's birthday celebration. Once you have the supplies, you'll be all set to travel to the human world."

"Sounds good. Happy birthday to Adelyn, by the way."

"Thanks. She went through her immortal change a few years ago, so she'll always 'appear' to be twenty-five,"—he made quotation marks with his fingers—"but my bonded loves to throw a party and it's a nice excuse to get the family together."

"Well, have fun at the party, and I'll be ready to go once I have everything from Heden."

"You should come," Latimus said, striding around the desk and patting him on the shoulder. "Everyone would love to see you, and Kenden can update you on the intel on Dakath from the scrolls before you head to the human world. He's studied them extensively."

"Sounds like a plan," Jaxon said, happy to be invited. He'd met Lila on a few occasions and had worked many times with Kenden throughout his spy career after the War of the Species ended. "Thanks, Latimus."

Once they'd said their goodbyes, Jaxon headed home, determined to study the notes Latimus had compiled so he'd be ready for the journey ahead. Thanking the goddess for bringing purpose back in his life, he vowed to find Tatiana and do his best to keep the Elf king from meddling with Esme and Tordor's plans.

Chapter 6

E sme felt somewhat refreshed after showering and resting. After donning the new clothes Tordor left hanging on the doorknob, she headed downstairs and found him sitting in the outside courtyard.

"Hey," she said, strolling over and sitting beside him. "Did you talk to Latimus?"

"I did. He has some ideas about sending an investigator to track down Tatiana and ask for her help. He's going to keep us updated."

"Okay." Rubbing her arms in the late afternoon sun, she warded off a chill even though the breeze was warm. "Tracking her down is a viable option in a situation where we don't have many available. I know the immortals are sick of war, and starting one against my father in the human world isn't feasible."

"War is never feasible," he said, shaking his head. "But finding Tatiana and asking for her alliance against Dakath would give us a powerful ally. Not all battles have to be fought with physical violence. Hopefully we can attack him here." He tapped his temple.

"Hopefully."

Tordor's thick arm glided over her shoulders and he gently pulled her into his side. "Is this okay?" he asked softly, his lips barely grazing her hair. "I feel like you might need a hug."

Sighing as her heart trembled at the comforting gesture, she nodded. "I swear, I'm pretty tough. Seeing my friend taken down in cold blood has really shaken me though."

"You're one of the strongest people I know." His hand caressed her shoulder, the strokes soothing as she relaxed against his side. "I'm so thankful you're helping my people." Gazing into her eyes, he murmured, "*Our* people."

"They were never mine," she said, her voice gravelly as she shook her head. "You're the heir, Tor. You have such a bright future."

"And you don't?"

Lowering her gaze, she wondered if he would ever truly understand. Someone like him, who had loving parents and a path blazed for him since birth. "It doesn't matter. I'm an old lady compared to you. Once we begin the implementation plan, I'm going to trust the team to run it effectively so I can get some damn rest."

His fingers slid under her chin, warm against her skin as he tilted her head. "You don't plan to stay?"

"I can't," she whispered, shaking her head. "You see what happens to people I form connections with." Tears welled as she thought of Clayton.

"I need you, Esme," he said, dragging his thumb over her cheek. "I can't do this without you."

"Once we place the first wave of immortals in the human government, the plan will be in motion. I'm going to assign Brienne and Larkin to lead the mission from our base in Rausch Gap. This was never a permanent assignment for me, Tor. I don't have the luxury of permanence in my life."

Disappointment clouded his eyes as they darted between hers. "What if you chose a different path? One where you at least tried to put down roots. My parents and I have discussed purchasing the land that comprises Rausch Gap under a human LLC and building a village where immortals and hybrids living in the human world can find shelter. It fits perfectly with your goal of protecting our species."

"I think having a safe haven in this realm is a fantastic idea, but I would never settle there. I'm too restless and only know how to live on the move."

Cocking a brow, he said, "More like *on the run*. Don't you ever want to stop running?"

With a frustrated laugh, she ran a hand through her hair. "You'll never get it, Tor. Someone like you will never understand what it's like to be hunted by the very person who created you." Shifting, she stared deeper into his eyes. "And I'm so glad. I don't want that for you. You deserve better."

"Esme—"

"You have a whole kingdom to inherit," she interjected. "Once I'm gone and Brienne and Larkin are running point, you have no future in this realm. This discussion is rather pointless."

"What if I told you I wasn't sure I wanted to rule?"

Silence stretched between them as she digested his words. Realizing he was serious, her eyebrows drew together. "Do you have a choice? I thought it was your destiny."

"I think we always have a choice if we're strong enough to push through the fear of making it."

Breathing a laugh, she grinned. "You're an optimist. Should've guessed from your handy-dandy diplomatic skills. Have you ever seen a situation you can't find a solution to?"

Squinting one eye, he pondered. "I don't think so. And my optimism will come in handy since you're a very determined pessimist."

"If you're not determined, what's the point?"

"Fair enough." Tightening his hold, he resumed stroking her shoulder as she pressed her cheek to his chest. Esme was rarely comforted by others, and although she knew it was dangerous to rely on her handsome companion, for some reason, she couldn't find the will to extricate herself from his embrace.

"Tell me about Clayton."

Closing her eyes, she settled against him and began telling stories about her friend. He'd been such a bright soul, and they had shared some fun and poignant times. When she spoke of the brief time they'd dated, Tordor's muscles tensed. It shouldn't have mattered that he was jealous, but something in his possessive reaction elicited a visceral response deep in her bones.

"Our relationship was only romantic for a short time, but he was a good friend," she said, unable to quench the need to reassure him. "I've never had space for romance in my life."

"I haven't had much either," was his soft reply.

Glancing up at him, she arched a brow. "You? Mr. Handsome Slayer-Vamp who's heir to a kingdom? I would've bet my left pinkie the girls threw themselves at you." She held up her pinkie and wiggled it.

Chuckling, he gave the wiggling digit a playful squeeze. "You assume a lot of things about me, Esme. Instead of assuming, maybe you should get to know me. On a deeper level than as your partner in the ITU. I'd certainly like to get to know you better." His voice was husky as he tucked a strand of hair behind her ear. Blood pounded through her veins as she gazed up at him.

"I didn't mean to assume," she said, curious about the secrets floating in his eyes, "but I've never allowed myself to grow close to people. In case you haven't noticed, I'm kind of a loner and I don't want anyone to get hurt."

"Oh, I've noticed—" he droned as her phone rang. Startled, they both shifted, and Esme lifted it to her ear.

"Hello? General Markson?"

"Hello, Esmerelda. Clayton's body has been cremated and his ashes are ready for pickup. My men left them in locker #737 in the south corridor of the Union Station train terminal. The code to locker's keypad is 3763, which corresponds to 'ESME' on a phone keypad. Do you need me to text it to you?"

"No, I'll remember. Thank you for doing this, General. That was fast."

"These matters require urgent attention. The media is reporting that a homeless man was shot by a stray bullet that resulted from an argument between two unidentified armed tourists. It explains the occurrence and creates a plausible story."

"Thank you," Esme said, realizing how powerful Clayton's contact truly was. Not only did he have access to the highest levels of US government, but he apparently had contacts at media outlets as well. "We're going to return to the abandoned town in Pennsylvania we've been using as a base camp. I need a day to regroup and strategize against my father. Then I'll be in contact to implement our plan."

"I'll await your call. Be safe, Esme."

The phone went dead and she glanced up at Tordor. "As much as I was enjoying our rather serious discussion, I think we should hit the road. I'd like to get back to Rausch Gap and check on the team before it gets too late."

"Agreed, but I reserve the right to resume our serious discussion at a later date," he teased. Extending his hand, he asked, "Want me to drive?"

Plucking the keys from her pocket, she handed them to him. "Sure. You can double park while I retrieve Clayton's ashes from the train terminal."

Empathy crossed his features. "Okay."

They headed out, Esme overcome with equal parts sadness at retrieving her friend's remains and gratefulness for the steadfast immortal at her side.

J axon attended Adelyn's birthday party and had a great time chatting with Latimus, Kenden and the rest of the royal family. Heden attended with his wife, Sofia, and their twins, both of whom had just graduated high school in the human world. An hour after Jaxon had settled into the festivities, Heden pulled him to the side to give him the materials he'd prepared.

"Here's your ID, credit card, passport, cash and all the other essentials," he said, pointing to them as he placed them atop the wooden picnic table. "In the human world, you'll be Jaxon Trammell, since that was your father's name."

"It was a good one," Jaxon said, looking over the items before placing them in the bag he'd brought. "I'll do my best to find Tatiana and figure out how to deter Dakath. I'm thankful to have a mission again and looking forward to it."

"You don't hate the human world like some other immortals I know," Heden said, curiosity simmering in his ice-blue eyes. "Did you learn that affinity somewhere, or were you born with it like my annoying big sister?"

"I'll pretend I didn't hear that," Arderin droned from several feet away, rolling her eyes as she sipped her drink. "And *you're* the most annoying sibling. Everyone knows that."

"I'd argue you're both exasperating," Sathan said, uttering an *"ouch"* when Arderin punched his arm. "Stop hitting me. I should be your favorite brother for letting you go to the human world and become a doctor."

"No one ever *lets* my wife do anything," Darkrip interjected, sliding an arm around her waist. "I learned a long time ago she'll just drive you insane until you capitulate."

Arderin landed a resounding punch on her husband's arm, causing him to scowl before nipping at her lips. "Careful, princess. I fight back. Or maybe you'd like that—"

"Okay, chill with the lovey-dovey shit before I puke," Evie chimed in, jutting her finger to the back of her throat and fake gagging. "Plus, Lila's about to have a heart attack we're discussing something as improper as *sex* at her daughter's party." Dramatically lifting the back of her hand to her forehead, Evie sighed. "*Oh goddess...bring me the vapors...*"

Haughtily lifting her chin, Lila huffed. "I'm doing no such thing. But I do think we should keep the conversation light and fun since this is a party." Tossing Evie a haughty glare, she pivoted and trailed to the punch table.

"Our parents are weird," Evie's daughter Rinada said, rubbing her chin as she spoke to Callie, Jack and Adelyn.

"For real," Callie said. "Thank the goddess we're all perfectly normal."

Jack snickered, causing them all to devolve into laughter as Jaxon and Heden observed the reverie.

"Gotta love my family," Heden said. "Every strange and crazy one of them." Facing Jaxon, he grinned. "Anyway, your supplies are here and you're good to go. If you need anything once you're over there, I'm only a phone call away. Sofia, the twins and I are heading back to Italy in a few days."

"Thanks, Heden," he said, shaking his hand. "I plan on heading to the human world tomorrow morning and will be sure to call you if I need anything. I spoke to Kenden earlier about the lost Elven scrolls and he mentioned you have a close relationship with Tatiana. Any pointers?"

"Eh, maybe closer than some, but she's still an enigma to me. I still don't understand what her motive is in the big scheme of things. It was important to her to help Callie fulfill the prophecy and eradicate the ether, and we now know she's half-Elf, but..." Drifting off, he rubbed his bearded chin. "I just can't figure out her angle...what she truly wants to accomplish. If you can, you'll be my hero." Patting him on the back, Heden smiled. "She's a very valuable asset, but she's also squirrely. Good luck. You're going to need it."

"Thanks. I've always loved a challenge." He gave a good-natured salute. "For now, I'll enjoy the rest of the party and head home to catch some Zs before I depart in the morning."

"Before you go, you have to hear this new playlist I put together," Heden said, dragging him to the DJ booth he'd set up for the party. "Dude, it's epic. You're going to love it."

"I'm not really a fan of human music, but I'll give it a try."

Heden removed his phone, hooking it up to the sound system and pressing play. Loud, booming music began to blare from the speakers and Miranda and Arderin both covered their ears before yelling, "*Heden!*"

"I know you two love my sweet jams," he yelled over the music, pumping his fist in time to the music. "Come on, ladies. You have to dance to this!"

Overcome with laughter, Jaxon watched Sofia rush over and tug the cord from the phone before grabbing her husband's sleeve and dragging him behind the house. It was a while before they reappeared, Sofia's curly black hair extending in several various directions it hadn't been in before they vanished.

"Still glad you came?" Latimus asked, arching a brow as he stepped into place beside him. "My family's a little much."

"Honestly, it's really cool to see. I'm kind of a loner, but you all make companionship look good. Thanks for inviting me, Latimus."

"Anytime. I look forward to your first report, Jaxon. Safe travels."

Jaxon stayed until the festivities wound down and then walked home under the setting sun, invigorated for the mission ahead.

Chapter 7

D akath, King of the Elves, rested his thin, pale fingers on the windowsill, methodically tapping his nails in a rhythm that was both pleasing and grating as he stared at the mountains below

Pleasing because the rhythm had structure, and Dakath was an immortal who thrived on structure.

Grating because each subsequent tap of his nails mimicked the passing of time and the inevitable consummation of yet another Elven hybrid.

And if there was one thing Dakath hated, it was an addition of impurity to the bloodline he was tasked with keeping pristine.

Eons ago, Dakath had been an Elf like any other in their small haven of the immortal world. There had been no need for kings or leaders, not with a species as simple and loving as the Elves. But their simplicity had been their downfall; their inability to comprehend danger and destruction their ultimate weakness.

The flood had washed away their innocence, ripping away their families and children as if they'd never existed. The scant few who escaped through the ether to the unknown world beyond were shaken to their core. Dakath had recognized the need to build anew, and he'd been determined to build a better, stronger species from the dust the flood left behind.

When he'd declared himself king, the others had gladly pledged their allegiance. Together, they built a village far away from the prying eyes of humans, and then another village, and more...until they had an interconnected web of Elven settlements throughout the European continent.

Perhaps that was why the Carpathian Mountains of Romania had always felt like home, he thought, gazing over the rugged mountaintops as he scanned the horizon. The Carpathians weren't his favorite place in the human world—that designation would always belong to Denmark, where he'd met Dyana—but they were "home" as much as any place he'd known since his world was destroyed.

Never in his most vivid nightmares had he envisioned a world where Elves wanted to procreate with humans. After all, the species was so inferior Dakath considered them ants to be stepped on when the need arose. By the gods, they were *mortal.* Procreation between the infernal beasts and his pristine species should've never been possible. Unfortunately, biology seemed to have other ideas, and his kinsmen and women couldn't seem to help themselves.

Dakath remembered the day the first human-Elven hybrid was brought before him, here in this very castle. The guards had dragged the simpering human female as she clung to her child, its slightly pointed ears a clear representation of its heritage, pushing her to stand in the middle of the circle comprised of Dakath and his nine council members. The woman trembled as he leaned forward in his throne. It was imposing, much bigger than the other council members' tall chairs, although they still emanated a formidable vibe. One that indicated anyone who stood before them was subject to the fate and will of the council.

"Who fathered this child?" Dakath asked, rising as he pointed to the mother. Sobs emanated from her throat as she held the baby with shaking arms. "Speak now, or your human and her spawn will perish!"

Silence pulsed through the room, the Elves that had gathered to watch in the wings both terrified and awed by the display of power.

"One last chance," Dakath droned, stepping forward and lifting his hand. It began to glow a dark green, comprised of the powers he'd been gathering for centuries as he'd traveled through the human world. Few of his kinsmen had figured out their kind could generate magic in the human world if they only dedicated the time to study and wield it. Yet another reason Dakath considered himself the superior being in his species; the perfect leader to mold them into the immortals they were meant to be.

"No one has the courage to claim them? To stand up and admit what you've done?" Spittle flew from his lips as he spoke with rage. "So be it." Opening his fingers wide, he concentrated on the glowing energy, condensing it into a tight ball on his palm.

"It was I!" an Elf yelled, stepping forward and rushing to the woman's side. "I met Yilani in the village and we fell in love. I am sorry, King." Bowing, the Elf appeared contrite as he stepped in front of the woman and child. "Please spare them. If anyone must die, it should be me."

"I appreciate your willingness to *finally* come forth, Wallace," he said, arching a brow. "I knew all along it was you."

Fear entered the man's eyes. "You did, my king?"

"Yes. But your willingness to step forward—to claim this abomination—will actually help me. Perhaps I can show you some grace for that."

"I have no wish to defy your orders or disappoint the council. I just want to live a quiet life with my wife and child."

"Your *wife*?" Dakath sneered. "You know marrying outside the species is forbidden."

"I cannot help who I love, sire."

Making a *tsk, tsk, tsk* sound, Dakath leaned forward, shaking his finger in the man's face as he trembled. "I will kill you swiftly to thank you for the opportunity you've given me to demonstrate appropriate punishment."

Fast as lightning, Dakath plunged the ball of energy into Wallace's temple, backing away and extending his fingers, directing the energy field to expand and envelop the woman and child as well. Once they were surrounded, Dakath slowly touched the pad of his middle finger to his thumb. With one ominous snap, the small family was incinerated as the energy field disappeared, leaving a pile of ashes on the cold stone ground.

Lifting his arms, palms facing the domed ceiling, Dakath addressed the room, voice booming as he reveled in the power of wielding lives in the palm of his hands. "Don't look away, my people. This is what becomes of those who mingle with humans. We were cast from our world once by an angry god who wished to exterminate us. Now that we have been given a second chance, do you really wish to ruin it by diluting our bloodline?" His breath formed soft, angry pants as he gazed into the crowd. "With *mortals*, no less?"

Grumbles of, "No, *my king*," and "No, *we don't, sire*," permeated the chamber.

"Good. Go forth and remember this day. Know that if you associate or procreate with humans, this will be your fate. Council is adjourned!"

The subjects scampered back to their surrounding homes with many of the council members disseminating thereafter. Most had kept their eyes averted, but one had glared at him straight on, seemingly unafraid of Dakath's powers.

"What, brother?" he asked, sliding back into his massive throne. "It is imperative we train the people to keep the species cohesive and separate."

"Careful, brother," Gillam said, rising from his seat to Dakath's right. "Small displays of power create respect, but large displays of heartlessness create dissent."

"No one will dissent from me," Dakath snapped. "I am the leader of our people and have their best interests at heart. Comingling with humans will do us no favors."

"Humans are evolving quickly, brother. They evolved from Bronze to Iron in a matter of centuries. In a few more, they could become the dominant species."

Scoffing, Dakath waved a dismissive hand. "Impossible."

Gillam had only cocked a derisive eyebrow before giving a firm nod and exiting the chamber.

Now, all these centuries later, Dakath admitted his brother had been right. Clenching the windowsill, he could almost feel the foundation crumble beneath his fingers as the mountains below seemed to mock him. All this time, the rolling mountaintops had remained the same, much as Dakath and the Elves had, but humans had evolved.

And by the gods, Dakath hated them for it.

He would always consider them inferior with their infernal wars, their bumbling mistakes and their cursed mortality. Anyone worth his salt knew immortals were superior to those whose time was limited. Even the Slayers and Vampyres, blundering idiots they were, had managed to end their war and unite their species. They would never hold the same reverence as the Elves, but at least they weren't *human*.

Of course, humans had some good qualities. Their knowledge of ancient mystical potions, curses and dark magic rivaled the soothsayers, but those who wielded them were often outsiders in human society. That worked perfectly for Dakath, who could study and steal their knowledge and usually kill them without anyone mourning the loss.

Their scientific advancements had also been vast over the past century, and Dakath had implemented that technology to ensure he could travel stealthily across the globe and remain hidden.

And lastly, the humans were...in a word...*beautiful*.

Relaxing his grip on the windowsill, Dakath closed his eyes and allowed *her* face to form in his mind. Thick, golden hair atop light green eyes surrounded by a button-tipped nose and freckles the color of autumn leaves...

"*Dyana...*" he whispered to no one but himself and the haunting memories.

It had been centuries since he'd last seen that face, although he was sure the vision would never fade. He'd been obsessed by her beauty...entranced by her laugh. He'd murdered her for it and to this day continued to punish her by torturing their daughter with the endless game of cat-and-mouse he now thrived on.

The game brought him sick pleasure, knowing Dyana was watching from the Great Beyond...knowing she couldn't stop him...hurting each time he inflicted arduous pain on Esmerelda.

Did he feel guilty? Absolutely not. Esmerelda was the vestige of the only terrible decision he'd ever made. In a strange way, he needed her, if only to remind himself of the consequences of weakness. In that vein, he would continue to torture her, reveling in her anguish and relishing the pain it caused her mother as she inevitably watched from afar.

"Sire?" his servant, Trembly, called, interrupting his thoughts as he strode into the room.

"Yes."

"The Slayer Clayton is dead, as you requested. Shot in front of her. As you anticipated, she contacted the human general and he secretly disposed of the body."

"Good," Dakath said, steepling his fingers as he leaned against the sill. "And has she gone into hiding to lick her wounds? I do always enjoy when she hides away from the world like the rodent she is."

Trembly worked his jaw, appearing to search for words. "I regret to inform you that we lost their trail, sir. I was sure our men would track her to the site where they've been hiding, but we still haven't found it."

Bristling, his features contorted. "Unacceptable. I thought that once we located Clayton, he would lead us to their base."

"We will continue to track the human, General Markson. His security detail makes it difficult, and he sometimes uses decoys, but she will eventually meet with him."

Narrowing his eyes, Dakath slowly pivoted to stare out the window. "In the meantime, where are we with the poisonings of the human-Elven hybrids targeted this month?"

"Eight down and two to go. As you know, our only unsuccessful target in the past year was the boy in the Arizona desert because Tatiana intervened. Otherwise, our kill stats are perfect."

Dakath gritted his teeth at the mention of the woman's name. She was a meddling thorn in his side he'd never been able to vanquish. "Good. No more failures, do you hear me?" He lifted a finger. "And once we eliminate the identified targets, we'll need to send investigators to find more Elven hybrids. I know Tatiana has done her best to hide many of them from me. I won't rest until they're all exterminated."

"Yes, my king." He bowed and clicked his heels before exiting the room.

"Well, well, daughter," Dakath muttered, running his fingertip along the window frame. "You eluded my men. How stealthy." Scowling, his nostrils flared as he formed a tight fist. "Have you finally decided to grow a backbone? Perhaps the immortal heir is filling your head with delusions of grandeur you don't deserve."

Scowling, he observed a hawk fly above the tree line as he pondered.

"No matter," he said, flicking his wrist, his eyes lighting with desire when the hawk caught a smaller bird in his beak mid-flight. "For I am the hawk and you are the prey, dear daughter. Forgetting that will take you down an unreturnable path. I thought you'd learned that lesson, but perhaps I need to remind you."

Stepping away from the window, Dakath headed to his chambers as anger at his daughter and rage for his twisted, enduring, indomitable love for the long-dead human who'd borne her burned in his chest.

Chapter 8

Esme was quiet as Tordor drove them home. She held the small box that contained Clayton's ashes in her hands the entire way, and the poignant image tugged at Tordor's heartstrings. Although he was comfortable with the silence, he decided to try to lighten the mood. Switching on the radio, he searched until he landed on a human pop station.

The DJ announced the song and Madonna's voice echoed through the speakers. Closing her eyes, Esme began to sing...softly at first, but growing into the melody as "Crazy for You" hit the first chorus. Unable to control his grin, Tordor watched her from the corner of his eye, taken with the wistful expression on her pretty features. Looking over at him, she continued to sing, head lolling on the headrest as she sang in perfect tune to the final chorus.

"Wow," he said, impressed. "That was good. Didn't know you liked human pop music."

Wrinkling her nose, she shrugged. "I'm a damn sucker for it. What can I say? I've lived a long time and was stuck with classical music for centuries." She mimicked gagging. "So *boring*. At least pop music has a beat and some melody."

"How old are you anyway? You look like you went through your immortal change in your late twenties."

"Early thirties," she corrected. "But flattery will get you everywhere."

Chuckling, he winked. "Noted."

Absently gazing at the dashboard, her fingers slowly stroked the wooden box in her lap. "I was born sometime in the Middle Ages, in Svendborg,

Denmark. Record keeping wasn't that great back then, but I was probably born in the year 950 or 951 A.D."

"Wow," he said, pursing his lips. "You're really old."

Tossing back her head, she broke into joyful laughter. "Not nearly as old as most immortals, but considering I'm a human-Elven hybrid, I'm old as molasses for humans."

"You must've seen so much," he said, awed by how much time she'd spent on the planet. "I love my realm, but it's not particularly exciting."

"Maybe not to you, but perspective is in the eye of the beholder. I thought it was lovely when I stayed at Uteria before we left to travel here. Your parents were very generous hosts and I really enjoyed meeting them."

"They're pretty awesome. I'm wise enough to know how lucky I am to be their son. And if they have their way, I might have a sibling soon."

"No way," she said, mouth opening in excitement. "Are they trying to have another kid?"

"Yeah," he said, excited at the thought. Not only would it add to his rather large, close-knit family, but his parents would be thrilled.

And it might take the pressure off to take over the kingdom...

Brushing away the inner dialogue, he continued. "I hope it happens for them. Being pregnant with me was tough for my mom, and I think my dad is slightly terrified. But he's willing to risk it because Mom wants another baby and he'd do anything for her. It's kind of cute in a barf-worthy way."

"True love," she sighed, leaning back on the headrest. "So rare, but I guess some people do actually find it."

"Well, little Elf, I hate to tell you this, but it's hard to fall in love if you insist on traveling the world alone. You do know that, right?" He scrunched his features to soften the words.

"I might not be an expert in love, but I *do* understand that," she droned, sticking out her tongue in an adorable gesture that made his heart flip. "That's *why* I travel alone."

"Touché," he teased, loving their playful banter.

"Oh, this is a good one!" she exclaimed, reaching forward to turn up the volume. "'Careless Whisper' by George Michael. So angsty. Sing with me." Closing her eyes, she leaned on the headrest and began to croon. Tordor had never heard the song before, but as he observed her wistful expression, he decided it was the best damn song ever invented. She was achingly beautiful when she sang, and he vowed to find opportunities to have her do it more in his presence.

Thirty minutes and nine soulful pop songs later, they arrived at Rausch Gap, and Tordor drove down the winding dirt road that led to their camp. Their team had decided to set up large tents for shelter and privacy. All that remained of the town that had thrived there in the late 1800s were a few stone foundations from former homes and businesses. The dense woods and remote location offered the perfect hidden base for their team.

As they exited the car, Tordor eyed the box in her hands. "Do you want to spread Clayton's ashes?"

Nodding, she tenderly caressed the box. "I'd like to do it in the morning as the sun rises over the creek." She tilted her head toward the direction of the creek that ran behind the site.

"Do you want to do it alone?" Cupping her shoulder, he gazed into her eyes. "I want to support you, but I don't want to impose."

Her nostrils flared slightly as she contemplated. Finally, she gave a firm nod. "I'd love to have you there. I'll text the team, and they can come too if they want." She glanced at the tents where the others were sleeping.

"Perfect. I'm so sorry, Esme."

"Me too. He didn't have any family that I knew of, so I'm honored to send him to the Passage…or heaven…or the Great Beyond. Or maybe all three."

Lowering his hand, he let her go, although every cell in his body was screaming with the need to comfort her. She uttered a soft, "Good night," and trailed into her tent.

Entering his own, Tordor prepped for bed and lay down, sliding his hands under his head on the pillow. Allowing the anger to surface at the senseless loss of life, he vowed to succeed for his people and for Clayton, the first victim in their effort to amalgamate the two worlds.

T he next morning, Esme burrowed into her sleeping bag, squeezing her eyes at the faint sound of chirping birds. Wishing with all her might she'd dreamed yesterday's events, she rolled over and spied the wooden case that contained Clayton's ashes. As her eyes welled, she acknowledged he was gone.

Wanting to be strong for her friend who'd made the ultimate sacrifice, she rose and dressed before picking up the ashes and heading outside.

Breaking into a soulful smile, her heart leaped at the sight before her. Her entire team was waiting, lined up in a show of silent support, ready to walk with her to the creek.

Swallowing the lump in her throat, she acknowledged them with a nod before beginning the walk to the water. Tordor fell into step beside her as the others walked quietly behind them. When they arrived at the creek, they lined up alongside the gently gurgling water as Esme removed the bag that held the ashes.

"Thank you for connecting us with General Markson, Clay," she said, holding the bag over the water. "He's a valuable asset, and your contribution to our cause will never be forgotten. May you have a fantastic journey in your next voyage. We send you all our love and gratitude." Gently shaking the bag, she dispersed the ashes over the water.

They floated away, mingling with the leaves and small branches that floated atop the creek. Tordor's strong arm surrounded her shoulders, and she closed her eyes, reminding herself not to get used to his unwavering support. It would make it that much harder when their inevitable separation arrived.

And yet despite knowing her reliance on him could be disastrous, she settled into his firm body and soaked up his energy. He was such a calm, kind presence in a life that had rarely experienced either.

After a few minutes, she drew away and turned to face the team. "Thank you all for coming with me. Clay wouldn't want us to spend time mourning him. He fought with the humans to secure peace in their world, and the best way to do that is to continue our mission."

Tordor's phone chimed and he stepped away to answer it.

"Head back to camp and we'll be there shortly," she directed the others. "We'll sit down and discuss next steps."

After they departed, she waited for Tordor to finish the call.

"Good news?" she asked.

"Definitely. Latimus is sending Jaxon Trammell to Arizona to track down Tatiana. He's an extremely competent investigator."

"Excellent. Let's update the team, and we'll form a plan. They're waiting for us at camp."

Energized from the touching ceremony and good news, Esme felt a small bit of tension release from her shoulders as they began their trek back.

"**I**f anyone can find Tatiana, it's Jaxon," Tordor said, updating the team as they sat around the woodpile used for cooking dinner each night. "Latimus will keep us updated."

"In the meantime, I'm open to discussing other ways we can diminish my father's efforts," Esme said, rubbing her thighs. "Since physical combat isn't an option, considering we don't want to start a war, we need to strategize other possibilities." Lifting her brows, she looked between the members of her team. "Tell me what you've got, guys."

"As I said yesterday, I might have a lead," Larkin said.

Esme nodded, urging him to continue.

"I know an immortal in the human world who is proficient at making formulas and potions that can interfere with immortal powers, but I'll have to locate him. I have an idea of where to look, but I'm not sure how long it will take."

"Is he a friend?" Brienne asked, crossing one long leg over the other as she leaned on her palms atop the soft grass.

Larkin arched a sardonic brow. "I threatened to kill him if I ever saw him again, so I'd say 'friend' is a stretch. He worked with Bakari until he realized he was on the wrong side of the battle. Ultimately, he chose to defect from Bakari at the end. I'm not sure if he could be swayed to help us, but it's worth a shot."

"You think he could concoct some potions to counteract my father's poisons?" Esme asked.

"Yes. If your father is targeting us and one of his preferred methods is poison, it seems invaluable to have an ally who can create something to counteract his methods."

"You'd have to vet him and make sure he can be trusted."

"Absolutely."

"You had me at the whole '*I told him I'd kill him*' thing," Brienne said, making quotation marks with her fingers. "Sounds hella interesting. I'll go with you to find him."

"Fine with me as long as everyone agrees."

The team gave their unanimous consent, and Esme breathed a small sigh of relief. "Okay, you two will track down this immortal..."

"Dr. Tyson," Larkin said.

"You two will find Dr. Tyson," she continued, ticking her fingers as she spoke. "And Jaxon is going to locate Tatiana."

"In the meantime, we need to fortify our camp here to ensure we stay safe," Tordor said, gesturing around the site. "So far, this has been temporary, but I want to talk to my parents about making this place permanent. We can purchase the land and build fortified homes and buildings."

"I like the sound of an immortal safe haven," the spunky soldier Larissa said, stretching out her legs. "This realm is a lonely place for us. I ended up here after my father deserted the Slayer army centuries ago. He only survived a few years longer than my human mother."

"I don't have anyone either," a male soldier named Nikolas said. "I like the idea of building something permanent here."

"I have a brother who's great at construction," their team member Frederick said. "He lives in California with my Slayer parents, who escaped the immortal realm during the War of the Species. He has no desire to be a soldier, but he could build us some damn fine houses."

"Let's keep that in our back pocket once we accomplish the tasks we've discussed here this morning," Esme said. "For now, you all can hold down the fort here while Tordor and I head back to DC to begin the process with General Markson."

"I'd like to volunteer as one of the immortals who infiltrates the human government," Larissa said, raising her hand. "I've passed as human for decades and think I could help the cause."

"Then we'll make sure you're able to enter the vetting process," Esme said. "The immortal royals have already nominated some candidates from their realm. Between our team and their candidates, I have faith our first fifteen placements will pave the path for future success."

"For now, I'll keep an eye on these vagabonds," Larissa said with a crooked smile at the team. "We've got your back, boss."

Esme grinned, admiring her leadership and affable demeanor. "Thank you. Please stay safe, guys. I can't lose you. Every one of you is valued and important. Remember that."

The team returned the sentiment, rising and wishing those who were departing well on their journeys. Facing her, Tordor pointed to his tent. "Want to call my parents first? Then we can contact Markson and let him know we're coming to DC."

"Sure." Following him, she stepped into his tent and sat on the soft sleeping bag. He lowered beside her and opened his laptop on his thick thighs, his shoulder touching hers so they could both see the screen. Pulling up the video chat app Heden and Sofia had developed years ago, they initiated the call with Miranda and Sathan.

Chapter 9

Miranda sat beside her husband on their massive four-poster bed, allowing him to take the helm during the video chat with Tordor and Esme. While Sathan discussed purchasing and developing the Rausch Gap site, as well as the plans to track down Dr. Tyson and Tatiana, Miranda watched her son...and the *very* interesting interplay with the woman at his side.

Esme sat beside him, dwarfed by his large frame, much as Miranda was by Sathan's muscular body. As they spoke, Esme often looked to Tordor for confirmation, her body swaying toward his almost imperceptibly. Tor would smile back, his gaze tender and affectionate toward his partner, and Miranda's heart almost burst wide open.

Her son was falling in love.

It was strikingly obvious to her in the reverence with which he spoke and the way he unconsciously touched her arm or brushed her hair behind her shoulder. Miranda didn't even think he knew he was performing the actions, but *she* knew, and goddess, if it didn't just make her want to weep and laugh with joy all at once.

Sathan poked her arm and she winced, covering the spot and scowling. "Ouch! What the hell, blood-sucker?"

"Are you even pretending to listen?" he asked, arching a sardonic brow. "Our son just said that he and Esme will be in DC for at least a week to meet with General Markson."

"Of course I was listening," she lied, rubbing her arm. "You two better stay safe, you hear me? I don't want anything happening to you."

"Yes, she's obviously racked with worry, as evidenced by her attention to this call," Sathan droned.

Rolling her eyes, she gave a *pfft* before continuing. "I'm on board with buying Rausch Gap and the surrounding land. We'll work with Heden to hire a lawyer and form the LLC so we can expedite the process."

"Latimus will also keep us updated on Jaxon's progress," Sathan said, gliding his arm over Miranda's shoulders and absently rubbing her upper arm. She leaned into him, bursting with anticipation at discussing Tordor's crush as soon as they ended the call.

"Hopefully Tatiana will be willing to help us strategize against my father," Esme said. "I'd feel terrible if he compromised the mission. If his interference becomes too meddlesome, I'll leave the team. I won't be responsible for the integration between the realms failing. We have to get this right."

"Absolutely not," Tordor said, shaking his head. "I've tried to tell her she's stuck with us, but she's stubborn."

Esme shot him a good-natured glare. "I like being stubborn. And I won't jeopardize the mission."

"I knew I liked you," Miranda said, resting her head on Sathan's shoulder. "Stubborn women are my jam."

"Coming from the woman who once tried to murder me, that's a solid endorsement," Sathan muttered.

"Oh god, that again?" she exclaimed, rearing back with an incredulous expression. "I didn't even *try*. You do know that if I wanted you dead, we'd be having this video chat at your gravesite, right?"

Sathan's lips thinned. "Let's leave the dramatics to Arderin, dear."

"Don't you 'dear' me," she said, straightening and pointing her finger in his face. Sathan just nipped her finger, causing her small flare of anger to wither away. "Stop being cute," she pouted. "I'm trying to tell our son how tough I am and how I let you live because I needed your stupid royal blood."

Laughing, Tordor shook his head. "Okay, this is where they start flirting and it gets weird," he said to Esme. "Time for us to cut out. I'll call you from DC to let you know we're safe."

"Thanks, sweetie," Miranda said, sparing one last glance at the tender smile he gave Esme. "Talk soon."

Ending the chat, Sathan closed the laptop and stood, setting it on the dresser. Turning to her, he tilted his head. "I swear, woman. Decades into this marriage and you could still drive a saint mad."

Rising, she approached him and patted his face—a bit *too* hard—just to remind him who was boss. "Well, then, my dear bonded, it's a good thing you're nowhere near sainthood."

His arm snaked through the air, grasping her wrist as she gasped. Chuckling in that deep timbre that always drove her wild, he leaned down, the tip of his nose brushing against hers. "You little minx. Something's got you riled up. What is it?"

Feeling her lips curve, joy emanated from her frame as she gazed into his eyes. "Can't you see it? He's falling in love, Sathan. Our baby is falling in love."

Those dark eyes considered for a moment before the corner of his lips ticked up. "You think so?"

"I know it. The way he gazes at her...the admiration in his voice when they talk. It's so sweet..." Tears burned her eyes as emotion overwhelmed her.

"Don't cry, sweetheart," he soothed, pulling her close and stroking her hair. "This is a good thing." Drawing back, he assessed her. "Right?"

Laughing, she wiped her nose and nodded. "Yes, I think it is. And I love when you ask me what to think."

"I did no such thing," he said, gently pushing her toward the bed. "I'm just trying to understand which of your thousand moods you're in. They can be quite overwhelming."

The backs of Miranda's legs met the bed. "Careful, blood-sucker," she warned, lifting her inner thigh to slowly caress his. "I can lodge my knee in so many creative places right now—"

His arms weaved around her, cutting her off as he lifted her and dropped her on the bed. Stifling a giggle, she shook her head. "Oh, no. You do *not* get to kiss me after telling me I'm moody—"

Looming over her, he stole a kiss as he straddled her. Resting his palms on each side of her head, his eyes flared with lust. "Oh, dear wife, I'm going to do much more than kiss you."

Lifting her arms above her head, she flashed the sultry grin that set his body on fire. "So, what are you waiting for?"

A desire-laden breath exited his lungs as he gently caressed her cheek. "Miranda," he whispered, fangs glowing in the sunlight that filtered through the curtains. "How are you still so fucking beautiful? I love you, sweetheart."

Tears filled her eyes like a damn sap as she brought her hands to cup his cheeks. "*Sathan...*"

And then all words ceased to exist as her bonded ripped away their clothes, tossing them to the floor as he bared their heated skin. His lips caressed every inch he'd revealed, kissing her neck...then her collarbone...toward the valley between her breasts...before taking one of her taut nipples deep in his wet mouth.

"Yesss..." she hissed, threading her fingers in his thick hair.

Each time with him was a combination of old and new, and she reveled in the way he loved her, as if he cherished her more than anything upon Etherya's Earth. After so many years together, he played her body like the finest instrument—in tune with her desires but always reaching for the next level of perfection.

Kissing a trail down her abdomen, he took his time at her C-section scar, peppering it with kisses as she stroked his hair. Debating whether to interrupt their sexy times, she pondered as he gazed up at her.

"What is it, sweetheart?"

Gently twining his hair in her fingers, she grinned. "I'm late. Almost a week now. And my cycle is pretty damn regular."

His eyes widened, glowing with pleasure and a slight twinge of the possessive pride she found so attractive. Spreading his palms over her belly, he caressed her with reverence. "Are you sure?"

"I don't know, but if you think I'm moody now, I'd stock up on patience just to be safe. It's been a while since I was pregnant, but I remember being a beast."

Tossing back his head, he gave a joyful laugh. "You were a complete nightmare," he teased, eyes glowing as he kissed her stomach. "And I can't wait to see you that way again. When can you take a test?"

"I'm going to have Sadie give me one tomorrow." Pushing his head farther down, she arched an eyebrow. "In the meantime, let's keep practicing just in case."

His sultry chuckle surrounded her as he continued his way to her core. Widening her thighs, she tossed back her head, offering herself to him as his tongue worked its magic, bringing her to her peak.

After her release, as she lay sated and quivering on the mattress, her strong, loving Vampyre rose over her, sliding his fingers in her silky hair as the blunt head of his shaft found her deepest place. Staring deep into her eyes, he began to ease inside...to ease *home*...joining their bodies as deeply as their souls...

"After all this time..." she whispered, overcome with emotion. Perhaps it was from seeing her son falling in love. Perhaps it was from the hormones coursing through her body. Even though she'd told him she wasn't sure, Miranda knew deep in her bones she was pregnant. Overwhelmed with love for her bonded mate, she undulated against him, so thankful for her strong, stoic Vampyre.

"I know," he rasped, trailing kisses over her cheeks as he worked his cock deep into her shuddering frame. "We're so lucky, Miranda." Lowering his mouth to her neck, he licked her, preparing the soft skin for his invasion.

She braced for it, already anticipating the pleasant sting that would result from that first bite. The points of his fangs pressed into her vein and she arched, begging him for more. Groaning, the pace of his hips increased as he loved her, his soft grunts as he drank urging her toward another orgasm. Lowering his hand, he rubbed the swollen nub under her mound as his shaft ceaselessly pounded her.

Claimed by her mate, she gave everything over to him. Her muscles grew lax as he pummeled her spent body and drank her essence. Growling against her neck, his body tensed, stilling for a moment before it began to jerk. Hot, sticky jets pulsed into her core as he claimed her for what felt like the thousandth time and the first time, rolled together in an intimately pleasurable experience.

Afterward, they lay sweaty and sated, Sathan's fingers trailing through her hair as it fanned over the mattress. Small swipes of his tongue rasped against her neck as he closed her wounds with his self-healing saliva. Eventually, he rose, dragging her sleepy body to the bathroom so they could wash up.

Returning to the bed, she crawled inside, reaching for him as he slid in beside her. Tossing her leg over his broad thighs, she rested her cheek on his chest as he slowly stroked her shoulder.

"Do you think she'll break his heart?" Miranda asked, worry creeping in now that the excitement of realizing Tordor's feelings had died down. "I like Esme a lot, but she seems like a loner who's built a lot of walls."

"I'm not sure," he murmured, kissing her hair. "I certainly hope she doesn't hurt him. But you need to consider something else, Miranda."

Lifting her head, she rested her chin on her fist as her elbow pressed against his chest. "What's that?"

"If he falls for her, he might not ever come home, sweetheart." He caressed the hair at her temple, trying to soften the blow of the realization. "He might not ever take the throne."

Biting her lip, she contemplated as her gaze trailed over the spiky hairs on his chest. "Well, we knew there was a strong possibility he wouldn't rule. He's been honest with us about that."

Sathan nodded.

"Would it disappoint you?"

He squinted at the ceiling as he pondered. "For centuries, I was consumed with having an heir to fulfill my duty. But then you came along and turned my whole damn world upside down—"

"You're welcome," she interjected, playfully rolling her eyes.

Chuckling, he lifted a shoulder. "I just want him to be happy, Miranda. I don't give a shit about anything else."

"Me neither," she said, placing a sweet kiss on his lips. "And since you're going to have another heir, maybe this one will want to rule."

"Maybe so. And if not, I'm happy to rule with you for eternity. Although I do most of the work, you *do* come in handy every once in a while."

"Most of the work," she muttered, tossing a frustrated glare at the ceiling. "I run this damn kingdom and everybody knows it."

Laughing, he shook his head on the pillow. "I think we *both* run this kingdom." He ran his thumb over her jaw. "And I can't imagine ruling with anyone else. You're magnificent, Miranda. My perfect queen."

"I pretend I hate it when you refer to me as *your* queen, but it's a lie because it sends all sorts of shivers through my body."

"I'm *your* king and happy to belong to you, sweetheart."

"Damn it, stop saying sappy shit. The pregnancy hormones are already raging. Let me take a nap, will ya? We've got thirty minutes before I have to get ready for the orientation ceremony of the new school at Takelia."

"Napping usually requires silence," he teased, urging her to lay against his chest. "So, maybe if you stop talking..."

"You're infuriating," she said against his pecs.

"Mm-hmm," he said, his deep chuckle vibrating through her.

After a moment, he spoke against the shell of her ear. "I'm happy for Tor. I don't know if she's going to hurt him, but we'll be there for him no matter what. We did our best, and I want him to find what we found."

"Me too," she whispered, nuzzling against him. "He deserves it, Sathan."

"I know, sweetheart."

Lulled by her bonded's smooth strokes against her skin, Miranda clutched onto the joy she'd felt at seeing her son glow in the presence of the woman he cared for, hoping his path to love wouldn't be too rocky or difficult. As with most things in the immortal existence, only time would tell.

Chapter 10

After the call with Miranda and Sathan, Tordor and Esme packed up everything they would need for their stay in DC. Brienne and Larkin had already hit the road, and they followed shortly behind.

Esme enthralled Tordor with another round of soulful singing as they navigated toward DC. Every so often, she would look over at him and smile, and he wondered when seeing those pretty lips curve had become the primary source of his happiness. She didn't smile nearly often enough, and he vowed to create opportunities that would remedy that.

As they approached the hotel they'd scouted, Esme scrolled through the website on her phone. "The hotel has suites, and it's probably easier if we get one of those. That way, we'll share a communal living space where we can strategize and video chat with General Markson but still have our own bedrooms."

"Why, Esme," he said, covering his heart, "are you asking to share a room with me? We haven't even been on a proper date."

"Nooooo," she said, playfully rolling her eyes. "I'm just trying to be practical. I figured your pragmatic ass would appreciate that." She poked him in the arm.

Laughing, he nodded as he maneuvered into the hotel parking lot. "A suite is a good idea. I'm in."

Grabbing their bags, they checked in at the hotel, reserving a suite for a week. Tordor urged her to lead as they headed up the elevator to the third floor. Once inside, she inspected the suite before pointing between the bedrooms.

"They both have a mini-fridge so you can store your Slayer blood, and both have queen-size beds, so you pick."

"Doesn't matter to me," he said, scoping out the rooms. "This one faces east and probably gets better light. You take that one in case you want to do your morning yoga routine while the sun rises."

A slight flush crossed her cheeks. "You know I do yoga in the morning?"

Embarrassment swelled as he realized he was busted. In truth, he'd discovered her yoga routine when they'd first moved to Rausch Gap. He'd heard rustling outside the tent and peered through the felt to look. She'd stood tall, arms stretched above her head as light filtered through the trees, before bending down to touch her toes.

Tordor's mouth had turned dry as sandpaper as he'd studied her cute backside in the black yoga pants she wore. Then he'd realized he was being a hundred shades of creepy and quickly closed the flap on his tent.

But the thought had lingered in his mind, and the next morning, he heard the rustling yet again. Unable to stop himself, he'd watched her, making sure his eyes remained on her *face* and the peaceful expression that covered her gorgeous features. He wasn't a creeper if he watched her face...right? Unsure, he only knew he didn't possess the willpower to stop.

"Man, I'm sorry, Esme," he said, uncomfortable as he rubbed the back of his neck. "I...I can hear you when you wake up in the morning...you know, since your tent is next to mine..."

Mirth sparkled in her eyes as she arched a brow. "Go on."

Clearing his throat, he wondered if his face was as red as it felt. "I... You just always looked so peaceful, and it helped me feel kind of calm and centered as I woke up." Scraping his hand over his face, he cupped his chin. "I'm really sorry—"

Lifting her hand, she flashed a sympathetic grin. "You should've asked to join me. Morning yoga is very Zen and it helps get the blood flowing."

Relief swished through him as he realized she was letting him off the hook. "I should have. I'd love to do it with you sometime."

Her brows lifted slightly as her grin deepened. "Would you now?"

Laughing at the double entendre, he expelled a deep breath. "I think I'm going to stop talking. I'm digging a really big hole."

Tossing back her head, she laughed, the sound filling him with joy. Thanking the goddess he'd made her smile, he figured a small dose of embarrassment was well worth it.

"You're doing just fine. And yes, you can do morning yoga with me anytime. I'll do it in here in case you want to join me." She gestured around their shared living room. "For now, I'd like to shower since we're living in a place with actual running water, and then we need to call Markson. Since he's insistent on meeting each immortal candidate to vet them in person, we need to put the profiles together so he can begin to comb through them."

"I'll grab a shower too. Our first video chat with Markson is set in an hour, right?"

"Yep. See you back here then."

Pivoting, she headed to her room and softly closed the door behind her.

Heaving a sigh of relief that she wasn't angry, he entered his room to unpack his bag and shower.

J axon stood encased by the red Arizona rocks as the two boys played in the distance. Their mother, Kasa, smiled and crossed her arms to ward off the chill.

"It will get dark soon and you're welcome to stay with us," she said, pointing to the natural cavern they called home.

"Thank you, ma'am, but I actually enjoy sunset hikes. Once it gets too cold, I'll stop off the trail, build a fire and camp for the night." He patted his backpack. "But the info you've given me about Tatiana is invaluable. I appreciate it."

"Any friend of Calinda's is a friend of mine. She saved Nuka and we're grateful."

"I don't know Callie that well, but she's got a good heart. And her Uncle Latimus is one of the best men I know. The royal family of the immortal kingdom is extremely gracious and kind."

Kasa trained her chocolate-colored gaze on him. "Are you worried now that the ether is destroyed? Humans and immortals are very different beings, and we haven't done well in this realm learning to live with each other yet. I wonder how we'll do when an entirely new set of species is introduced."

"I learned a long time ago there's no point in worrying," he said with a shrug. "What's meant to be will be and all that jazz. Tordor and Esme have a plan and a pretty solid team, and I'm going to trust them."

"Sadly, my people have seen the worst of both immortals and humans," she said, kicking the ground with the toe of her sneaker. "Our indigenous people have been persecuted and discriminated against since Europeans arrived here centuries ago. And the Elf king almost succeeded in poisoning Nuka. There's no shortage of evil in the world."

Jaxon gave a solemn nod. "True, but there's also an abundance of goodwill and hope if we choose to see it." Grinning, he lifted a shoulder. "I've always kind of been an optimist."

Laughing, she turned to fully face him and patted his arm. "Good. We need more of those."

"Kasa!" her husband, Lonan, called from inside the cave. "Dinner smells like it's almost ready."

"Coyote stew," she said, jerking her head toward the cavern. "You'd think he could learn to stir it on his own, but men are quite oblivious." She playfully wrinkled her nose.

"You won't get any argument from me on that." He showed her his palms before extending his hand. "Thank you, Kasa."

"You're welcome." Her palm slid over his, and he was impressed with her firm shake. "As discussed, I believe Tatiana is taking respite in the inn on the Northern California coast. She knew the respite might be short-lived, and she might be a bit...*salty*...when you show up. There's no love lost between her and King Dakath. They have a sordid history, of which I only know bits and pieces."

"Lucky for me, salty women are my specialty," he said, huffing on his fingernails and rubbing them on his chest. "I've got this in the bag, Kasa."

Chuckling, she flashed a brilliant smile. "I believe you do. Good luck on your mission, Jaxon Trammell. I will pray for you and ask my ancestors to protect you." Peering at the children, she rubbed her arms. "*All* of our ancestors. None were more surprised than me to learn that Nuka's immortal Elven genes will be expressed. He will become immortal when he goes through his change as an adult. It is...baffling, to say the least, since the gene is suppressed in the rest of our family."

"I'm always happy to keep an eye on him," Jaxon said, placing a hand on her shoulder. "You have my cell number and I hope you won't hesitate to use it."

"You are very kind," she said, eyes glistening in the slowly setting sun. "Thank you."

"Anytime. Enjoy the stew."

"Sure you don't want some?"

He scrunched his features. "Thank you, but I'll stick to Slayer blood."

Nodding, she turned and called to the boys. "Nuka! Adriel! Come and say goodbye to Mr. Trammell."

They ran over, full of energy, and wished him a safe journey. With one final wave, Jaxon began the trek back to his rental car, figuring he could hike for two hours before stopping to camp. He'd get a good night's sleep, and tomorrow, he would begin the drive to California.

Chapter 11

Esme emerged from her room, freshly showered and ready for the video call with General Markson. After setting up the laptop and pulling up the secure video app, she glanced at the time. Wondering if Tordor had fallen asleep, she trailed to his door and knocked.

He opened it, clad in gray sweatpants and...nothing else. *Gulp.* Her eyes ran over his sculpted chest, scattered with tiny black hairs that swirled over his copper nipples. Unable to control her gaze, she lifted it to his bottom lip, noticing it was slightly red. He held a Slayer blood canister, and the thought of him swallowing the thick liquid threatened to set her body on fire.

Had he ever used those sexy half-fangs to drink directly from a Slayer? Touched those full lips to someone's neck to wet the skin before he impaled it in an act of intimate desire?

And why was she envisioning *her* neck as the one he drank from?

"Hey," he said, wiping the blood on the back of his arm. "Am I late?"

"Uh, yeah." She felt like a dolt who'd lost the ability to speak. "The call's in four minutes."

"Sorry. That warm shower felt good. You don't know what you've got until you live in the woods for a few weeks. Be right out."

He slightly closed the door, giving her an opportunity to back away and try and wrangle her hormones into something that didn't resemble a puddle of melted desire. God, but it would be so damn sexy to have him drink from her...

"All set," he said, exiting his room and padding to sit in front of the laptop. He'd put on a black T-shirt—which she found *slightly* disappointing—and she mentally chided her libido to calm down as she lowered beside him. Reaching toward the laptop, she initiated the video call with General Markson.

His face appeared, strong and stoic with russet skin and deep brown eyes behind glasses. His black hair was shaved short, which she knew was characteristic of soldiers in human armies. Straightening, she waved as Tordor leaned in beside her.

"Hi, General Markson. Nice to see your face."

"You too, Esme. And I assume this is the Vampyre royal heir, Tordor."

"Yes, sir," he said with a salute. "Pleasure to meet you."

"I'm sorry Clayton's not here with us. He was a good man, and I aim to carry out the plan we conceived together."

"Thank you, sir," Esme said. "On that note, we thought it best to begin with visual contact to establish trust."

Smiling, he nodded. "You don't look like evil beings who are going to decimate our world, but I've been fooled before."

Breathing a laugh, she looked at Tordor. "I think we're pretty harmless. The immortals have been involved in war and conflict for over a thousand years and they've finally secured peace. They are adamant the transition goes smoothly and wish to avoid any more war."

"The greatest accomplishment of soldiers and leaders is to prevent war," he agreed. "We'll do our best to ensure success."

"The first thing we're going to do is compile profiles on the fifteen immortals and hybrids our team is considering as candidates for the first wave of infiltration."

"Excellent. Once you've compiled them, I'd like you to load everything on a jump drive. I'll set up an in-person meeting for us at a secure location where we can go over each candidate together."

"Will do. We also want to inform you that the immortal royals are going to create a human LLC and purchase the abandoned town of Rausch Gap, Pennsylvania. They want to create a safe haven for any subjects who need refuge in the human world."

Rubbing his chin, Markson nodded. "I see the logic. Rausch Gap is quite rural, so you'll be able to build a village there without much fanfare. Still, I might want to send an undercover unit there once the town is functional, just to ensure things go smoothly. We humans have a penchant for conspiracy theories,"—he grinned and ran his hand over his shorn hair—"and I don't want people thinking something nefarious is going on in central Pennsylvania."

"We're open to that," Tordor said. "We appreciate your help and want this to be a seamless process."

Markson arched a brow. "Seamless is a word we don't hear often in the US military, but I'll remain optimistic."

"Optimist here too," Tordor said, pointing to his chest. "I like the sentiment."

Markson's smart watch chimed, and he glanced at it. "I have to go. Stealing time to conference with you is difficult but a priority I'm committed to. Please contact me when the profiles are ready."

The screen went dark and Esme closed the app. Facing Tordor, she lifted her eyebrows. "Well, my friend, I think we have work to do."

"At your command, boss."

Shivering at the deep tone of his voice, she got to work.

L arkin leaned over, tying his sneaker before rising and pushing the chair under the desk. The hotel in the St. Louis suburbs was functional, and he felt rested after a good night's sleep. Glancing at his phone, he realized he had ten minutes until he needed to meet Brienne in the lobby. After brushing his teeth, he stuffed his belongings into his backpack and unzipped the inside compartment. Reaching inside, he drew out the faded letter. Sitting on the bed, he read it for what must have been the thousandth time.

Larkin,

I'll never know why Latimus chose me to lead the troops he stationed at Uteria. It must've been a divine act of Etherya herself because it led me to you. In our realm of deep tradition and latent prejudice, I wondered if I would ever find a mate. But you, my strong, loyal partner, are everything I always dreamed of.

Positions as great as ours require immense sacrifice, and the chance that both of us will survive long enough to see Crimeous defeated is small. Whether our time together is brief or lasts an infinity, know that I loved you with my entire soul.

Yours,

Takel

Swallowing thickly, Larkin blinked away the wetness, wondering if his eyes would ever remain dry when he read the letter. Did the pain of losing your mate ever truly fade? And when that mate died to save you, wasn't it exponentially more excruciating?

He and Takel had been fighting against the Deamons during one of their raids on Uteria. They always fought so seamlessly together, his massive Vampyre anticipating his moves before Larkin knew he would make them.

Until...well, until they didn't. The battle that night had been particularly bloody and a Deamon had gotten the upper hand, training an eight-shooter directly at Larkin's heart. In those last moments before his imminent demise, Takel's face flashed through Larkin's mind, and he felt profound sorrow that he'd never see him again...or kiss his full lips...or feel his fangs drag across his neck...

But Larkin hadn't died. Instead, Takel had thrown himself in front of him, saving him at the last moment. The poisoned bullets had ravaged Takel's body upon impact, and he'd perished on the muddy ground.

Running his hand through his tawny brown hair, the old rage formed in Larkin's gut as he railed at the world. A soldier as prolific and respected as Takel deserved better than to die on the cold, unyielding ground. Larkin had wanted to comfort him. To throw his body over his lover's and hold him as the last breaths left his lungs. But they'd agreed to keep their relationship secret since old prejudices ran deep in the immortal realm. A Slayer loving a Vampyre was scandalous. A gay interspecies couple was unheard of. Sadly, Takel had died before he could see the kingdom begin to evolve, thanks to new rulers who were much more progressive and accepting.

Larkin had watched his mate perish as Latimus yelled with fury before murdering the Deamon who'd killed him. Larkin wasn't proud to admit it, but watching Latimus stab the bastard in the chest with a sword multiple times had soothed something in his soul, if only slightly.

In honor of his service, King Sathan and Queen Miranda named the newest compound after his former mate: Takelia. It was a small token of honor Larkin carried with him as he continued in his immortal life, knowing he could search for eternity and never find anyone like Takel.

In the bleakest moments, when he missed his mate so vehemently he thought his heart might crumble in his chest, Larkin would hear Takel's deep voice in his head.

You made an oath to your queen, Larkin. The realm needs you, and your people need you.

It was because of this oath, and Larkin's inherent sense of duty, that he didn't take his own life. Although he wished for nothing more than to reunite with Takel in the Passage, he understood his people needed him. Miranda had bestowed her trust upon him all those decades ago when he'd helped her defeat her father, and then Crimeous, and he wouldn't dishonor her by neglecting his duties.

So, he carried on, and eventually, the pain began to fade. It crept from a constant ache in his soul to a dull burning in his heart. Now, many decades later, it was just a latent pulsing. Strong enough to remind him of Takel's role in his life, but not smothering as it once had been. And for that, Larkin was grateful.

"Well, lover," he said softly, folding the letter and tucking it back in his bag, "I think I've taken long enough to remember you today. Hope you're at peace in the Passage. This old soldier has to get to work." Slinging his bag over his shoulder, he headed downstairs to find Brienne.

She gave him a curt nod when he approached, and Larkin inwardly admitted how much he liked the female Slayer-Elven hybrid. He didn't know her well, but she possessed an innate tactical knowledge and a brisk, no-nonsense attitude. It was a perfect complement for someone as focused as he, and they made a good team.

He also suspected that Brienne was gay, creating another silent tether that bonded them. Although immortals had become much more progressive under Queen Miranda, Governor Evie and Princess Arderin's tutelage, there were always more advancements that could be made. Of course, Brienne had been born in the human world, and Larkin found himself curious about her past. How had her immortal parents ended up in the human world, and how had they met to create her? Were they still alive? Did she have any siblings or perhaps a lover she visited when she wasn't on assignment for the Immortals Transition Unit?

They were all interesting questions that Larkin would ask her eventually. For now, they had a job to do, and both of them were ready to accomplish their task.

"I settled up for you too," Brienne said, clutching the straps of her backpack. She was almost as tall as his six-foot height, and he liked the fact he could look her straight in the eye when they spoke.

"Thank you. Do you want to drive, or should I?"

Arching a sardonic brow, she held up the keys to their rental car. "Since you purebred immortals lived in the stone ages for the majority of eternity, I think you should let the hybrid with the human-world experience drive."

Chuckling at her snarky sense of humor, he nodded. "Fine with me."

Falling into step, they headed to the rental car. Once inside, Larkin strapped on his seat belt as Brienne revved the engine.

"What are the chances Dr. Tyson is going be at the location?"

Larkin's features drew together as she pulled out of the parking lot. "Fifty-fifty. He used to live in the house we're heading to when he began working for Bakari years ago. We did a lot of reconnaissance on Bakari's associates before he was defeated, and thankfully Heden kept it all on the immortal servers."

"Handy," she said, adjusting the radio so a heavy metal song played low in the background.

"I wasn't sure if he would return to a place he'd already inhabited, but the land records show the property has been owned by the same landlord for over a century. It might be a family home where the danger of him returning has lessened now that Bakari has been defeated. Regardless, it's the best place to start looking."

"Hey, if we come up with zilch, at least we ran down a lead."

"Agreed." Grasping the handle above the window, Larkin peered out, studying the landscape. As the trees and buildings whizzed by, his thoughts drifted to Dr. Tyson, or Quaygon, which was his immortal name.

When he'd encountered Quaygon in the woods during the final battle with Bakari, his first impulse had been to kill him. After all, he'd aligned with the enemy who'd wrought much death and destruction upon the kingdom. But something had lurked in Quaygon's deep brown eyes, and Larkin had hesitated. Recalling the fear and remorse he'd seen in the hybrid's expression, Larkin thought of their brief exchange in the forest beside the raging battle.

"Go, Quaygon, before I change my mind. I don't want to see you anywhere near the immortal kingdom in the future, understood? If I do, it will be your last day in our realm. Are we clear?"

"Crystal," Quaygon said with a hurried nod. "Thank you."

He'd scattered from the forest so quickly Larkin sometimes wondered if their exchange truly happened...and wondered why he'd felt compelled to spare the man's life.

"What are the chances he'll help us if we *do* find him?" Brienne asked, interrupting his thoughts.

Thinning his lips, Larkin shrugged. "Well, he owes me one, so I'm betting one hundred percent. If not by choice, then by force."

"Fun," she quipped, tightening her fingers on the steering wheel. "Let's try to lure the bee with honey before we kick the hornet's nest. I'm not in the mood to bash someone's head in today."

Resting his fist on his lips to stifle his laugh, Larkin nodded. "I'll do my best. Hopefully, he'll be amenable."

Tuning in to the electric guitar strumming in the background, they relaxed into comfortable silence as Brienne drove toward their destination.

Ten minutes later, they entered a sparse residential neighborhood. The dilapidated houses were scattered far apart, and Brienne squinted to discern the house numbers.

"That must be it," she said, pointing toward the house at the end of the street. It was barely visible behind a thick growth of trees and brush. She maneuvered the car down the gravel driveway parallel to the home and pulled to a stop before cutting the engine. "I've got the mini eight-shooter loaded just in case." She patted her belt.

"Hopefully we won't need to use it," Larkin said, opening the door. They both did a final check of the weapons secured to their belts before walking over the overgrown sidewalk to the front door. After climbing the two steps that led to the concrete front porch, Larkin pulled open the screen and knocked on the main wooden door.

Stepping back, he waited, his ears perking up when he heard the sound of several locks being disengaged. The latch clicked and the door slowly swung open, revealing an anxious Dr. Tyson.

"Hello," Larkin said, noticing the fear in his eyes behind his wire-rimmed glasses. "I'm—"

"Larkin," he said, his gaze trailing to Brienne before landing back on Larkin. "I remember. Have you come here to kill me?"

"Not yet," Larkin said, lifting an eyebrow, "but it's still early. We have something to discuss with you, Quaygon."

The man's throat bobbed before he shook his head. "I wasn't expecting company, so it's a bit of a mess, but you're welcome to come in." Stepping back, he opened the door wider, and Larkin shot Brienne a look that said, "Stay alert," before he crossed the threshold. She entered behind him, and Quaygon closed the door.

"Is it too much to ask you to call me Dr. Tyson? Or Quinn? Quinn is the human name I use. Sadly, the name Quaygon is laced with memories I'd rather leave behind."

Since Larkin had his own memories that remained buried deep in the past, he took pity on the hybrid and nodded. "Fine. Quinn, we'd like to sit and talk for a few minutes."

He led them to the dim living room, gesturing for them to sit on the couch before he opened the curtains. Sunlight filtered through the room, which looked like it hadn't been cleaned in some time.

Dr. Tyson sat on the chair opposite the couch and crossed an ankle over his knee. Steepling his fingers, he touched them to his lips as he warily regarded them. "How can I help you, Larkin?"

"I wasn't sure you'd come back here after returning to the human world," Larkin said, curious for some reason.

"It's obvious I chose the wrong side when I chose to work with Bakari," Quaygon said, lowering his hand to pick a speck of nonexistent lint off his khaki pants. "I've never really belonged anywhere, and I was quite angry at the world when he found me. I thought I might finally be able to use my skills to further a cause. Sadly, it was the wrong cause. But"—he lifted a finger—"with Bakari's defeat, I realized there wasn't a huge threat upon me if I came back here. King Dakath is hell-bent on destroying Elven hybrids, but he's going after human-Elven hybrids first. I think a Vampyre-Elven hybrid such as me is lower on his list."

"So, you're familiar with the Elf king and his council?" Larkin asked.

"I am," he said with a nod. "Tatiana and I discussed it, and I also did some research when I returned to the human world." Grinning, he lifted a shoulder. "It's amazing what you can find in the archives of human libraries and the internet. Immortals and hybrids have inhabited the human realm for eons. If one chooses to look, they will find many accounts of their footprints across time and history."

"Most humans attribute immortal sightings and incidents to supernatural experiences," Brienne said, stretching her arm over the back of the couch. "They've never understood that a realm of immortals lived beyond an invisible wall of ether they didn't know existed."

"Ah, but it doesn't exist anymore," Quaygon said, arching a brow. "And I surmise that is why you're here."

"It is," Larkin said, shifting to face him. Leaning forward, he rested his forearms on his thighs. "You said you chose the wrong side before. What if I gave you a second chance? An opportunity to choose the right side. Would you take it?"

He gnawed his lip, contemplating. "That depends on what I have to do. Will it put me in jeopardy?"

"Possibly," Larkin said, wanting to be honest, "but putting oneself in jeopardy for a noble cause carries much honor."

Quaygon digested his words, rubbing his chin as he pondered. Finally, he inhaled a deep breath and nodded. "I haven't embodied honor in quite some time and appreciate the opportunity to change that. What do you need me to do?"

"The Elf king possesses powers similar to Crimeous, Darkrip, Evie and Tatiana. You are the only immortal I know of who was able to concoct a potion that bestowed powers upon someone else."

"I've studied the history of immortal powers in depth," he said, rising and walking over to a bookshelf. Pulling a notebook from a shelf filled with dozens of others, he returned to the chair and began flipping through it. "The truth is, many immortals could develop powers if they truly wished, but it requires much study and patience. Even Galredad did not possess powers when he was merely an Elf. Only after many eons of research and practice, fueled by his hate of Etherya, did he develop his *gifts* and become Crimeous," he finished acerbically.

"And we know Tatiana has lived for many centuries and has studied the supernatural and black magic associated with many cultures," Brienne said.

"Yes, Tatiana is powerful indeed," Quaygon confirmed. "Her Elven bloodline must be very pure, as I've discerned the purer an immortal's bloodline, the easier it is for them to learn to wield supernatural powers."

Larkin glanced at Brienne. "This makes sense considering Evie and Darkrip's bloodline as well."

"Correct," Quaygon said, flipping through the scrawled notes on his pages. "Plus, Evie was infused with the blood of Etherya, and we all know there is nothing more potent upon the Earth."

Brienne waved her hand back and forth, gesturing to his notebook. "I see you've kept a note or two on this," she said, flashing a sardonic grin. "That's why we're here. King Dakath is powerful, and he's interfering with our mission to integrate the humans and immortals."

Quaygon's eyebrows drew together. "Interesting since he sees humans as insignificant. I thought his true desire was to eradicate human-Elven hybrids. He's obsessed with keeping the Elven bloodline pure."

"Unfortunately, the two are intertwined for a myriad of reasons," Larkin said, holding up a finger. "First, his daughter is a human-Elven hybrid and he has a strange obsession with tormenting her."

"Why doesn't he just kill her?" Quaygon asked.

"Dear ol' dad's in it for the torture," Brienne muttered. "Death would be too quick, although he doesn't mind murdering her friends."

Quaygon ran his fingers through his shaggy hair, which hadn't seen a haircut in quite some time if the tussled, uneven ends that rested against his neck were any indication. "They're all the same," he said, collapsing back and rubbing his eyes. "All these demigods are the same. They crave torturing others, and I fear we'll never be free of them."

"Not all immortals who possess powers are evil," Larkin said. "Evie and Darkrip have proven that. But Dakath is focused and quite patient from what I've surmised. Esmerelda, Dakath's daughter, is the leader of our implementation team." He held up another finger. "Second, we can't have dead hybrid bodies lying around for our human counterparts to clean up. It's too dangerous."

"I get it," Quaygon said, holding up a hand. "You don't need to explain every detail. I'm a chemist and a genius, according to the human Mensa society, so I do have some deductive skills." Glancing down at his notebook, he tapped the page several times. "You want me to create some potions to diminish the effects of Dakath's poisons."

"And to cure anyone injected or exposed to them," Larkin said. "The human implementation plan will take decades, and we need antidotes if we're going to succeed."

Rubbing his bottom lip with his finger, Quaygon considered. "I can do it, but I'd need a lab. I have a small homemade one here, but I'd need access to something more advanced."

"We're working on that. The immortal royals are in the process of purchasing a permanent base for immortals in Pennsylvania. We'll be hiring contractors to build the site, and your lab will be top priority."

Intrigued, Quaygon considered. "And this includes security?"

"Yes," Larkin said. "As long as you agree to relocate to Pennsylvania. To be clear, this is an extensive mission, Quaygon—"

He opened his mouth to correct his name, and Larkin held up a hand.

"Sorry...*Quinn*. This won't be an easy or short mission. But if you help the immortals succeed, not only will you have helped many on Earth, but you'll be welcomed with open arms in the human and immortal worlds."

Glancing down, Quaygon closed the notebook and ran his palm over the weathered front cover. "I can't remember the last time I belonged somewhere. Being a Vampire-Elven hybrid hasn't been easy. I've never met another, although I'm sure more must exist." His thumb trailed back and forth over the notebook. "As I said, immortals and hybrids roam the human world whether we acknowledge it or not."

"Hey, I'm a lesbian Slayer-Elven hybrid, so I feel your pain, man," Brienne said, straightening on the couch. "I've never fit in *anywhere*—until I found Esme, that is. She's cultivated a team of immortals who won't let this world turn us into bad people." Rising, she approached him and extended her hand. "Join us. Our team needs you, and we'll never make you feel as if you don't belong. That's a fucking promise."

Larkin watched the interplay of emotion on Dr. Tyson's face. The slight glimmer of hope gave way to a flash of pride at being asked to join the team before it morphed into full-on acceptance. Setting the notebook on the table, he rose, shaking Brienne's hand firmly before releasing it and extending his hand to Larkin.

Rising, Larkin engulfed his hand, a strange sensation shooting up his arm at the contact of the man's soft palm against his own callused one. Shaking it, he smiled. "Welcome to the team, Quinn. We're excited to have you on board."

"Thank you," he said, pumping Larkin's hand once more before releasing and looking back and forth between them. "So, what do we do now?"

Larkin pulled his phone from his belt. "I need to call Esme and tell her you're on board. Then you'll need to settle things here in St. Louis so you can begin the relocation to Rausch Gap. That's our base."

"I've been contemplating selling this home for a while," Quaygon said, glancing around the room. "This will definitely give me the push I need. I'll research real estate agents and begin the listing process tomorrow."

"You don't have any ties here?" Larkin asked.

Shaking his head, Quaygon shrugged. "I bought this house at the end of World War I. I wanted somewhere to settle in a world where I didn't belong. It's appreciated nicely, and I'm happy to contribute some of the profits to the cause."

"That's a noble offer, and I'll inform Miranda and Sathan," Larkin said.

"Then it's settled," Brienne said, craning her neck to the kitchen. "While Larkin calls Esme, I have a very important question for Quinn."

"Yes?"

"You got any food in this dump?"

Chuckling, Larkin observed them trail into the kitchen while he stepped outside to call his leader and inform her the first leg of their mission was complete.

Chapter 12

E sme and Tordor worked for hours creating the profiles for General Markson. Sathan and Miranda had vetted thirteen immortals from their realm to be the first wave of candidates who would infiltrate the US government. Esme called Larissa and informed her she could apply, as well as anyone else on their team. Nikolas also expressed an interest, and she emailed them the forms to complete so she could create profiles for them.

As she and Tordor worked in their shared living room, she received a call from Larkin informing her that Dr. Tyson had pledged his allegiance to their cause. After the harrowing events of the week, it was some welcome good news.

After creating several profiles for the candidates they would send to General Markson, Esme groaned and fell back on the couch cushions. "Can't. Take. Any. More." Harshly rubbing her eyes, she exhaled a deep breath. "I'm starving, and if I look at that laptop one more minute, my eyes are going to melt."

"I could eat," Tordor said, removing his fingers from the keyboard on his laptop and stretching them. "There are a few restaurants nearby."

"Let's go to the steakhouse. It's supposed to have an Australian theme. I haven't been to Australia in decades."

Laughing, he rose and stretched. "I think that's a kitschy thing to get more patrons, but I could handle a steak. Let me wash up and we'll head out."

Esme headed to her bathroom, splashing cold water on her face to get some circulation flowing. Gazing in the mirror, she observed her flushed cheeks and leaned forward. Tracing her finger under her eye, she studied the smooth skin. It had the barest hint of wrinkles that would never deepen thanks to her immortality. Still, the tiny lines were there, faint and permanent. Had Tordor noticed them?

Goddess, he was still so green in a world where she was so worn. Being surrounded by his youthful optimism and trusting nature was good for her, but she reminded herself to be careful. Allowing herself to become too entrenched in him would spell disaster for them both. She needed to be the mature one who kept a safe distance for both their sakes.

Stepping from her room, her eyes roved over his muscular body in a T-shirt and worn jeans. Visions of climbing him like a very sexy tree and doing all sorts of things to that strong body flooded her brain, and she clenched her jaw.

Safe distance, Esme. Jeez.

She needed to bring it down several hundred notches.

Approaching her, his lips formed that adorable smile that made her knees buckle.

"And what are you smiling at?" she asked.

"One day," he said softly as he gently tapped her forehead. "One day, you're going to tell me what you're thinking when you look at me like that."

"Like what?" she asked, playfully grabbing his finger. "You don't want to read my thoughts. Believe me."

He cocked a brow. "I want to read every single one...but we've got time."

Releasing his finger, she strode to the door. "Well, right now I'm think-ing about steak. Feed me, Tor. I'm starving."

His half-fangs squished his bottom lip as he smiled, following behind her as they exited the room. His broad palm rested on her lower back as they walked, and she basked in how natural it felt. When had it become so comfortable to have him touch her? She rarely initiated or received physical contact, but damn, she was woman enough to admit she loved being touched by him. Unwilling to dig deeper into the sentiment, she fell into easy conversation with him as they walked to the restaurant.

After waiting a few minutes, they were seated at a booth and promptly ordered two sirloins and draft beers. Once the waitress dropped them off, they clinked their glasses and Esme took a huge sip.

"Beer, huh?" Tordor said. "For some reason, I pegged you for a wine girl."

"Now who's prejudging?" she teased, arching a brow. "I do love a good glass of red. I don't discriminate against alcohol. If it's good, I'll take it, and I was craving a beer."

"Same." Drinking, he studied her. "So, I'm trying to come with small talk so I don't grill you."

"Why would you grill me?"

Affection entered his eyes as they roved over her. "Because I want to know everything about you. Your hobbies and things you hate. How you became such a good singer. What happened with your parents..." He trailed off, gently tracing the wooden table. "I want to know your story."

"Yikes." Grimacing, she took another gulp. "That's heavy, and I don't usually do heavy with people."

"I know," he said, frowning. "It's kind of a bummer since I think we're becoming friends. But friends actually tell each other things."

"Okay, BFF," she said, leaning forward and resting her chin on her fist. "You go first and show me how it's done. Then maybe I'll reciprocate."

White teeth flashed as he grinned. "Okay. What do you want to know?"

Leaning back, she spread her arm over the back of the booth. Narrowing her eyes, she asked, "Why don't you want to rule? You'd be so good at it."

He fanned his lips as he gazed at the table. "I'm not sure I'd be good at it, but that's not why I don't want to do it."

"Believe me, you'd be awesome." He seemed to glow under her praise. "But I'm intrigued. Go on."

Working his jaw as he struggled to find the words, he shrugged. "Are you familiar with human professional tennis?"

Her eyebrows drew together. "Somewhat."

"Uncle Heden loves it, and I've kind of absorbed it by being around him. Anyway, let's say someone told you you'd have to take over for Serena Williams at the height of her career and were expected to produce at the level she did."

"Um, she's the G.O.A.T. That's probably impossible."

"Exactly. Now imagine having parents who were born to rule and being told you're going to inherit their kingdom. No one asks you, and your individual strengths and skills aren't considered. It's just what you're expected to do."

"Your parents are kind of the Serena Williams of ruling, aren't they?"

Chuckling, he nodded. "They're exceptional, and I'm so proud of them. I know neither of them wishes to give up the throne, and they shouldn't have to, especially when I don't want it."

Squinting one eye, she mulled. "And you don't want to seem like an ungrateful prick for giving up something most would kill to have."

Lifting his glass, he emitted a hearty laugh. "Bingo."

"You're the last thing from a prick, Tor. I've rarely met anyone as compassionate as you."

"Thank you. It's important for me to be understanding and level-headed so I can see all sides of a situation. It makes me a strong negotiator and diplomat."

"And you've fallen into a situation in the human world that requires those skills in spades."

"Yep." Tilting his head, he grinned. "Integrating the species properly is extremely meaningful, and I'm committed to it for however long it takes."

"Even if that means staying here in the human world?"

Leaning his chin on his fist, he nodded. "It's why I'm excited about building something at Rausch Gap. I can have a home base in this realm instead of having to travel from the immortal world."

"Do you think your parents will accept you not taking the throne?"

"I think so. I've been honest with them, and they want me to be happy."

Esme's lips formed a sad smile as her mother's face blazed through her mind.

My sweet girl. Promise me you'll always choose happiness. Even if it ends in pain, it will be worth it...

"Esme?"

"Sorry." Raking a hand through her hair, she pushed the memory away. "Choosing your own path and your own happiness is noble, especially when you're turning down an entire *kingdom*." Flashing a cheeky grin, she leaned forward. "We should all be so lucky."

"Hey, I know how privileged I am," he said. "I want to take that privilege and use it for good in the best way I can. Does that make sense?"

"Absolutely."

The server arrived with their steaks, and Esme's mouth watered as she dug in. Chewing, she closed her eyes to savor the taste. "Oh my god... Why is it so good?"

His strong jaw worked as he grinned. Swallowing, he said, "I think it's because we've been existing on granola bars for several weeks."

"Truth." Taking another bite, she chewed as she contemplated. "How often do you need to drink Slayer blood? I thought hybrids drank once per week, but I realized I never saw you drink before today."

"Once a week is about right. I kept the canisters in my tent, and Sofia created this kick-ass thermos that can keep Slayer blood at the cooler storage temperature we need for months. Comes in handy when you're camping in the human world."

"And Jack will deliver more if you need it?"

"Yep. He delivered it to Arderin's family when they lived in the human world, so he's a pro at this point."

Narrowing her eyes, Esme's thoughts drifted to the future. "We're going to need to set up a Slayer blood distribution system in the human world as we integrate more immortals."

"One of the many things we'll need to implement down the road," he agreed, cutting the last pieces of his steak. "It's going to be a lot of work, but I'm excited about it."

"You'll do a great job. You might not be the king in the immortal world, but you'll be the king of the immortals and hybrids in the human world. Maybe it was the role you were born for after all."

"Maybe so." Taking the last bite, he slowly chewed as he studied her. Swallowing, he wiped his mouth and set his napkin on the table as Esme's heartbeat began to accelerate. Questions swirled in those luminous green eyes, and she struggled not to squirm.

"Uh...you just got weird." She rubbed her chin. "Is something on my face?"

Arching a brow, he leaned back and draped his arm over the booth. Lifting his glass, he studied her over the rim. "You always do that," he murmured, the silken tone causing bumps to rise on her skin.

"Do what?"

"Make a funny quip to reset the conversation. You know there's nothing on your face."

Feeling thoroughly called out, Esme dipped a fry in the ketchup and rubbed it on her chin, leaving a huge red blob. Mirth entered his gaze as she lifted a shoulder. "I mean, if there's nothing on my face, cool. Just making sure."

A challenge flared in his expression as he leaned forward. Picking up his napkin, he reached over. "Come here," he softly commanded.

Esme's muscles collapsed into a pool of jelly at his sultry tone, and she realized she'd made a grave mistake. Clumsily, she felt for her napkin on her lap, intending to use it to wipe her face.

"Let me get it." Urging her closer, he hooked his hand.

Wondering why she could feel her heartbeat inside her eardrums, she leaned forward, slightly jutting out her chin. Tordor touched the napkin to it, gently wiping off the ketchup. Lifting his thumb, he rubbed her chin, the rasp of his skin against hers causing her breath to hitch.

"Got it…I think. There might be some here…"

He slowly dragged his thumb over her lip…

"Okay, I think you got it," she said, recoiling as if his hand were on fire. "Well done. I'll remember not to 'quip' with you again." She made quotation marks with her fingers.

Laughing, he wiped his hand on his napkin before bringing his thumb to his lips. Ever so slowly, he sucked the pad clean, and Esme felt a rush of wetness at her core. Holy gods in heaven, but this man was sexy. Why wasn't there someone waiting for him in the immortal world? Someone with whom he could slate the very obvious lust burning in his gaze.

The waitress appeared, jolting Esme as she asked if they wanted dessert. They both declined but ordered one more beer to enjoy while they waited for the check. Once the fresh beers were in hand, she expelled a deep breath.

"Well, I'm wet…from the condensation dripping from the beer," she said with a cheeky grin as she lifted the glass.

Tossing back his head, he gave a joyful laugh. "The vow not to quip lasted about two minutes."

"It's a defense mechanism. Thanks for calling me out," she teased, drawing circles on the table. "How did we get on that subject anyway?"

"You were saying that ruling the immortals in the human world might be the role I was born for. And then I probably gave you a weird look."

"Why?"

Narrowing his eyes, he leaned forward. "Because I was thinking it might be the role *you* were born for."

She waved a dismissive hand. "I have no desire to rule anything."

"But you have a desire to help our people and you're a natural leader. Whether you like it or not, you might just be perfect for it, Esme."

Pretending her heart didn't slam at the sentiment, she shook her head. "I told you. Once we're done with Phase I of the immersion, I'm leaving the project to you, Larkin and Brienne. I'm happy to come back and help when we begin the other phases, but my place on the team isn't permanent. And to be honest, it will be better for you if I'm away from the project to keep it off my father's radar for a while."

He shot her a disbelieving glance.

"It's not running, okay? I have things I need to do and places I want to visit too, you know."

"Tell me," he said gently. "I can't believe there are places you haven't visited yet."

"I've seen a lot, but I still have a bucket list."

He arched his eyebrows expectantly.

"Okay, I guess this is where I start to get a *bit* personal." She playfully rolled her eyes. "I've been to several islands in Indonesia, but I've never been to Bali. There's this Hindu temple there called Ulun Danu Bratan. It sits on a beautiful lake, and if you find the right spot, the temple appears to float on the water." Closing her eyes, she envisioned how peaceful it must be. "One day, I'd like to spend some time there and meditate as the sun rises each morning."

"It sounds amazing," he said reverently.

Lifting her lids, she broke into a huge grin. "Doesn't it? I heard about it somewhere in my travels and it's taken up permanent residence in my head." She tapped her temple. "I just feel a calling to go there."

"Then you have to make it a priority after we finish Phase I and the fifteen immortals are implemented into the US government."

Her features scrunched. "I'm terrible at making myself a priority, but maybe this time I'll actually do it."

"You deserve that, sweetheart. I hope you do it."

Thankfully, the server showed up with their check, saving Esme from melting into a pool of lust at his tender endearment. They settled up and headed back to the hotel, his hand on her lower back again as they walked to their room.

Once inside, she lifted her arms and forced a wide yawn. "Well, I'm in a food coma. Going to head to bed. Thanks for dinner."

"Sweet dreams," he said, the slight pout on his full lips indicating he wanted to hang longer. "Maybe next time you'll tell me about your mother. I can spring for a fancier restaurant than the one we went to tonight if that will help."

Grinning at his teasing, she turned to walk to her room. "I'm usually a vault, but you might be able to entice me with a fancy restaurant. Only time will tell." Stopping in the doorway, she gripped the frame. "Good night, Tor."

His whispered "good night" followed her into the room long after she'd closed the door and prepped for bed. Drifting to sleep inside the soft covers, she could still feel the deep rasp of his voice surrounding her as she succumbed to the darkness.

Chapter 13

E sme squeezed her eyes, frustrated at the unseen force that wouldn't allow her to open them. Grunting, she tried to lift her hands to rub them, but she couldn't move, frozen by fear as the image formed behind her closed lids.

Her parents were arguing as they often did in the last days of their fateful courtship. Her father strode around the room, his long velvet cape almost touching the floor as it swished with his steps. Dyana stood tall, tears blazing in her eyes, as she pleaded.

"Darling," she said, stepping forward to clutch his arm. "You have become obsessed with keeping the Elven line pure. I understand it stems from fear that your people will be punished again if they change...if they evolve...but such is the way of life. Things must be allowed to change so they can grow."

"No!" Dakath screamed, ripping his arm from her grasp. "I have hidden here too long. Sheltered in a fishing village while the humans lust for war. They are an inferior species and not worthy of our Elven blood."

Dyana's features crumbled. "But I'm human. Your daughter is human—"

"Esmerelda is half-Elf, and that will always be the superior part of her. I was hoping the Elven gene would stay suppressed and she would die like the rest of your species, but alas, the points of her ears have started to form." Rubbing his forehead, he expelled an angry breath. "Her Elven gene will dominate and she will be immortal. It is an abomination!"

"My love," Dyana said, slowly approaching and taking his hand. "This does not have to be so dour. It can be your opportunity to change. To accept a new era for your species."

"A new era?" he asked incredulously. "I have killed hundreds of my kinsmen who procreated with humans, as well as their offspring." He gazed at Esme, who sat in the corner of the room, playing with the wooden dice she'd received for her last birthday. Fear at her parents' anger toward one another threatened to choke her, and she pretended she didn't hear them as they hissed with rage.

"I've created that which I detest." His shoulders sagged in frustration. "All because I couldn't deny my desire for you..."

"Darling," she soothed, sliding her arms around his neck, "we'll figure this out. What's most important is that we love each other."

Reverently gazing at her, he placed his hand on her cheek. "By all the gods, I've loved you since the second I laid eyes on you, Dyana."

Hope laced her mother's beautiful features as she stared up at him.

"But I cannot let this go on. Sometimes one must sacrifice their desires for the greater good."

Tensing, she released him and backed away. "What are you saying? That you'll kill her? Never!"

"It must be done," he said, shaking his head. "I cannot let an Elven-human hybrid—and one with my blood—exist on the earth. It negates everything I stand for."

Her mother's cheeks flushed with rage as she backed toward the small kitchen nook. Reaching behind her, she clumsily patted the counter until she found the large carving knife. Grasping it with white-knuckled fingers, she lifted it high as Dakath's eyes grew wide.

"I love you, Dakath. I have since the moment we met. You told me you were content to live here with me...with us...and take some time away from ruling."

"Your pregnancy was an accident, Dyana, and I never believed she would express the Elven gene."

"Well, she has, and I won't let you murder her! Do you hear me?" Her hand trembled as she held the knife high. "She's our daughter, Dakath! You cannot do this!"

"Put the knife down," he said, his voice laced with harsh steel. "I have no wish to hurt you, Dyana."

Armed with the deepest love possible—a mother's love for her child—Dyana lunged forward, swiping the knife through the air. Dakath dodged it, whirling around to glare at her. "For the goddess's sake, Dyana! Stop this!"

"She is everything precious in this world!" Dyana continued, advancing and attempting several more swipes with the knife. "I must protect her!"

Dakath blocked her arm, grabbing her as they struggled for the upper hand. Esme watched in slow motion, her ten-year-old heart beating in a furious rhythm she could feel in the depths of her bones. Opening her mouth to scream, only a soft puff of air escaped as she watched the events unfold.

Dakath took control of the knife, plunging it forward as they struggled. Dyana gasped, her back arching as she went limp. Her father held his lover, one arm behind her back as he gazed at his other hand with disbelieving eyes. Lifting his gaze to Dyana's, he shook his head.

"Oh god..." she sputtered, blood spurting from her mouth as she coughed. "You stabbed me...Dakath..."

As her voice trailed off, Dakath observed the knife lodged in Dyana's side. His expression showcased the knowledge that he'd impaled several organs and there was no chance of survival. Lifting his bloody hand to her face, he lowered his forehead to hers and began to weep.

Esme sat as still as a rock, overcome with shock and unable to move. Straining to hear their hushed words, she could only discern a few whispered words.

"I'm so sorry," he rasped, shaking his head. "Dyana..."

Her mother lifted a shaking hand, clutching the hair at his nape and pressing her lips to his pointed ear. She whispered something as her father wept.

Dakath murmured back before her mother expelled her last breath and the light left her eyes.

"Oh god," Dakath wailed, "what have I done?"

Dyana lay limp in his arms, his words wasted on her lifeless frame. Sucking in a breath, Dakath lowered her body to the floor before clenching his hands in his hair and wringing the thick brown strands.

Finally able to move, Esme rose and bolted toward her mother, lowering to the ground to shake her.

"Momma," she cried, her mother's face blurred by the hot tears in her eyes. "Momma, wake up!"

"What have you done?" a deep voice boomed from the doorway as heavy footsteps entered. Glancing over her shoulder, Esme observed her Uncle Gillam approach. "Dakath? What the hell?"

Lowering to Dyana's side, Gillam pressed two fingers against her neck. His features softened with grief as he realized she was dead. Gazing up at his brother, he shook his head. "For the love of all the gods, Dakath, you've taken this too far. She was your mate, brother!"

"A mate who would eventually die!" he screamed, crazed and angry. "And she left me with this...pestilence!" He pointed at Esme. "It's my duty to eliminate hybrids!"

Gillam rose and began a hushed conversation with Dakath as Esme crumpled over Dyana's body. Holding her mother's lifeless frame, she cried at the loss of the beautiful, vibrant woman she loved deep in her soul.

Eventually, Gillam gently eased her away from Dyana's body, lifting Esme in his arms and running a soothing hand over her hair. "Let's get you somewhere safe, sweet girl. I promise I'll come back and take care of your momma's body and bury her properly."

Turning to look at Dakath, Esme saw the hatred in his hazel eyes. "Father?" she called softly.

"Get her out of my presence!" he spat. "If you want her safe, take her."

Gillam's arms tightened around Esme. "Come on, sweetheart. Let's go."

Her body shook with each step of her uncle's strong legs as she buried her mouth against his shoulder and watched her mother's body grow smaller with each stride. And then she pressed her face into his chest, craving the darkness as pain threatened to strangle her. It was the blackest darkness she'd ever seen...sticky and thick as it wrapped its grizzled fingers around her throat and squeezed...

Gasping, Esme shot upright, arms flailing as she searched for a stronghold. Wiping her drenched forehead, she closed her eyes as she struggled to catch her breath. The memory was nearly a thousand years old, and yet it still plagued her nightmares like locusts devouring a fertile field. Goddess, but she hated that memory and wished for nothing more than to scrub it from her brain.

Tossing off the covers, she trailed to the kitchen located in the alcove of the main room of the suite. Clad in soft shorts and a tank, she didn't think of throwing on a bra. Tordor would be sleeping like a *normal* damn person who didn't dream of their mother's murder every other night. Reaching for a glass in the cabinet above the sink, she filled it with shaking hands and took a huge gulp. Resting her palm on her chest above her thrumming heartbeat, she took another sip...before her trembling hand lost the grip on the glass and it fell to the floor, shattering into what looked like a thousand tiny pieces.

Tordor's door swung open, his eyes heavy with sleep under his tousled hair as he searched the dim room.

"Esme?"

"God damn it!" she hissed, staring at the circle of broken glass that surrounded her bare feet. "I just dropped my water. Son of a bitch. I'm fine."

He moved toward her, clad only in boxer briefs, and she wanted to melt into the floor in a puddle of embarrassment. Feeling like a dolt, she glanced around to find a rag. "I just need to wipe it up—"

"Don't move," he commanded in that velvet voice. "I'm going to see if there's a broom in the closet."

Sure enough, he found a broom and returned, latching onto her with his green gaze and silently telling her to remain still. She nodded, and he began to clear away the glass. Esme stared at her legs, noticing they'd taken the brunt of a few small shards and small rivulets of blood trailed down her pale skin.

When he'd finally cleared the glass away, he set the broom against the counter and wet a cloth. Lowering to his knees, he began to wipe the floor.

"Let me do that—"

"I've got it," he said, wanting to ensure he collected all the glass. "I don't want you to cut yourself any more than you have."

He wiped the floor before rising and placing the cloth in the sink. After washing his hands, he reached for a clean cloth in the cupboard above and wet it. Tossing it over his shoulder, he leaned toward her and slid an arm over her shoulders before crouching and placing his other arm behind her knees.

"Tor, this isn't necessary—"

He lifted her as if she were a feather, carrying her to the couch and lowering her onto the soft cushions. Her back rested on the arm of the couch as he sat in the middle and positioned her calves atop his thighs. Removing the cloth from his shoulder, he began to gently clean the cuts on her shins.

"I don't like seeing you covered in blood, little Elf," he said, his movements slow and methodical as he worked. "This is twice now, and it twists me up pretty badly right here." Glancing at her, he tapped his chest over his heart.

Resting her temple on the high back of the couch, she watched him continue the careful ministrations. "I'm sorry. That was stupid and clumsy. I wasn't sleeping well, so I came out to get some water. Probably should've stayed in bed."

"I'm not saying that so you'll apologize," he said, studying her legs as he cleaned the last of the blood, ensuring all the tiny shards were removed. Setting the cloth on the side table, he encircled her calves, one with each hand, holding her in a supportive grip. "I'm telling you that so you know how protective I feel toward you. I've never felt it with anyone else."

Her heart shot straight to her knees at the tender words, and she swallowed the rather huge lump in her throat. "I don't need protection. I'm pretty tough."

"You are, but honestly, I just don't care, Esme. Whether you need it or not, something in me is determined to protect you. My mom taught me not to be a misogynist ass, but there are some things you just can't fight." Leaning closer, he rested his cheek on the back of the couch. "Some things you don't *want* to fight."

Lifting her hand to his face, she cupped his jaw, reveling in the feel of his slight stubble against her palm. "Tor..." she whispered. "We can't."

His eyes roved over her as he seemed to mull whether to respond or not. After several heavy seconds, he slowly caressed her leg as he spoke. "Why couldn't you sleep?"

She debated lying or making one of her famous quips, but the emotion in his eyes held her mesmerized. Licking her parched lips, she said softly, "I had a nightmare."

The soothing strokes on her legs continued as he processed. "About what?"

She exhaled a long breath. "My mother."

Nodding, he stroked her, letting the admission float between them as it settled.

"Do you dream of her often?"

Esme nodded against the couch.

Expressing his considerate nature, he didn't push for more. It opened something inside Esme—the fact he knew her well enough not to challenge her boundaries, especially when she felt so vulnerable.

"I'm here whenever you want to tell me," he continued, his tender strokes halting as he squeezed her ankle.

Fear surged deep within as she realized she wanted to tell him everything. To lean into him and explain how her world had gotten so fucked up. Licking her lips, she wondered where to even begin.

"The first murder I ever saw was my mother's," she said softly. "I was ten years old and she and my father got into a terrible argument. She didn't survive it."

Expelling a heavy breath, his fingers tightened on her ankle. "That's awful."

"Clayton was just the last of a very long string of people I care about that he took from me." Her voice was scratchy as she continued. "So many friends along the way, a few lovers, and a few who were merely acquaintances. Sometimes, a poisoned arrow would lodge in their throat as I spoke to them. Those occurred mostly before guns became prominent."

His thumb slowly stroked her leg as he remained silent, absorbing her words as his features laced with empathy.

"One friend, Valentina, was a woman I'd gotten close to in Spain centuries ago. She was a lovely woman who would walk with me along the river where I lived in the sixteenth century. One day, as we stood under a tree soaking up shade, an arrow pierced her neck. I'll never forget her clutching her throat as she tumbled to the ground and died."

Wishing he could absorb her pain, he shook his head. "I'm so sorry, sweetheart."

"There was another man I encountered in nineteenth century Peru. I'd gone there to research the healing rituals of the ancient Inca, hoping to discover some plants that could combat my father's poisons. My guide was charming with a quick wit and determined to get in my pants."

Frowning, he muttered, "I hate him already."

Breathing a laugh, she bit her lip. "I'm not trying to make you jealous, but we did have a romantic relationship for a while before I decided to return to Europe. As I was about to board the ship, I saw the rats eating something out of the corner of my eye near the shoreline." Her chin quivered as the tears threatened to overflow in her stunning eyes. "It was him, Tor. My father's men had just left him there as a symbol that they were watching me. That I could never escape his reach."

"So you became a runner," he said softly.

She nodded, finally able to admit in the dark what she hadn't been willing to say in the light of day.

"I did my best to stay off my father's radar, but I also made sure to observe him every few decades. I felt it imperative to watch him interact with the Elves in the village below his castle. To see if he had the propensity to grow kinder."

"But he didn't change?"

"No," she said, gnawing her lip. "If anything, he grew more rigid and unyielding with his people. He would walk through the village, obsessed with finding anyone who'd mingled with humans. If he found someone, he would bring them back to the castle and murder them in front of the council."

"Did you observe him in the castle too?"

She shook her head. "I hired a spy for several centuries who informed me of my father's cruelty. Eventually, I stopped paying the spy for information because I gave up hope my father would ever change. But observing him helped me learn his habits. It's how I anticipate his moves when he begins to hunt and torture me again." A resigned laugh exited her throat. "Sometimes he gets tired and takes a break for a few decades, but he always resumes the hunt." Opening her mouth in a wide yawn, she settled further into the couch. "It's fucking exhausting."

Tordor's deep eyes studied her as they fell into silence, his smooth strokes on her skin never easing. Finally, he shifted, realizing her eyes were drooping.

"Okay, sleeping beauty, I think you're ready for bed." Running his fingers over her cuts, he smiled. "And I think the crisis is averted, so you won't bleed out. I won't push you any more tonight, but I'm honored you trust me enough to talk to me about your past."

"Trust comes so easily with you," she said wistfully. "I'm not used to that."

"Best diplomat in the immortal world," he boasted, pointing at his chest. "Don't even try to evade my skills. I can win over the crabbiest immortals you've ever met. You're not even close to ol' Luna who hates her neighbor's dog."

Breathing a laugh at his teasing, she slowly removed her legs from his lap and planted her feet on the floor. "On that note, I'll reclaim my buttoned-up status and try to get some sleep." Standing, she pushed her hair out of her face as he rose and steadied her.

"Okay?" he asked.

"Yeah." Craning her neck to look into his eyes, she grinned. "Maybe you were born to be a doctor instead of a king. You've got a great bedside manner."

Something flared in his eyes as he arched a brow. "I'd be honored to be anywhere near your bedside, sweetheart."

Wrinkling her nose, she disengaged from his grasp. "Too cheesy, but I appreciate the sentiment." His deep chuckle followed her as she padded to her room. Turning to face him, she smiled. "Thanks, Tor. Sorry I woke you up."

"It's okay. I'm just glad you're not hurt. If you need me, I'm right there." He pointed to his room. "I mean it, Esme."

"Thanks."

Her eyes were glued to his heartfelt expression until the moment she closed the door. Striding to the bed, she sat and examined her legs, realizing they were fine. Stroking them, she mimicked the caress of Tordor's thick fingers, closing her eyes as she imagined them working higher...

Emitting a huff, she plopped on the bed and pulled up the covers, determined to get some sleep. Tomorrow would be another long day, and she wouldn't let old memories deter her from her objective.

L arkin and Brienne got on the road early the next morning to tackle the twelve-hour drive back to Rausch Gap. They would leave Dr. Tyson behind for a few days so he could settle his affairs, and then he would join the team at Rausch Gap.

After a long day of travel, Larkin and Brienne arrived at camp around midnight. Several members of the team were still awake, sitting around the campfire, and they welcomed the weary travelers with open arms.

"Hey, guys," Larissa said, grinning as she saluted them with her beer. "Plop down and open a cold one. Nikolas and I are sharing old war stories. Oh, and Frederick is telling us about his brother, who we're recruiting to move here and build our site." Leaning over to whisper to Brienne, she held her hand up to the side of her mouth. "And he's single, so I'm grilling Fred."

"I heard that," Frederick said, tilting his head. "Topher hasn't dated anyone since he lost his wife several decades ago, but you never know."

"Whoa," she said, showing her palms. "No one said anything about dating. Some people just need to scratch an itch sometimes."

"TMI," Frederick droned.

"I'm probably moving to DC anyway," Larissa continued. "I'm heading to a coffee shop in East Hanover tomorrow to use their Wi-Fi and send my application to Esme." She snapped her fingers. "Don't want to chance sending it with our spotty connections here. The immortal royals are awesome to equip us with mobile technology, but you can't beat a good ol'-fashioned café Wi-Fi connection."

"I'm going with you to send mine in too," Nikolas chimed in.

"Fine with me, but you're buying the coffee."

Nikolas shot her a good-natured glare as the banter continued.

After catching up with everyone, Larkin rose and addressed Frederick. "Next time you speak to your brother, ask him if he's comfortable building a chemical lab. If he's going to move out here to help us, one of the first things we'll need is an efficient lab for Dr. Tyson."

"I'm sure he'll be amenable if Dr. Tyson is willing to help him with the specs."

"I'll see to it. Good night, everyone."

Heading into his tent, Larkin lay down and settled into his sleeping bag. As the soft lull of the fireside chat echoed several feet away, he closed his eyes and thanked Etherya for Quaygon's acquiescence. Or rather, *Quinn's*. He would be a valuable asset to their team as he created concoctions to null and cure the effects of King Dakath's poisons.

As the thoughts lingered, Larkin realized he was doing something he didn't do very often. He was *smiling*. Strange that it would occur while the vision of Quinn's angular features and cavernous brown eyes behind wired glasses stared back at him. Too practical to analyze it, Larkin gave in to exhaustion and allowed himself to sleep.

Chapter 14

E sme awoke the next morning slightly embarrassed at the previous night's events before telling herself to chill out. If anyone would understand, it was Tordor. Hell, he was the epitome of compassion and understanding. Tossing off the covers, she dug through her bag to find her yoga pants. Pulling them on, she donned her bra and slid her tank top back over it. Heading into the living room, she pulled open the curtains and stared across the meadow behind the hotel. Inhaling some deep breaths, she centered herself before moving to an open spot on the carpet. Reaching high, she began to stretch.

She moved for a few minutes before Tordor's door slid open and he peeked his head out.

"Morning yoga," he said with a sleepy grin.

"Yep. You're welcome to join me."

"Be right there."

The door clicked, and she smiled as she continued to move. After a few poses, he walked toward her, taking his place at her side. They began to move, her eager student following her lead, and she pursed her lips to keep from laughing.

Her handsome companion was absolutely *terrible* at yoga.

Still, he exerted great effort through the bends and stretches, and she took pity on him by keeping the poses easy. Lifting her arms high, she clenched her hands above her head and pointed her index fingers.

"Reach up," she directed, glancing over at him as he mimicked her. "Then slowly bend until you're pointing at the floor."

She began the pose, showing him as he watched her.

"And don't stare at my ass," she quipped.

His deep chuckle enveloped them as he began to bend. "Busted."

As they both hung upside down, she grinned. "Great stretch, right?"

"It feels good," he gritted as his fingers grazed the floor. "And you're kind not to make fun of me because I'm awful."

Laughing, she began to rise as he followed beside her. Reaching to each side, she slowly dropped her arms and patted her sides.

"Okay, I think that's a pretty good warm-up for today. How do you feel?"

"Awesome," he said, shaking out his arms. "I've never been too flexible, but maybe if I work out with you every morning I can fix that."

Arching a brow, she shot him a playful glare. "Not even touching the insinuation in that statement," she teased, skimming a hand over her ponytail. "We've got a lot of work to do today."

After showering, they both sat down, coffee and bagel from the downstairs lobby in hand, and resumed putting together the profiles for General Markson. Larissa and Nikolas emailed their applications around noon, and Esme was proud they'd chosen to represent the cause by joining the implementation team.

"Should we send Nickolas and Larissa's profiles to your parents so they and Latimus can vet them like they vetted the other candidates?"

Tordor's eyebrows drew together. "We can, but they'll trust my recommendation."

"And you're comfortable recommending them?"

"Yes. If you say they're a good fit, I am."

"They're a good fit," she said with a nod. "Both extremely smart and loyal."

"Then I'll wholeheartedly recommend Larissa and Nikolas."

Tilting her head, she studied him. "You know, we've only known each other a few months. That's a lot of trust to place in me."

"I trust you," he said, squeezing her knee as his other hand clicked the portable mouse and he squinted at the screen. "Some things are just intrinsic, sweetheart."

Swallowing thickly, she tried not to focus on the heat from his hand that burned through her pants.

"Sorry," he said, drawing his hand away. "My hands and my mouth have a mind of their own around you."

"I don't mind," she rasped, wondering when someone had dumped a pile of gravel down her throat. "You're one of the least creepy guys I've ever led a team with."

Tossing back his head, a laugh bellowed from his chest. "I've never received such a glowing endorsement. Thank you."

With a warm grin, she resumed the focus on the profiles, and by five o'clock, they were nearing the finish line.

"The fifteen profiles look good," she said, leaning back on the couch and rubbing her eyes. "I think we need to read over them all once more in the morning with fresh eyes. Otherwise, this phase is almost complete. Thank the goddess," she moaned, stretching her legs to rest on the coffee table. "I'm not cut out for paperwork. I'm more of an 'action' girl." She made quotation marks with her fingers.

"Our own little superhero," he teased, leaning back beside her.

"I'd be pissed you called me *little*, except you dwarf me by a foot, so I guess from your perspective it's true."

"Wow, I really step in it sometimes with you," he teased. "Before I die from foot-in-mouth syndrome, I'm going to need some food. Are you hungry?"

"Starving." Leaning forward, she flashed a cagy grin. "In case you haven't realized, I'm *always* starving. It takes a lot to maintain this superhero energy." She pointed to her chest.

"No doubt. Maybe we can..."

"Yes?"

His lips formed a shy grin. "Maybe I can take you on a date?"

"Tor," she said softly, drawing her knees to her chest and burrowing into the corner of the couch. "If things were different...if I were different, I'd take you up on that in a second. Unfortunately, I'm...me." She shrugged.

"Um, yes, I was rather sure I knew that when I asked."

Giving him a droll look, she sighed. "I can't form attachments, Tor. I told you that. I wish things were different, but they're not."

Turning to face her, he rested his ankle on his knee, his foot ticking as he contemplated her.

"I don't think you do," he finally said.

"Huh?"

"I don't think you wish things were different. If they were, you'd have to actually *depend* on someone."

Bristling, she clutched her knees tighter against her chest, the defensive action mimicking the thick wall she'd built around her heart. "People who care about me get killed, Tor. If you didn't learn that from Clayton, I don't know what to tell you."

"Clayton's death was tragic, but it wasn't your fault. Blaming yourself is beneath you, Esme."

Gritting her teeth at the infuriating conversation, she ran a hand through her hair. "I don't want to talk about this, and I don't want to fight with you."

"Were we fighting?" he asked sincerely. "I think I was just challenging you."

Frowning, she glared at him. "Well, read the room, but I don't really like being challenged."

"Oh, I got the message." Leaning forward, he said in that deep, silken voice, "But maybe it's time you met someone you can't push away."

Thankfully, Esme's stomach took that moment to growl so loudly they both began to laugh. Encircling her wrist, he squeezed. "I'm sorry. I just feel this strange urge to push you to open up, along with a visceral need to protect you. I'm doing my best here. This is new for me."

Empathy swelled in her gut and she reminded herself she was supposed to be the practical, mature one between them. Hard to do with all the feelings surging inside, but she could at least be gentle with him.

"Okay, take me on a date. What should we do?"

The excitement in his eyes sent shards of pleasure through her frame.

"Well, first we need to eat," he said.

"Definitely."

"Then maybe we could try..." He flashed a sheepish grin. "This might sound weird, but I've always wanted to try bowling. We don't have that game in the immortal world, but humans seem to enjoy it. If I'm going to spend time in this realm, I need to learn human activities."

"I love bowling," she said, shifting on the couch and waving her hands as she spoke. "I haven't done it in a while, but last time I finished over 200. And I got two turkeys!"

"I have no idea what you're talking about," he said, lifting a shoulder.

"*Ohmygod*, this will be so fun! Let's eat and find a nearby bowling alley." Glancing at the laptop, she maneuvered forward and saved all the open work before shutting down. "We deserve a fun night, right? We can take one night off from saving the world."

Rising, he extended his hand. "Yes, ma'am. I'm excited for you to teach me."

"Make sure whatever you wear is comfortable."

"Meet you back here in five minutes."

Esme hurried to her room, giddy at the excitement coursing through her. She hadn't had fun in…honestly, she couldn't remember the last time. Determined to relax and let herself enjoy the evening with her thoughtful companion, she tugged on some jeans and touched up her makeup. Not because he might kiss her. Of course not. She wouldn't let that happen…

As she stood under the staid light of the bathroom mirror applying the soft red lipstick, she gazed into her eyes as one word repeated over and over in her head…

Liar.

For if Tordor took her in his arms and gazed at her with those soulful green eyes, she knew she'd never deny him if he pressed his full lips to hers…

Tordor dressed in jeans, a polo shirt and sneakers. Combing his hands through his thick hair, he studied his reflection in his bathroom mirror. Thanking Etherya he was a confident man, he blew out a breath. After all this time he'd waited to meet the right woman, he knew he'd feel it in his bones when she blazed into his life, and he knew without a doubt that woman was Esme.

But damn, if the woman didn't have some nearly impenetrable walls. Grinning at the reflection, he leaned forward.

"Mom told you love wasn't easy, Tor," he murmured, observing the challenge that lit his expression. "If you've learned anything, it's that she's usually right."

Miranda's face flashed in his mind, accompanied by the deep love he felt for her and his father. Inhaling as his chest rose, he vowed not to be deterred. Yes, his little Elf had some thick walls, but he'd never shied away from a challenge, and he wouldn't start now.

Nerves ticked in his gut as he acknowledged it was time to lose his virginity. Esme was the one—he knew it as sure as his next breath—and he would never forgive himself if he squandered their time together and didn't make love to her. It was impossible to tell if they would go the distance since their relationship was still new, but he knew hers was the face he wanted to see for eternity when he remembered the first time he made love.

It was all a bit daunting, even with his confidence, but he reminded himself how comfortable he felt with Esme. Rarely did one cross paths with someone who just *fit*. There was such an ease to their comradery and playful banter, and he knew she would accept him just as he was.

The thought was extremely profound, causing Tordor to rub his hand over his heart. Was he falling in love? Hell if he knew. He'd certainly never experienced the sentiment, but his desire to protect and cherish her—and to be with her as much as possible—left little doubt. Somewhere along the way, he'd begun falling for the venerable leader of their ambitious initiative, and he had no desire to go back.

Heading to the living room, his eyes latched onto her as she trailed out of her room. She'd done something to her makeup, causing her lips to appear full and red, and he felt unsteady on his feet as she approached.

"Ready?"

The scent of her perfume wafted through his nostrils, along with the barest hint of something else. Inhaling it, he realized it was her arousal. It smelled of honey and spring, and his mouth watered as he anticipated palming her smooth thighs and pressing her legs open before touching his tongue to her deepest place and tasting the dewy essence…

"Tor?"

"Ah, yeah." He cleared his throat, inwardly scolding himself for being a horny creeper. "Ready."

Placing his hand on her lower back, he escorted her from the room, anticipation buzzing at the fact he was going to spend the entire night hearing her laugh and seeing her smile. And if he was lucky, he might be bold enough to steal a kiss at the end of the night…

Would she let down her walls enough to kiss him back? Ready to find out, he led her to the nearby restaurant, reveling in their comfortable conversation the entire way.

T wo hours later, Tordor was embroiled in the most epic bowling match of his life. Granted, it was his *first* bowling match, but he doubted he'd ever experience one to rival it. Esme resembled a Tasmanian devil as she jumped up each time to take her turn. She would grab her eight-pound ball, spend almost a minute lining up her shot with deep concentration...and bam! Most frames she got a strike or a spare, and Tordor was enchanted by her precocious competitive spirit.

"Okay, you're going to get a strike this time," she said, grabbing his wrist and dragging him to the ball chute. "Pick it up and let me help you with your stance."

Grasping his ball, he took the stance he'd been using for the previous frames, and she shook her head. "No, you need to back up a foot so you have ample room to approach the pins." Clenching his hips, she drew him back. "Here, this is better. Your legs are really long, so you need to use the entire walkway. When you release it, remember to let your arm naturally take the arc. It will help guide the ball."

Taking her instruction, Tordor concentrated with all his might. Sticking his tongue between his teeth, he strode forward, releasing the ball in a smooth motion. Straightening, he watched it slam into the first pin and knock all the others down.

"Woo hoo!" she said, jumping up and down and clapping. "You've got it! I'd be worried, but I'm already severely kicking your ass, so let's help you get over 100 at least."

Laughing, he chucked her nose. "Do you have to exclaim to the whole place how awful I am?"

"Oh, who cares? Man, this is fun. Okay, my turn!" Reaching for her ball, she began the ritual she took before each turn to position herself.

Tordor watched her, overcome with her innocent joy, and wondered how many times in her long life she'd truly been able to let go. She'd been on the run since she was ten years old, building a life in a world where her mother was murdered by her father. And yet, with all those obstacles, she'd evolved into a strong, confident, feisty woman. One with almost impenetrable defense mechanisms, but who could blame her? Observing her infectious laugh as she made another strike, Tordor vowed to ensure the next chapter in her life wouldn't be filled with heartache. It was a lofty aspiration, but he figured one made those sorts of declarations when they were on the precipice of falling in love.

"Wow," she said, breathless as she hopped over to him. "This is so fun. Thank you for taking me on a date and for not letting me screw it up." Cupping his shoulder, she squeezed it. "Maybe I did need someone to challenge me after all." His heart slammed as her lips curved into a tentative grin. "I'm glad it was you."

Placing his hand on her neck, he reveled in her soft skin beneath his palm. "Me too, little Elf," he said, unconcerned with the multitude of sounds and people in the background. He was too consumed with her to notice anything but her flushed cheeks and the swirling emotions in her eyes. He cataloged them all: arousal...fear...lust...tenderness. Each sentiment dwelled in the honey-flecked orbs, and he felt the magnetic pull he always experienced around her.

"One frame to go," she said, her voice raspy as she licked her lips. They shone under the bowling alley lights, and he almost groaned with the need to taste them. "I'm going to cream you, but let's try to get you one more strike."

Nodding, he begrudgingly released her and reached for his ball. He ended up getting a spare, and Esme did too, before they sat down to remove their bowling shoes and tug on their sneakers.

"Great game, Mr. Slayer-Vamp," she said, rising and extending her hand. "You improved a lot as we progressed."

Shaking her hand, he tilted his head. "Thanks for the instruction. You're a good teacher."

Her smile drifted away as her gaze lifted over his shoulder. Noticing her shoulders tense, he began to turn to see what had caused the change in her mood.

"Don't turn," she said softly, her nostrils flaring. "There's someone suspicious in the corner watching us."

Yearning to assess the situation, he held himself in check and followed her directive. "What do you want to do?"

"Act normal. Let's return the shoes and get out of here. We'll need to make sure we're not followed back to the hotel."

Nodding, Tordor grabbed both pairs of shoes, striving to remain calm. As they walked to the counter, he glanced at the man with dark hair dressed in black and situated in the back corner. After settling up, he led Esme to the car and slid behind the wheel.

"Who is he?" he asked, revving the engine and looking in the rearview mirror as he exited the parking lot.

"I don't know, but he's got the mark of my father's council." She tapped her neck. "It's a three-pronged tattoo, similar to a pitchfork. All the council members and supporters have one. My father has many spies he sends throughout the world."

Reaching over, he squeezed her thigh. "Good job spotting him. It's possible he already knows where we're staying, but it doesn't hurt to make sure we're not followed. I'll take some rural roads and keep an eye out."

Nodding, she pulled her leg up, hugging it to her chest in the defensive posture Tordor was coming to recognize well. "I can't let my father interfere in our mission any more than he already has, Tor. After what happened to Clayton...maybe I should leave the team."

"No," Tordor said firmly. "I need you, Esme. We're not letting Dakath deter us. We'll figure it out."

Her throat bobbed as she stared out the window, and he ached to comfort her. He drove for over half an hour, ensuring they weren't being followed, before pulling up to the side entrance of the hotel and heading to the room. Once inside, he pointed to the kitchen.

"Want me to bring you a glass of water?"

She shook her head. "I think I just want to go to bed and process this. That guy's face seemed familiar, but I can't place it."

Striding toward her, he placed his hands on her shoulders. "Don't process it alone. Let's talk. Two heads are better than one."

"I don't want to involve you—"

"I'm already involved, Esme!" he interjected, frustration in his tone. "And honestly, I'm getting tired of you leaving me out of the fucking loop. I can't help you if you're closed off to me."

Jerking away from his touch, she jabbed a finger in his face. "I never said I needed your help! I've always done everything on my own, and I like it that way."

"Not anymore," he countered, grabbing her finger. "It's time to stop running and trust someone. Your need to do everything alone is going to get you hurt, and it might get one of our team members killed. Do you want that?"

Her mouth fell open. "Of course I don't want that! How could you accuse me of wanting to hurt our team?" Her face crumpled as tears flooded her eyes. "All I've ever done is try to help immortals..."

"I know, sweetheart, but you can't do it on your own. We're stronger united—"

"I knew I should've stayed away from you," she interrupted, swiping tears from her cheeks. "I never asked for this!"

"Asked for someone to care? To want to know what's really inside? That's bullshit, Esme, and I didn't know your mother, but I can bet she'd be pissed you're living a solitary life. She'd want more for you."

Rage and pain contorted her features into a mask so torturous Tordor wanted to reverse time and take back the words. Hating that he'd hurt her, he reached for her.

"Esme—"

"You're right," she said, backing toward her room. "You didn't know my mother. You don't know anything about her!"

"Because you won't *let* me." Stepping toward her, he pleaded, "Let me in, Esme. Let me show you that it doesn't have to hurt when someone cares about you."

White-knuckled hands clenched the door as she glowered at him. "Leave me alone, Tor. I mean it." Firmly shutting the door, she ended the terrible conversation.

Overcome with frustration and guilt for the way he'd spoken to her, Tordor ran a hand through his hair. Cursing the gods, he trailed to his room and plopped on the bed. Sliding his hands beneath his head, he gazed at the slowly whirling ceiling fan, hoping he hadn't blown it.

Racked with emotion, he allowed his heartbeat to settle before prepping for bed. After stripping down to his boxer-briefs, he climbed under the covers, determined to apologize to her tomorrow and set things right.

Chapter 15

As soon as Esme drifted to sleep, she fell into the nightmare. Visions of her parents arguing flooded her brain as she relived the last moments of her mother's life. As always, before her last breath, Dyana strained toward Dakath, whispering something unintelligible to Esme's ears...

Shooting upright, Esme gulped down air as she struggled to calm her beating heart. Patting her damp forehead, she seethed with annoyance at the ever-occurring nightmare. For once in her damn life, she wanted to be free of the wretched memories.

Closing her eyes, she focused on the palpable yearning she felt to be comforted by Tordor. The feeling was compounded by the argument they'd had and her belief she'd royally fucked things up between them. She'd been shaken by the ominous man watching them whose face seemed familiar but she couldn't place. It had left her unsettled, and she'd been unable to control her temper when Tordor challenged her.

Goddess, she hated pushing him away, but Esme was terrified of the alternative...even if she craved it with every fiber of her being...

Her gaze lifted to the door, knowing Tordor was only steps away. A severe longing throbbed in every cell of her skin as her pulse quickened. It would only take seconds to tread to his room and have him hold her with those thick, strong arms.

Her tender half-Vamp would pull her close, soothing her as she so rarely allowed.

As the yearning grew, her legs unconsciously moved as if detached from her brain. Her feet touched the carpeted floor, and suddenly she was drifting across the darkened living room. Arriving at his door, she reached for it with shaking fingers.

Fiddling with the knob, she slowly turned it, pushing the door open as a waft of light from the bulb above the kitchen stove shone over his bed. His gaze seared into her, and she realized he'd been awake. Was he waiting for her? Did he know she would find her way to him?

Goddess, could he *feel* her craving for him?

Focusing on her with those striking green eyes, he gripped the covers and lifted them, extending an invitation to climb inside and take the comfort she desperately needed.

She'd never given in to that need before.

But for some reason, tonight, she capitulated.

Closing the door behind her, she approached the bed and slid under the soft covers. Gliding her arms around his neck, she buried her face in his chest, nuzzling as she settled against him. Gliding her leg around his waist, she snaked around him, holding on for dear life. Throwing caution to the wind, Esme decided if she was going to lean on someone, she might as well lean *all* the way.

Tordor drew the covers up, tucking them around their entwined bodies. Sighing with contentment, Esme allowed herself to take comfort from someone for the first time in so very long...

Tordor's eyes snapped open as soon as he heard the jiggling doorknob. As his heart jumpstarted in his chest, he observed Esme push the door open. Tears glistened under long lashes in the dim light as she stared at him, a heart-wrenching expression covering her stunning features. She looked so vulnerable in the moonlight, cheeks flushed as a vein pounded in her neck, and he lifted the covers, offering her a silent invitation.

Relief flooded him when she took it, sliding in and wrapping herself so tightly around him he didn't know where she ended and he began. Overcome with the joy of holding her, he stroked her hair and waited.

She curled into him, warm and soft in her cotton shorts and tank top, and he gently kissed her temple as she nuzzled his neck. His other hand caressed her back over her shirt, and he strove to keep his breathing steady so she would remain relaxed. Difficult, since having her wrapped around him was his ultimate fantasy.

She hooked her leg around his waist, clutching him tighter, and Tordor clenched his jaw. Tamping down his desire, he realized her proximity would lead to an inevitable physical response the longer he held her. Determined to focus on comforting her, he relaxed his muscles, hoping to keep the erection at bay.

"I'm sorry," she mumbled against his chest.

"It's okay, sweetheart," he said, stroking her golden hair. "I'm sorry too."

They lay there, hearts beating in tandem with each shallow breath. Closing his eyes, he reveled in her smell and the soft tendrils of hair that brushed his nose. Content with the silence, he waited, giving her complete control.

Finally, she sighed against his chest. "I have the same nightmare almost every night," she said softly, gently sifting her fingers through the tiny black hairs atop his pecs.

"Of your parents?"

Nodding, she burrowed deeper into his body.

"I just stood there, frozen, when he hurt her," she warbled, her voice thick with emotion. "Why didn't I try to help her? Why didn't I save her?"

Compassion flooded him as he finally realized where her deep-seated need to protect and save other immortals originated. "You couldn't have done anything, Esme. You were a child."

"I could've *tried*," she said, pressing her face into the valley of his chest. "Why didn't I at least try?"

Sliding his fingers under her chin, he forced her to meet his gaze in the moonlit room. "Because you were a *child*, Esme. You need to forgive yourself."

Her tongue darted out to bathe her lips, wetting them as they glistened under his gaze. "What if I can't?"

He ran his finger over the bridge of her nose. "You can, Little Elf. You're so strong. It's one of my favorite things about you."

She frowned slightly, causing him to chuckle.

"Are you laughing at me?" she asked incredulously.

"I'm just laughing at your frown. It's cute. Sorry."

Sighing, she slid her palm over his jaw, caressing the stubble as blood surged to his crotch. Accepting the inevitable, he gave in to the desire, feeling himself harden as she touched him.

Gasping, her eyes widened as his cock swelled, nestled in the juncture of her thighs.

"Sorry about that too," he said, feeling his cheeks flush. "I can't really control it." Sliding his hand down her back, he gazed into her eyes as his palm glided down to cover her bottom. Gently squeezing, he drew her closer. "I've never wanted anyone like this, Esme. Somewhere along the way, you invaded every thought I had, and I never want you to stop."

A shudder ran through her at the words. "My romantic half-Vamp," she teased. "Somewhere along the way, I forgot what it was like to be young and romantic."

"The great thing about being immortal is that I have lots of time to show you, hon." Threading his fingers through her hair, he drew her close, grazing her lips with his. "I don't want to push you, sweetheart," he rasped, brushing his lips back and forth over hers. "But, goddess, I want to kiss you so badly—"

She pressed her lips to his, inhaling his deep moan as she writhed against him. Her breasts pressed into his chest through her thin shirt, and Tordor could feel the tight points of her nipples against his heated skin. It drove him wild as he surged his tongue inside her mouth...testing...tasting...finally touching her as he'd so often imagined.

"*Tor...*" she whispered into his mouth, her body arching into his as they licked and played with each other. Sliding his tongue across her lower lip, he sucked it between his teeth and gently nipped her with his fangs. Her groan shot to every crevice of his body, causing his cock to swell as she undulated against him.

"Not fair," she teased, nipping him back. "I don't have fangs."

"You can still bite me, little Elf," he rasped, licking her lip to soothe the sting. "Anywhere and everywhere you want."

Breathing a laugh, she rubbed the tip of her nose against his. "I don't think that would be pleasurable in *some* places." Gliding her hand down his side, she slowly began to inch toward his shaft.

Tordor encircled her wrist, drawing her hand to his chest as he resumed kissing her. Extending his tongue, he coaxed her, licking her wet tongue until she surged it deep in his mouth. Tightening his arms, he groaned as their tongues battled and mated.

Eventually, she drew back and stared at him, desire rampant in her glassy eyes. "I can take care of this for you," she said, pushing her mound into his swollen shaft as she grinned. "If you want me to."

Although it sounded amazing, she'd come to him for comfort and he didn't want to add sex to the mix quite yet. He still needed to tell her he was a virgin and wanted to do it thoughtfully so she understood how special she was to him.

Plus, he thought with an inward grimace, if she touched his cock with her soft palm, he might explode on the spot, and that would just be fucking embarrassing.

Armed with that knowledge, he rested his forehead against hers, pleased her breathing was as rushed and jagged as his. He was extremely attracted to Esme, and her resulting attraction bolstered his confidence since he was vastly inexperienced compared to her.

"Not tonight," he said softly, placing a reassuring kiss on her lips when they formed a slight pout. "I just want to hold you and have you talk to me, sweetheart."

She expelled a wistful sigh. "You're determined to worm your way inside, aren't you?" she asked, tapping her chest over her heart.

"Now you're catching on," he said, beaming as she chuckled. Shuffling on the bed, he drew her across his body, urging her to rest her cheek on his chest as he ran his fingers through her hair. "Tell me more about your mom."

"We really should talk about the creepy dude who was watching us tonight. He didn't seem startled that I spotted him, and he didn't harm us. I'm not quite sure what to make of it."

Tordor contemplated. "Let's talk about him in the morning."

"Tor—"

"I promise we'll make it a priority. We need to figure it out." Kissing her hair, he pulled her closer. "For now, tell me about Dyana. Did she sing like you? Is that where you got it from?"

Sighing, she snuggled into him and nodded. "She had such a beautiful voice. God, Tor, she would sing lullabies to me every night, and I adored listening to her. Her voice was haunting, but in a good way. Kind of ethereal."

"What was her favorite lullaby?"

"Hmm..." Her voice drifted as she pondered. "She often sang one she called 'Havfruens Hærlighedssang.' In Danish, it means 'The Mermaid's Love Song.'"

"Very romantic and imaginative for a human."

"Hey, I'm half-human," she said, playfully swatting his chest.

Chuckling, he rubbed his cheek against her hair. "No disrespect. I like your human half...and your immortal half."

Tordor felt her smile against his chest.

"Did Dyana look like you?"

"Yes," she said, plucking the tiny hairs on his chest. "I got my blond hair and fair complexion from her, but I have my father's eyes." Clutching him tighter, she stiffened. "I hate them. I have to see him every time I look in the mirror."

Tordor stroked her back, soothing her as she continued.

"Mother was radiant. She was always smiling or laughing. My father is quite serious, as you can probably imagine, but from the stories she told me, they were smitten with each other the moment they met."

"In Denmark?"

Nodding, she trailed her fingers over his pec. "My father heard about an outpost of Elves living in the fishing town of Svendborg. He came to scope it out and met my mother. From what she told me, they fell in love through a whirlwind courtship and she begged my father not to return to Romania."

Tordor's eyebrows drew together. "With how much he detests humans, she must've really had some sway over him."

"I think they truly loved each other those first few years. Interestingly, many stories circulate in Svendborg about an immortal king who couldn't deny his love for a human," she said in a soulful tone. "Most think they're fairy tales. Very few know they're true, or that the story ends in tragedy."

"The tragic ones are always the most memorable," he said softly.

"So true. Anyway, my father took a break from ruling and stayed with her, and eventually, I was conceived. She tried to convince him I wasn't the abomination he feared, but ultimately, my existence was too much for him to bear. He became crazed with the notion that he'd borne a hybrid. My mother did all she could, but they were doomed."

"Such a sad story. No wonder you don't believe in love."

Lifting her head, she placed her elbow on his chest and rested her chin on her fist. "I certainly didn't have the best example," she said, arching a sardonic brow, "but I also believe love requires sacrifice. If I can save someone by leaving them, I'll do it every damn time, Tor. I've never minded sacrificing my happiness to keep those I care about safe."

Tracing his finger across her jaw, he studied her. "And what do you think your mother would say about that?"

Her chest rose as she inhaled deeply, contemplating. After several seconds, she shrugged. "I think she would say I sacrifice too much sometimes. That I let fear prevent me from having a full life."

Tordor's expression turned sentimental as he acknowledged the truth of her statement and her willingness to be honest.

"She wanted me to be happy," Esme continued, "but I'm so damn scared. I don't want anyone I care about to be put in jeopardy. To be hunted and tormented. It's a terrible existence."

"Maybe, and I'm just spit-balling here..." he said, flashing a tender grin, "but maybe if someone cares about you, they won't give a crap about the risks. Have you ever considered that, sweetheart?"

Lowering her gaze, she shook her head. "It's not worth it—"

Sliding his fingers under her chin, he forced her gaze to his. "*You're worth it, Esme.* I wish you'd allow yourself to accept that people want to be in the trenches with you."

Her throat bobbed in the silver moonlight as it wafted through the windows. "What if I allow that and they die like my mother? Or Clayton...or the other bodies my father has left in my path? It's excruciating, Tor..." Her voice cracked, the sound breaking his heart wide-open, and he surrounded her with his arms, pulling her into a strong embrace.

"I know," he soothed, smoothing his hand over her hair as she squeezed him. "It's okay, hon."

Resting her face on his chest, she burrowed against him. "You have so much life ahead of you," she murmured against his pecs. "I won't let you sacrifice that for me."

"Well, little Elf, I hate to tell you, but it's not your decision. I'm pretty stubborn, and I make my own choices."

Sighing, she pressed her nails into his chest, causing him to hiss.

"Watch the claws," he teased, inwardly reveling at the possessive touch. Sliding his hand to her butt, he lightly smacked it.

"Hey!"

"You're not always a picnic either. You're so committed to being a lone wolf. I can't wait to break through those walls, and I definitely love a challenge."

"It's not happening," she muttered.

His deep laughter surrounded them. Settling further into the mattress, he resumed stroking her back. "Tell me more about your mom. It's nice to see her through your eyes."

She melted into his body and began to tell him. About Dyana's laugh, and her dreams, and her deep-seated love for Dakath. Eventually, her words began to drag as she drifted atop his chest.

There in the moonlit room, they crossed the abyss together, falling into slumber entwined and content. Before the last vestiges of consciousness scattered, Tordor thanked the goddess for Esme's openness and vowed to ensure her walls continued to part with each passing day.

Chapter 16

E sme's eyes fluttered as the first rays of dawn filtered through the window. Lifting her lids, she turned her head on the pillow to observe the large body sleeping beside her. Tordor must've shifted on his side sometime during the night, and he was snoring as if he were in a contest with a freight train to see who was louder. Covering her mouth with her fist to halt her giggle, she studied his back, debating what to do.

Suddenly, he mumbled something incoherent and flipped on his back. Throwing his arm over his eyes, he continued snoring as Esme tried not to devolve into a fit of laughter. Seeing him like this was adorable, and it shifted something deep within to see his vulnerability as he slept.

Glancing down, she noticed the bulge under the covers, situated directly above his crotch. Feeling her mouth water, Esme took a moment to wonder... After all, Tordor was huge, so it made sense he'd be *endowed* in all the right places. Glancing at her hand, she flexed it, trying to imagine the feel of his length between her fingers. Was he a gentle lover? Passionate? Dominant? Judging by the light slaps he'd given her backside last night, he certainly seemed like a playful and ardent lover. Wanting to find out, she reached for the covers, slightly gasping when she pulled them away.

His cock swelled beneath the fabric of his black boxer-briefs, firm and ready as her eyes grew wide. Dying to touch him, she reached toward his torso, touching her fingers to his side and grazing them down to the hem of his underwear...

His hand snaked around her wrist, halting her as his eyes snapped open. Gazing at her with half-lidded eyes, he swallowed thickly.

"Sweetheart," he whispered, "not yet."

Rising to balance on her shins, she regarded him, wondering why he wanted to wait. She'd had her fair share of lovers, and none had ever turned down an opportunity to enjoy some morning delight. Gazing at his swollen cock, she lifted a shoulder.

"You just seemed...*ready*. I wanted to make you feel good."

Breath hissed from his lips as he seemed to steady himself. "Well, it *is* morning, hon. I usually wake up ready."

Biting her lip, she grinned. "Then let me touch you."

He appeared frustrated as he rubbed his eyes. "I have to tell you something, and I was waiting for the right moment. I'm not sure this is it since I'm barely awake."

Curiosity swelled in her belly. "Well, you *have* to tell me now."

Chuckling, he gazed at her from the pillow, his expression reverent and a bit hesitant. "Crap. I should've prepared better for this."

"What the hell are you going to tell me? You inherited self-healing abilities from your dad, so I don't think we have to worry about STDs."

"That's not it. I definitely don't have any STDs."

Arching her brows, she breathed a laugh. "Said with confidence. Okay then. What is it?"

His chest lifted as he inhaled a deep breath. "I'm confident because I've never been in that type of situation."

"What type of situation?"

His throat bobbed. "A sexual situation."

Esme opened her mouth then shut it, working her jaw as she processed. "You've never...had sex?"

His lips formed the cutest pout she'd ever seen, melting her heart as he slowly shook his head. "Nope. It just never felt right with anyone else, and, well, when you're the son of two people who intensely love each other, you kind of want the same for yourself."

Compassion filled every crevice of her soul as she took a moment to realize how hard it must've been to tell her. Tordor was extremely confident, but his admission was one that required vulnerability and openness. Moving closer, she glided her leg over his stomach, straddling him but ensuring she didn't touch his burgeoning erection. Cradling his face, she smiled.

"You're a virgin?"

"Yeah." He playfully rolled his eyes. "It's awkward, but I wanted you to know before things turned sexual between us."

Arching a brow, she formed a sultry grin. "Pretty sure of yourself, *hmm?*"

Laughing, he ran his hands over her arms in a soft caress. "*You* came to *my* bed last night, sweetheart. So, yeah, I guess I'm feeling confident."

"Touché."

His gaze was soulful as he spoke. "The thing is, Esme, I think I knew the moment I saw you that you were the one I'd been waiting for. It took some time to grow into it, but it's been there since you ate my lunch on the battlefield."

She grinned, taken by the sweet words. "I did no such thing. You were just being way too formal and I had a job to do."

"You put me in my place," he said, playfully tugging a lock of her hair.

Squinting, she bit her tongue. "Okay, maybe I did. But you liked it."

"I loved it," he said reverently. "I have no idea what the future holds, but I know I want to make love to you." His cheeks flushed. "If you don't mind that I'm a virgin. I'm *very* good at taking instruction."

"Goddess, you're so cute," she said, running her thumb over his reddened cheek. "Of course, I want to make love to you, Tor. I mean, I'm terrified, because I think it's going to generate a bunch of unwanted *feelings*,"—she circled her hand over her heart—"and I don't really let myself experience those."

"I'll protect your heart, Esme," he whispered.

Tears burned her eyes as she recognized how magnificent he was. A generous, protective, soulful man who cared for her despite her best efforts to push him away. Leaning down, she brushed his lips with hers. "I know you will. I can't promise forever, Tor, but I can promise today and tomorrow...and maybe a few days after that. We'll see how eager a student you are."

Delight twisted his features as he squeezed her arms. "Oh, I'm eager. Believe me. But we have to look over the profiles and try to figure out who was watching us last night. I'd rather focus on that first so we can really enjoy being together our first time. Is that okay?"

"Yes. Plus, I'm pretty sure I have some super unsexy eye crust going on right now." She pointed to her face as he chuckled. "Also, you snore like a foghorn. What gives?"

Rolling his eyes, he shook his head on the pillow. "I know. It's awful. You have permission to smother me with a pillow if it gets too loud."

"Ohhh, fun." She chucked her brows. "Okay, let's get crackin' so we can move onto the fun stuff." She kissed him before rising.

"Wait," he said, gripping her wrist. "Thank you, Esme. I wasn't sure how you'd feel about my...*situation*. I don't want to make it weird."

Sliding her hand in his, she squeezed. "Then we won't make it weird. I'm sure I'm going to start freaking out in the shower once I have time to process." His lips thinned. "Not because of you," she assured him. "Because of me. Being someone's first is meaningful, and the little voice in my brain is going to tell me it's going to make me even more attached to you."

She sat on the edge of the bed and shrugged. "But the thing is, I'm already becoming attached. I think that was clear when I came to *your* room last night," she teased, parroting back his words. "If I freak out about it, I'm going to psych myself out, so let's just agree we both won't make it weird. We're adults and we want to be together. Let's stay in the moment and take comfort from each other."

"And what if I want more than the moment?"

Kissing his hand, she shook her head. "Too much. That's definitely making it weird, and I just can't right now."

Nodding, he accepted her terms. "Okay. I'll relent...for now."

"Thank you." Giving a nod, she rose and trailed out of the room. "I'm going to throw on yoga pants and do some stretches before I shower. Join me if you want."

Five minutes later, dressed in her yoga clothes, she stepped into the living room to find her sexy half-Vamp waiting for her. Deciding it was going to be a good day, she strode to the window to begin her poses.

A few hours later, Tordor saved the last document on the laptop and gave a firm nod. "The profiles look great. I think we can confirm with General Markson that we'll be ready to hand them over tomorrow morning."

Picking up her cell, Esme typed a text to the general.

Her phone chirped in response, and she showed him the screen. "Confirmed to meet at the secure location," she said, grinning. "Holy shit, Tor. We're doing it. Once he vets our candidates, the first wave of immortal integration will begin."

"And once they're settled, we'll implement more waves until we're ready to reveal ourselves." Sitting back on the couch, he laced his fingers behind his head. "Man, I hope it works. We won't know for decades, probably."

"Better than us showing up and saying, 'Hi, *we're immortal beings who live with you now, so get used to it,*'" she teased, waving her hands like a cheerleader. "This plan has the strongest chance of success, and we'll do our best to make it happen."

Glancing at the laptop, his eyes narrowed. "In the meantime, I'd like to try to track down the guy from last night, especially if he looked familiar to you. We need to figure out why he was watching us."

Sliding the laptop closer, she pulled up a browser and typed in "Elven council tattoo." "Well, here's the tattoo I was telling you about." Pointing at the screen, she showed him countless images of the three-pronged tattoo.

Scooting closer, Tordor studied the various pictures, some of men's necks with the tattoos and others as drawings. "I can't believe it's just there for everyone to see. How have humans not discovered that Elves have been living among them for ages?"

"People only see what they're capable of seeing," she said with a shrug. "And the Elves blend in pretty well. We look human except for our ears." She rubbed the slightly pointed tip of one ear. "And I'll remind you that the Vampyres and Slayers had no idea Elves existed until your mom and Kenden found the scrolls at Restia."

"Fair point. They were too busy fighting each other to realize another species of immortal existed."

"And there are probably more species—who knows? But that's a discussion for another day." Clicking through the pictures, her expression grew pensive. "So, creepy dude from last night definitely is or was on my father's council. I say *was* because it's possible he defected along with my uncle."

Tordor lifted his brows. "Well, that seems relevant. You've mentioned your uncle helped you as a child, but I didn't realize he dissented from your father's council. How long has it been since you've seen him?"

She frowned as her expression grew sad. "Several centuries. He was kind to me after Mother died, but he also maintained distance between us. I think it was his way of showing loyalty to my father. Gillam was still on the council at that time, and I think he felt that showing me too much affection would anger my father. He hired a caretaker for me named Pedrene and left me in Denmark so she could raise me."

"Did he come to visit you?"

"A few times over the years until I turned seventeen and left to branch out on my own. I observed Gillam a few times when I visited Romania to gather intel on my father, and eventually, my spy informed me he dissented from my father and left the council."

"Better late than never," Tordor said, arching a derisive brow.

"True. It's likely he became disenchanted with Father's methods. I think he would've preferred the Elves stick to their own, but he couldn't justify the killing of hybrid Elven children. From what I know, several Elves dissented along with Gillam, and they haven't been seen since. I assumed they all went on with their lives and weren't involved with Elven matters anymore, but I could be wrong."

"So, perhaps creepy dude was watching us to gather intel for your uncle."

"Maybe," she mused, rubbing her chin. "Gillam was always quite compassionate toward me. Maybe he heard about Clayton and decided to send someone to check on me."

"Or maybe the guy is just waiting for the right time to take us out."

"How very *unoptimistic* of you," she teased, squinting one eye. "When you've lived as long as I have, you learn to listen to your gut. I freaked last night, but once I slept on it, I realized I didn't get any nefarious vibes from him. If he'd wanted to hurt us, he could've shot us in the parking lot, even if we did a good job of evading him. Anyone with my father's mark is skilled in surveillance."

"So, what's our plan of action?" Tordor asked. "Do you want to try to track him down?"

"There are some underground immortal channels," she said, typing as she pulled one up. "See? This one's called IM-Chat. Let's post some anonymous feelers on these message boards and see if anyone bites."

"Immortals using human internet technology to surreptitiously connect with each other," he said, shaking his head. "It's amazing how many are hiding in plain sight here."

"For sure." She pulled up a different chat site. "This one has an anonymous posting of an Elf who lost her husband and is looking for other immortals to connect with." Glancing at Tordor, she lifted a shoulder. "Even more reason to build a safe haven at Rausch Gap. I'd love to offer immortals like her a place to go."

"I couldn't agree more."

She pulled up another screen and continued to type. Finally, she turned and smiled. "Okay, I just made a few anonymous posts asking if anyone knows of an Elf matching the description of creepy dude. I'll check later to see if we get any hits. In the meantime, should we call your parents to get an update on purchasing the site?"

Glancing at his watch, he nodded. "Let's do it. They should be around."

Pulling up the video chat app on the laptop, Tordor scooted closer to her, inhaling the fragrant scent of her shampoo as they called Miranda and Sathan.

Chapter 17

Jaxon stood atop the cliff overlooking the Pacific Ocean in the small coastal town outside San Francisco. He'd taken the day-long road trip from Arizona and promptly passed out once he arrived at his hotel. Now, freshly rested, he was ready to track down Tatiana and ask for her help.

Inhaling the salty breeze, Jaxon closed his eyes, admitting the human world was quite beautiful. The immortal world had its beauty too, but its landscape consisted mostly of rolling hills instead of magnificent oceans and red-rocked deserts. Surprised at his affection for a land that wasn't his, he allowed it to bloom as he stood firm and tall above the sea.

"Breathtaking, isn't it?" a feminine voice chimed beside him.

Jaxon's lids snapped open as his head jerked toward the woman beside him. Long, black curls extended down her back, framing her amber eyes under the blue sky. Her russet skin was flawless and wrinkle-free, although Jaxon knew she'd lived for centuries. Perhaps even eons.

"It's absolutely stunning." Facing her, he crossed his arms and grinned. "You know, I was really looking forward to hunting you down. A good investigator enjoys the challenge more than the result."

Her lips twitched as her expression softened. "I understand, but I don't like wasting time, Jaxon, son of Trammell. Heden should've told you this."

"I'm sure he did, ma'am, but I'm still a bit shocked to see you appear out of thin air."

"Very few of us can transport," she said, gazing across the ocean. "I learned how long ago, as did Crimeous and Dakath. Calinda is the most recent to acquire the ability, although I don't think she truly understands it yet." Latching onto his gaze, she spoke solemnly. "Each step forward is a small brick laid on a path forged long ago."

"Prophetic," he said, arching a brow.

"Just reality." Placing her hands in the pockets of her leather jacket, she studied him expectantly. "So, Jaxon, you are here to ask for my help. A noble request, but it is not time for me to join Tordor and Esmerelda's cause yet."

"Dakath has already killed one of their counterparts in cold blood," Jaxon said. "We thought you might want to intervene so more don't get hurt."

Something dark and laced with agony flashed through her eyes before it disappeared. "Pain and death are part of the journey, even for immortals. I support the immersion of the species, but the two heirs need to blaze the path."

Jaxon drew his features together, slightly confused.

"Esmerelda is heir as much as Tordor is. One is celebrated and one is tormented, but it doesn't negate their birthright. They are both children of kings and will learn to become great rulers."

"So you don't want to help us because you want them to learn?" He rubbed the back of his neck. "I get learning from experience, but they have no idea how to combat Dakath's powers."

"Dr. Tyson will be helpful in that regard. I'm glad Larkin spared his life and tracked him down. Quaygon needs a purpose that is not motivated by evil. He has never felt love or acceptance. Perhaps his ability to help the cause will provide the opportunity."

"I've been briefed on his abilities as a chemist," Jaxon said. "If he can make antidotes that counteract the effects of Dakath's poisons, it will certainly help." Sparing her a look, he asked, "Should I even be surprised you know Larkin approached Dr. Tyson?"

Chuckling, she shook her head. "No. But remember I have powers similar to Dakath's. If I'm aware of the workings of the ITU, so is he."

"Noted." Kicking the soft ground with the toe of his boot, he slipped his hands into his back pockets. "I'm not thrilled to return empty-handed. I thought you might agree to help us."

Lifting her chin, she arched a brow. "Then don't return empty-handed."

"Why do I feel like you're going to send me on a mission to retrieve something?"

Grinning, she asked, "Well, isn't that your job?"

"I guess it is. Lay it on me."

Turing to him, she lifted her palm and began to trace it with her finger. "Before the great flood, the Elves lived in their own section of the immortal world." She circled the spot where her pinkie met her palm. "Afterward, the Deamons eventually lived in their caves,"—her finger trailed toward the center—"and Vampyres and Slayers lived in the lush valleys." She circled the broad area where her thumb met her palm.

Displaying the palm of her other hand, she shook it. "Humans always lived separately, but there was always spillover." Clapping her hands together, she "meshed" the two worlds. "But did you know there were fairy tales of another species of immortal living on the undiscovered border between the human and immortal worlds?" She flipped her hands and wiggled her fingers. "Here, where no one thought to look."

Jaxon studied the smooth skin of the back of her hands. "Well, I'm thoroughly confused, but go on."

Her throat shone under the sun as she threw her head back and laughed. "You're almost as funny as Heden. I enjoy the ribbing." Refocusing, she continued. "This species disappeared from the scrolls and soothsayer manuals eons ago, but their traditions have been passed down to those of us who remember."

"I'm guessing there's a point somewhere here," he teased, arching a brow.

"The ancient species were called Nymphs, and they were fantastic healers. One of their favorite healing properties came from the barks of ancient trees."

"Okaaaaay…"

"The oldest tree in the human world sits not far from here in the Inyo National Forest of California. It is aptly named Methusela after the oldest living man in the human Bible." Stepping forward, she tapped his forehead. "Don't return empty-handed, Jaxon."

Realization dawned as he finally understood. "You want me to retrieve some bark from the tree and deliver it to Dr. Tyson at Rausch Gap."

"Yes. I have used the bark in some of my potions, but Dr. Tyson wouldn't know of its power. It will be helpful for creating antidotes against Dakath's poisons."

"I don't mind getting some samples of the bark. I assume the tree is guarded, but I've been known to be stealthy."

"Ah, yes, the infamous bed-hopper. I relish the day when you meet a woman who will end that streak."

Grimacing, he waved his hand. "Not likely...unless you want to take advantage of this romantic setting..." He waggled his eyebrows.

White teeth flashed as she laughed. "I'm not the woman who will break your streak, Jaxon, but trust me when I say, it will happen."

Plugging his ears with his fingers, he muttered, "Not listening."

"All right, I'll relent. But take my advice on the bark samples. They will help the cause."

Lowering his hands, he fisted one on his hip. "Are we going to pretend you didn't just drop a bomb on me by indicating another species of immortal existed? We should probably discuss that, no?"

Gazing wistfully across the gently breaking waves, her teeth toyed with her lip. "The Nymphs have not been seen for eons."

"But that doesn't mean they don't exist. It could mean they don't wish to be seen."

"Agreed," she said with a nod. "And we'll leave it that way for now."

"What do they look like? When I hear 'Nymph' I think of hooved feet and horns over their ears."

Wrinkling her nose, she shook her head. "They rather look like the rest of us, as all the species share similarities." Lifting her finger, she cocked a brow. "But Nymphs did share one distinct feature no other immortals possessed."

Jaxon circled his hand, rapt with curiosity.

Leaning forward, she spoke softly as if to increase the dramatic effect. "They all had lavender eyes."

Straightening, Jaxon felt his eyes grow wide. "Lila and Adelyn have lavender eyes."

"Yes. The only two immortals still alive known to express the lavender eye color gene. Rather remarkable, is it not?"

Stunned, he nodded. "Does that mean they're part-Nymph?"

Lifting a shoulder, her lips formed a shuttered grin. "I can't say for certain, but it's an interesting question."

"Sure is." Running a hand through his hair, he looked to the sky. "How far is Inyo National Forest from here?"

"Less than five hours. If you leave now, you can make it by sunset and camp in the park. It might be easier to obtain the samples once it's dark."

"*Steal* the samples," he quipped.

"Semantics," she retorted with a shrug. "But if it saves lives, I think Methusela would happily donate his bark. He is a relic of days long past and a good reminder that things can stand the test of time."

Facing her, Jaxon extended his hand. "Sure I can't convince you to come with me? It's shaping up to be a fun adventure." He flashed a cheeky grin.

Sliding her palm over his, she shook. "I've had enough adventures for a while. Rest assured, I'll join the fray again when necessary. Give Esmerelda my best and remind her she is valued and important. Tordor will help you with this."

Releasing her hand, he narrowed his eyes. "Are they more than partners?"

Her resulting grin revealed the answer.

"Well, all right then. A pleasure to meet you, Tatiana."

"The pleasure is mine. Until we meet again, Jaxon." Stepping back, she lifted her hands and turned her palms to the sky. "Don't get arrested obtaining the bark. The team at Rausch Gap needs you more than you know." Closing her eyes, she began to chant as the wind churned and whirled around her, lifting her curls in a vibrant swath of color against the horizon. And then, in the blink of an eye, she was gone.

Resting his hands on his hips, Jaxon studied the spot where she'd stood, noticing the slightly bent grass. Facing the ocean, his nostrils flared as he inhaled the salty breeze and marveled at the sea. Then he pivoted and walked to his car, determined to make it to Inyo National Forest by sunset.

Chapter 18

Sathan spoke to Tordor and Esme as Miranda puffed her cheeks, rocking back and forth beside him. Their son's face shone on the laptop screen as it sat on the desk in their royal office. They'd turned it to face the room so he and Miranda could sit in the comfortable leather chairs that faced the desk, but Miranda looked anything but comfortable as her skin glistened with a slight sheen of sweat.

"Mom?" Tordor called. "You okay? You look...*green.*"

Visibly swallowing, she nodded. "I'm good. As your father said, the sale of Rausch Gap is in progress. We'll be in touch when everything is complete."

"Awesome. Thanks for your support on this, guys. I'm going to let you go because this one's starving as usual," Tordor teased, pointing his thumb at Esme as she chuckled. "We'll call after we meet General Markson tomorrow."

"Bye, son. Stay safe." Sathan closed the laptop and turned to Miranda. "Holy shit, I see it. He can barely take his eyes off her."

Rising, she covered her mouth. "Told you!" she mumbled behind her fingers. Gagging, she shook her head. "Damn it...gotta go."

Rushing from the room, she ran up the grand staircase to their private bathroom.

Sathan followed close behind, worried by the terrible sounds emanating from the bathroom. He found Miranda hugging the toilet, violently ill as she emptied her stomach. Fear shot down his spine, almost crumbling his large frame as he remembered her pregnancy with Tordor. It had been volatile, and he'd almost lost them both in childbirth. Icy rivulets of anxiety wrapped around his heart at the prospect of her suffering through that again.

"I'm here, little Slayer," he soothed, lowering beside her and wrapping his arms around her trembling body. "What can I do to help?"

"Don't touch me," she moaned, leaning her forehead on the toilet seat. "I swear to the goddess, I'm never letting you near me again. I know I said that last time, but I mean it."

Relieved she was still able to tease him, he combed her dark hair from her temple as she struggled to breathe. "I was worried this would happen, but we made our decision, sweetheart. Please don't make me feel worse." Kissing her neck, he nuzzled the soft skin. "I wish I could absorb your pain. I'd do it in a heartbeat."

"Stop being sweet," she droned. "It's going to make me want to have sexy times with you, and I told you it's never happening again. *Ever.*"

Unable to control his grin, he held her as the retching died down and eventually ceased. Helping her stand, he led her to the sink and poured her a glass of water. Drinking it, she studied him with those glorious eyes that still held him entranced after all these years.

Finishing the water, she set down the cup. "That helped. Thanks." Reaching over, she grabbed her toothbrush and paste and began to brush her teeth. "My mouth tastes like a warm garbage dump," she garbled as she moved the brush back and forth.

"Sexy," he teased, leaning on the counter so he could assess her. Although her face was still pale, a touch of color was returning to her cheeks, causing him a slight bit of relief.

When she finished brushing, he led her to the bed and kicked off his shoes before sitting and placing his back against the headboard. Reaching for her, he drew her close.

"I literally just told you I'm never doing that again—"

"Come on, Miranda," he said, his tone still filled with slight worry. "Let me help in the way I can."

Taking pity on him, she kicked off her shoes and slid on the bed. Pushing her butt into the juncture of his thighs, she leaned back and sighed in contentment when he cupped her shoulders. Hoping to soothe her, he began to massage her tense muscles. Joy flooded him when she moaned in contentment.

"Oh, yeah...that's the spot." Tilting her neck, she allowed him greater access. "How am I going to do this for ten more months? Of course, you blood-suckers have longer gestation periods, so the real torture hasn't even started."

Working his thumbs along her shoulders, he pressed his lips to her ear. "We'll take it day by day. And our kingdom is finally at peace, so we won't have to worry about fighting a war while your ankles are swollen."

"Keep it up. You're sooooo funny I forgot to laugh."

Chuckling, he began to massage her upper arms.

After several minutes, she craned her neck to stare into his eyes. "He's not coming home, is he, Sathan?"

"I don't think so, sweetheart. He's found a purpose, and we need a leader in the human world. It's a perfect fit."

Tears welled in her eyes. "Our little prince, ruling over our people in the new realm."

"He's not really *little*, but I get your point. And I'm sure you'll nag him enough that he'll visit often."

With a *harumph*, she faced forward as Sathan grinned. "Nag, my ass."

Remaining quiet, as he'd learned to do over several decades of marriage, he allowed the knowledge to wash over him that their son would most likely remain in the human world.

Finally, he spoke as his hands kneaded her. "He looks at Esme the way I imagine I probably look at you."

"Aw," she said, snuggling into him. "Do you look at me like that?"

"You know I do, woman. I think it's a little late to play coy. You *are* pregnant with our second child." Moving his hands to her stomach, he softly held her. "And I love you more every day. The next year isn't going to be easy, but we'll do it together, like everything else." Placing a reverent kiss on her temple, he tightened his embrace.

Miranda's lips fanned as she expelled a huge breath.

"What was that for?" he asked, incredulous.

"Because I'm totally going to let you bone me again. Damn it. I was so resolved, but you go and say the exact right thing and I know it's only a matter of time."

Breaking into joyful laughter, he nuzzled her neck. "I hope so, little Slayer. I very much enjoy making love to you. But for now, I'll just hold you and hope you don't puke on me."

"Ahhhh, so romantic," she sighed, settling further into him. "Tell me more."

Sathan whispered silly nothings in her ear, comforting her as her stomach settled. Then they headed downstairs, hand in hand, to the weekly scheduled council meeting, ready to attend to their kingdom's business.

Although they were finally free from war, the knowledge of Dakath's intent to harm immortals worried Sathan. It was imperative they tread carefully so Tordor, Esme and their team could remain safe.

Together, he and Miranda updated the immortal council on their call with Tordor before everyone dispersed home to their families. As he and Miranda headed to dinner, she slipped her hand in his.

"We need to tell the council about the baby, but we need to tell Tor first."

"We'll tell him on our next call."

Beaming, she bit her lip. "He's going to be happy, right?"

"He knew we were trying and he's going to be ecstatic."

"And it gives him another reason to come home often," she said.

"That it does." Leading her into the kitchen, he picked up the bottle on the counter. "Glarys bought this for us from the winery she and Sam visited for their anniversary. Sadie said you can have a glass once a week. Want some?" He shook the bottle.

Striding to the wine rack, she retrieved two glasses. "Hell yes. Make it big since it's my only one this week."

Chuckling as he opened the bottle, Sathan poured them a glass, content to share it with his favorite person on Etherya's Earth.

Chapter 19

E sme walked beside Tordor, soaking in the warmth from his palm as she steadied herself. Nerves swam in her belly, causing quiet discomfort. What the hell? Why was she nervous? She wasn't the virgin after all...

"Dinner was good," Tordor said. "I liked the chicken parm."

"Mm-hmm..."

"And the house wine was pretty good."

"Yep."

"And I thought the aliens who sat with us were great company."

"Uh-huh..."

Drawing up short, he grinned down at her. "Wow, you're not even trying to listen. Am I that boring?"

Biting her lip, she shook her head. "Sorry. I'm just..."

"Yesssss?" He cocked a playful brow.

"Come on, I don't want to talk about this outside. We haven't seen the guy from last night, but that doesn't mean he isn't watching us." She tugged his hand, leading him the extra two blocks to the hotel. Once they were inside his hotel bedroom, he encircled her arms and crouched to stare into her eyes.

"Okay, I'm dying to know what's running through that busy brain."

Her lips fluttered as she exhaled a huge breath. "I'm...well, I'm nervous. It's weird. *You* should be the one who's nervous." She poked his chest.

"Ouch!" he teased, grasping her finger. "Of course I'm nervous." Pulling her closer, his body heat seemed to emanate through his clothes. "But

I've waited to find the right person." Sliding his arm around her back, he drew her against his body. "And I know it's you, sweetheart."

Her heart slammed in her chest, forcing her to admit the truth. "And that's why I'm nervous," she said, palming his cheek. "Because I'm afraid to mean something to you."

A tender expression marred his features before he leaned down and lifted her in his arms. Esme squealed, laughing as she threaded her arms around his neck. "Is the whole 'caveman' thing supposed to turn me on? Because it's working."

Laying her gently across his bed, he chuckled as he brushed tendrils of hair from her forehead. "I hate to break it to you, but you already mean a lot to this caveman."

Swallowing thickly, she shook her head. "This is a bad idea. I need to renege."

"Okay," he said, forming a cute pout. "But let me kiss you one more time..." Leaning forward, he captured her lips in a soft kiss. Slowly and reverently, he moved his lips against hers, sparking every cell of her skin to burn as he nipped and licked her. Sighing into his warm mouth, she decided kissing him back wouldn't hurt...

His tongue met hers, sliding and sucking, as he settled deeper between her thighs. Moving his broad palm down her side, he glided his hand under the hem of her shirt. Moaning into the wet depths of his mouth, she arched into his palm as he slid it up to her bra.

His fingers searched, nudging under the material until he found her breast. Covering it, he cupped it as he kissed her before sliding his thumb back and forth over her rapidly pebbling nipple.

Emitting a frustrated grunt, Tordor drew back, gripping her shirt and dragging it over her head. Esme watched, her body frozen, as he reached behind her and fiddled with the clasp of her bra. Eventually, he figured it out and slowly dragged the garment from her body. Licking those full lips, he gazed at her breasts as he cupped one in his hand.

"Just one more kiss..." he whispered, leaning down so his warm breath rushed over her nipple. "And then you can renege..." Rimming her nipple with his lips, he stared at her with desire-laden eyes as he hovered over the pert bud. Then he opened his mouth and sucked her deep.

"Goddess..." she hissed, thrusting her fingers in his hair and squeezing. "Oh, that feels good..."

His cheeks hollowed as he sucked her taut bud before drawing back and flicking it with his tongue. A rush of arousal shot to Esme's core, and his Vampyre half must've immediately sensed it. His cock swelled against her thigh, and she felt it press into her soft flesh.

"God, sweetheart, I can smell you," he rasped, a muscle in his jaw twitching. Kissing a path to her other breast, he grinned, sly and sultry. "You must like this."

"Less talking, more kissing," she teased, lifting her budding nipple to his mouth. "*Please.*"

Taking pity on her, he drew her other nipple into his mouth, sucking it deep as he studied her reaction. Esme's fingers twined in his hair as she tried to remember what she was doing before he took her shirt off. Oh…right. She was leaving. She had to leave because being his first would signify something meaningful and she didn't want to hurt him—

"Turn it off, Esme," he murmured against her breast. "Stop thinking and let me love you."

Flicking her nipple with his tongue, he brought it to a turgid peak before he sucked her deep once more. Feeling her eyes roll back in her head, she gave in to the pleasure, unable to stop writhing underneath him.

Once both nipples were thoroughly ravished, he trailed a row of kisses down her abdomen. Nearing the waistband of her jeans, he tapped the button and grinned. "I could give you one more kiss here before you run away. Do you want me to kiss you here, Esme?"

Her body visibly shuddered as blood pounded in her veins. Unable to break his heated stare, she felt herself nod even though she hadn't consciously made the decision to do so.

His half-fangs flashed as he fiddled with the button, unclasping it and drawing her zipper down. Rising between her legs, he shimmied off her jeans after she kicked off her shoes. Hooking his finger under the lacy top of her panties, his lips curved into a sultry smile. "Can I take these off?"

Lifting her hips, she gave him silent consent. Grasping the sides of her underwear, he dragged them down her legs and tossed them on the nearby chair. Lowering to his knees, he drew her to the edge of the bed, resting one leg over each shoulder as he gazed into her eyes.

"I've never kissed anyone here before," he said, leaning down and closing his eyes as he inhaled her arousal. "I'll need lots of practice."

Tossing her head back, she expelled a blissful laugh. "You drive a hard bargain, but I might allow it."

Lifting his lids, he grinned. "Tell me what feels good, okay? I don't want this to suck. Well, figuratively, at least."

Biting her finger, she watched her tender virgin learn the ways of her body. Touching a finger to her core, he ran it through the slick wetness, breath rushing through his lips as he panted.

"So wet..." he rasped, lifting both hands to her deepest place and spreading her folds. His large body shuddered between her legs, and she thanked the goddess she wasn't the only one affected by their burning attraction.

"I'm usually this way around you," she said, marveling at his wondrous expression as he gazed at her most intimate place. "You're so hot, Tor."

"You're beautiful, Esme," he whispered, sliding his finger to her drenched opening. "Look at you..." Lifting his eyes to hers for approval, he waited for her gentle nod. Returning his focus to the mission at hand, he began to gradually nudge inside her.

Hissing, his shoulders tensed with every jut of his finger, culminating in a deep moan when it rested fully inside her. Licking his lips, he began to move in and out of her tight channel, mesmerized by the small claiming.

Esme allowed him to play, knowing it was his first time...*honored* to be his first. Removing his finger, he held her open as he buried his nose in her wet folds. Lust mingled with embarrassment as he inhaled the scent of her deepest place. It was a primal urge for Vampyres, but it was still so intimate for someone like her who rarely let anyone break through her walls.

"I could stay here forever," he moaned against her slick core. Extending his tongue, he touched it to her wet skin, licking her in one long stroke as she groaned.

"Oh...yeah...keep doing that..."

Her eager student followed her command, licking and stroking her slit...tasting her essence as if she were the finest delicacy. Needing more, she slid her fingers to her clit and began to rub.

Tordor watched, rapt with attention as he memorized the movements and placement of her fingers. After a minute, he touched her hand, stilling her. "Can I try?"

"Yes," she said, nodding. "I like slow, even circles."

"Okay," he said, his face a mask of concentration as he placed two fingers on her nub and began to circle. Esme closed her eyes, taken with his efforts although they weren't honed. His touch was too rough in some moments and too soft in others, and she realized he would need more experience to bring her to the peak.

Not wanting to embarrass him, she gently stopped his movements. "Kiss me while I rub myself. Women's bodies are like an instrument—you have to practice. For now, I just want you to kiss me while I finish. Then we'll do you. Sound good?"

Disappointment crossed his features. "Did I blow it already?"

"No," she said, lifting to cup his cheeks. "You're fine, Tor, I promise. Uteria wasn't built in a day, right? Now put that talented tongue to work. You got me all jazzed up, and I need a release."

Chuckling, he leaned down and nudged the wall of her sex. "Okay, sweetheart. I can definitely kiss you..." His mouth and tongue resumed their lascivious actions as she reached for her pleasure-filled bud. Stimulating it with concentric movements of her fingers, she reveled in the rasp of Tordor's tongue across her quivering flesh.

Rushes of arousal coated her core, and her lover lapped and licked as he tasted every drop. A tingling resonated in her lower back and she realized she was nearing the peak.

"Goddess, your tongue..." she cried, arching her back as she reached for it. "So good, Tor...*oh, god, I'm coming...*"

His deep groan vibrated against her wet core as her back snapped, sending her headlong into a crushing orgasm. Waves upon waves of pleasure filtered through her frame, spurred on by Tordor's primal grunts and moans against her core. He might not be experienced, but holy hell, the man sure knew to use his tongue. Lucky her.

Emitting soft laughs as she crashed back to earth, Esme let out a long moan and pressed her hand to her forehead. "Man, that felt good. I need to get myself off more."

Lifting his finger, he grinned between her legs. "I volunteer as tribute."

"Okay, Hunger Games," she said, giggling. "I got it. You like tasting me or whatever you Vamps call it. It's kind of raw and primal, but I'm here for it."

Resting his cheek on her inner thigh, he gently caressed her leg. "Sorry I couldn't figure everything out. I want to be the one who makes you come, Esme."

He looked so sweet, balanced between her thighs as he yearned to please her, and her heart turned to mush.

"We'll have a training session then," she said, waggling her brows. "It will be fun. But not tonight." Rising to rest on her elbows, she tilted her head. "Right now, it's time for *you* to come."

His nostrils flared as he licked his lips. "Are you sure? You said only one more kiss."

Cocking a brow, she said, "I wouldn't argue if I were you. I rarely concede."

Rising to his feet, he gave a quick salute. "Yes, ma'am." Esme broke into joyous laughter as he all but ripped off his clothes. Once naked, he strode toward the bed, his cock semi-aroused as it jutted from the nest of black hair.

Sliding up the bed, she fanned her hair out over the pillow and extended her arms. Tordor slowly crawled over her, looming above as his breath grew heavy. "Holy shit," he whispered, reverently caressing her cheek. "I'm finally here."

Clenching her arms behind his neck, she beamed. "You're finally here. Make love to me, Tor."

Tordor gazed into Esme's eyes, overcome with the emotion that simmered beneath the hint of desire. His thick muscles trembled in anticipation as he reveled in the gravity of the moment. Over the years, there were times he'd questioned himself, wondering if he was searching for something impossible. Craving a connection like his parents had even though he knew it was rare.

He'd been loath to settle, clutching onto the inner hope his mate would appear. After the battle with Bakari, Tordor had turned to find a gorgeous, spitfire imp ready to help him initiate the next phase for his people. Running his thumb over her lips, he gazed at her, thanking Etherya he'd listened to his gut and waited.

She was everything he'd never found.

Everything he wanted to build his future around.

Overcome with sentiment, he accepted the fact that he was falling in love with Esmerelda... Hell, was probably already knee-deep in love with her. Swallowing the huge lump in his throat, he basked in the overwhelming realization.

Her lips formed a cheeky grin as she returned his gaze. "You know, you *do* have to move at some point if we're going to bang."

"Is that how it works?" he teased, nipping her lips. "I thought we just lay here and I gave you the best sex of your life."

Tossing her head back on the pillow, she laughed. "We do need to expend *some* effort." Gliding her hand down his side, she slipped it between their bodies, searching for him. Lust flared in her eyes when she reached his cock, encircling it with her fingers and gently squeezing.

Tordor sucked in a breath, reveling in the feel of her soft palm against his skin.

"Let's get you ready," she whispered, tenderly stroking him as he swelled beneath her fingers. "I'm slightly terrified because you're huge, but I know you'll take care of me."

"I'll always take care of you," he whispered, undulating his hips into her tender strokes. "Goddess, Esme, that feels so good."

"Wait 'til you're inside me," she said, biting her lip. "Now, kiss me with that talented tongue so you can slick me up again. I love kissing you, Tor—"

His lips stole her words, swallowing them as his body moved in tandem with her skillful caresses. Groaning, he plunged his fingers in her hair, twining the soft strands to anchor her beneath him. Surging his tongue into her mouth, he searched, his large frame shuddering when he found hers, wet and slick as they licked and sucked. Lifting her leg, she wrapped it around his waist, pulling him closer.

"Do you want me to grab a condom?" he whispered against her lips.

Shaking her head, she stared at him as the flecks in her irises seemed to glow. "I have an IUD and you're self-healing, so we're good on both fronts. As long as you're okay with not using one. I haven't done this in a while, and my last physical was clear."

Thrilled at the idea of loving her skin to skin, he brushed her lips with his. "I'm definitely okay with not using one."

"Okay then." Widening her legs, she released his cock and lifted her hand to cradle his cheek.

"Esme," he whispered, kissing her palm as he probed her wet opening with the head of his shaft.

"You need to guide yourself inside me," she instructed, arching her back to deepen the contact. "Slowly, so I can get used to you."

Nodding, Tordor gripped the base of his shaft, aligning the tip with her slick opening. Instinctively, he dragged his cock through her wetness, coating himself with her honey. Nerve endings sizzled at the contact, and he hissed as he placed himself at her wet core.

Clenching his hand in her hair, he began to nudge inside...one inch...then another as her lips fell open in a silent moan. Desire clouded her gaze as she stared at him through slitted eyes.

"Tor..." she whispered, running her thumb over his bottom lip. "Oh, goddess...so full..." Closing her eyes, she tossed her head back on the pillow as he continued to ease inside.

Struggling to breathe, Tordor gritted his teeth as her warm, wet folds surrounded him. Every small jut of his hips pushed him deeper...into her most intimate place as emotion swelled within. Emitting tiny groans, he inched forward until he was fully seated.

"Don't stop now..." she moaned, fingers clenching his shoulder as she emitted a breathy laugh beneath him. "Fuck me, Tor—"

Rearing back, he withdrew, sucking in air as his length dragged through her wet core. Plunging his other hand in her hair, he held tight, anchoring her as he eased back inside. The feeling was overwhelming as her tight channel squeezed every cell in his swollen cock. Overcome with pleasure, he closed his eyes and vowed not to come too early.

"Harder!" the little imp cried, the directive in direct opposition to his vow not to come. If he increased the pace, he knew he'd only last a moment. Although virgins weren't expected to be perfect lovers, he wanted to last long enough for it to be memorable.

Drawing back, he began to move...in and out of her slick center...his anxiety growing with each moment as he felt the orgasm form. Every time he surged inside, her walls squeezed him, wrapping him in the most pleasurable vise. Resting his damp forehead against hers, he tightened his fingers in her hair.

"So fucking tight," he rasped, unconsciously increasing the pace of his hips with every thrust. "How am I supposed to hold back when you're wrapped around me like this?"

"Don't hold back," she said, claiming his gaze as she palmed his cheek. "I want you to come, Tor."

"Does it feel good for you?" Tossing back his head, he uttered a soft *ahhhh* as his body shuddered with pleasure. "I want it to feel good for you—"

"It does," she said, gently holding his jaw. "But you already took care of me. Look at me, Tor."

Focusing on her stunning eyes and flushed cheeks, he panted with labored breaths as he worked his hips. He was buried in her, the pleasure from her wet flesh so consuming he thought he might drown in it.

"Come," she softly commanded, her body arching to meet his frenzied thrusts. "I want to feel you let go inside me."

"*Goddess...*" he gritted, circling his hips as he burrowed deeper into her warmth. "I don't want to be a two-hump chump."

Laughter flowed from her chest, surrounding them as he loved her. "You feel so good inside me. Let go, Tor. We'll have plenty of time to practice."

"I need more time with you," he whispered, drawing her into a poignant kiss as his shaft surged in and out of her tight core. "I don't want to do this without you, Esme..."

"I'm here," she whispered, covering his lips. "Don't stop..."

Rearing back, Tordor balanced on his forearms as he began to fuck her in strong, smooth strokes. Feeling the base of his spine tingle, he knew he was only seconds from release. Gazing into her eyes. he settled into the moment, overcome with sentiment at finally losing his virginity to the only woman he'd ever considered making love to.

His beautiful, strong, kind-hearted half-Elf. The woman he felt an unassuageable need to protect and also felt extremely comfortable with. Nothing had felt right before her.

Until her.

Capturing her lips in a sweet kiss, Tordor closed his eyes, ready to claim her in the most intimate way possible. Breaths hitched against her lips as he reached the edge before his back snapped and he dove over the cliff. Drawn into the crushing orgasm, he gave in to the pleasure.

Esme laughed below him, the sound melodious to his ears as he shot his release into her core. The milky jets coated her deepest place, causing something animalistic to well in his chest as he growled.

"Stop laughing at me, woman," he teased, his body jerking as he buried his face in her neck. "*Oh god...it feels so good.*" His body quaked and shuddered against her as she tenderly stroked his back.

"I'm laughing because I'm happy," she said, smiling against his hair. "You make me happy, Tor."

Groaning as the last pulses of release shot into her flushed body, he slid his arms beneath her, wrapping them around her like a sated python. "*Mine,*" he whispered into her neck, tasting her salty skin as he sank into the delirious aftermath.

She shimmied against him, running her nails over his scalp in a caress so pleasurable his body shuddered. Wishing he could hold her against him for eternity, he slowly ran his thumb over her cooling skin.

"I'll last longer next time. That was lame," he muttered, shaking his head. "Sorry, sweetheart."

"It absolutely was not," she said, hooking her leg over his thigh and squeezing. "And you're an A-plus cuddler, so let's relax and enjoy it."

"Didn't peg you for a cuddler, but I'll take the win," he teased.

"I'm usually not. My brain has a tendency to lower all my defense mechanisms with you. It's slightly petrifying."

Lifting his head, he grinned, taken with the affection in her eyes. "Don't be scared, little Elf." Running his finger over her lips, he reveled in her slight shiver. "I won't ever hurt you."

Her throat bobbed as she gazed at him with glassy eyes. "For the first time, I think I actually believe those words." Shaking her head, her lips formed a heartbreaking smile. "It only took ten centuries."

Tordor's expression turned reverent as he continued to stroke her, delighted by her soft caresses upon his back. Eventually, their eyes began to droop and he felt himself slipping from her body. Rising, he strode into the bathroom in search of a washcloth. Gazing in the mirror, he noted his reddened cheeks and his expression of sated euphoria.

After so long, Tordor had finally shed his virginity.

Grinning at his reflection, he wet the cloth and cleaned himself before striding back to his lover. She stared at him, satiated and replete, as he tenderly cleaned away the evidence of his loving. Marveling at his milky release upon her skin, Tordor felt an overwhelming need to mark her again. It was primal, but he felt many primal urges toward Esme. Chalking it up to the fact he was most likely in love with her, he accepted his deep-seated need to claim her. It was archaic and raw but completely undeniable.

"What are you thinking up there?" she asked, grinning as she sprawled on the bed.

"Some caveman stuff that would probably severely disappoint my mother and most of the other feminists in my realm." Leaning down, he brushed a kiss over her lips. "I feel all these possessive urges toward you, and it's...strange, but I can't seem to control them."

"Eh, control is overrated," she said with a cheeky grin. Rolling over, she pulled up the covers and settled into the bed. "I shouldn't sleep here, but it's so comfy."

Striding to the bathroom, Tordor disposed of the cloth and turned off the lights. Sliding into bed beside her, he pulled her back against his front, spooning her as she cuddled into him.

"Why shouldn't you sleep here?"

"Because I'll get used to how warm and cuddly you are," she said, yawning. "It's a terrible idea."

"Hmm..." Settling his arm between her breasts, he spread his palm over her chest, allowing his thumb to skate over her skin. "Workplace hazard."

Chuckling, she shimmied her butt into his sated shaft. "Yep."

Minutes passed as they slowly drifted toward slumber. Resting his lips on the shell of her ear, he whispered. "Thank you, sweetheart. I waited so long for you."

Her heartbeat jumped underneath his palm at the reverent words.

"I'm honored to be your first, Tor. It's very meaningful for me too." Relaxing against him, she mumbled, "You tired me out. Don't snore in my ear, okay?"

Smiling at her teasing, he hooked his leg over hers to draw her closer.

"Good night, little Elf," he whispered, kissing her temple. Closing his eyes, he took one last moment to revel in the fact he'd crossed a momentous threshold with the woman who consumed most of his waking thoughts. Then he pressed his face to her skin, losing himself in her honeyed scent as he slowly drifted to sleep.

Chapter 20

Tordor awoke the next morning, stretching his arms as he yawned. Patting the bed, he realized Esme was gone and wondered if she was doing yoga. Rising, he donned some sweatpants and headed into the living room.

Sure enough, she stood by the window, arms high above her head as she stretched. He approached, positioning himself beside her so he could follow her movements. Glancing over, he caught her lips twitching as she continued to move.

"Don't come in here looking all cute and tousled. We have to meet General Markson in two hours."

"Me?" he asked, unable to suppress his grin. "I'm just doing my morning yoga. Don't distract me."

She uttered a teasing "*pfft*" before stretching to her left, arms high beside her head.

They moved in silence, Tordor sensing her desire to maintain a slight distance. Although he wouldn't mind a quick tumble before they showered, his little Elf had opened herself to him last night and was probably reeling from the intimacy they'd shared. Wanting her to feel comfortable, he stayed silent, mimicking her stretches until she pressed her hands together in front of her chest and murmured, "Namaste."

Dropping her hands to her sides, she turned to him and smiled. Lifting a shoulder, she said, "I'm trying not to freak out. It helps that you realize I'm trying not to freak out."

Grinning at how in tune they were, he nodded. "Nothing to freak out about. I'm going to show you that getting close to someone doesn't have to be a disaster, Esme."

Her chest rose as she centered herself. "A mighty challenge," she teased. Picking up her phone, she checked the time. "We need to leave in an hour and half. Let's shower and then load everything on the jump drive."

"Shower together?" he teased, loving her playful eye roll.

"You wish."

"I do, but I'll settle for a kiss." Stepping closer, he asked, "Can I kiss you, sweetheart?"

Nodding, she lifted to her toes and he placed a tender kiss on her lips. Drawing back, he licked his lips to savor her taste.

"Okay, I'll leave you alone until tonight." Lifting a finger, he arched an eyebrow. "But once we're back here, all bets are off."

"Deal," she said, biting her lip. "See you in a bit!" Turning, she waved as she headed into her bedroom and shut the door.

Returning to his room, Tordor threw on a shirt and shoes so he could head to the lobby and get breakfast. After placing it on the counter, he entered his room to prepare for the first day in the next phase of his life: the one where he would win the heart of his favorite half-Elf.

E sme stood under the spray of the shower, aware of the slight soreness between her legs after last night's poignant tryst. Washing the tender area, she thought of Tordor.

She'd woken that morning to the sound of his deep snoring in her ear. Surprisingly, instead of trying to bolt, she'd relaxed into him, craving his touch as he slept.

She'd enjoyed it for a few minutes before her eyes snapped open and her heart pounded with fear.

Never had she *craved* a man's embrace.

And never had she longed to linger in someone's bed.

The fact that she longed to with Tordor was deeply disconcerting.

Although she profoundly cared for him, their relationship had an expiration date and their lives were on different paths. Tordor had a duty and obligation to his people.

She had a duty too, and keeping her team safe was her highest priority.

Esme could only ensure that if she eventually left, allowing them to continue the mission without threat of her father's interference.

Sighing, she stepped from the shower and reached for the towel. Tordor had been cautious and mindful as he approached her earlier. Goddess, but he already knew her so well. Esme had rarely, if ever, experienced a connection like theirs, and it spurred the same old fears she'd combatted for centuries.

He'd read her mood and let her have her space. His deep understanding of her temperament and reservations was something she would miss when she inevitably left. It might lead to intense pain for both of them, but at least he would be safe. Alive. Fulfilling the duty he was born to accomplish.

After drying off, she dressed in black pants and a nice blouse, wanting to wear something dressier than khakis to meet the esteemed human general who was graciously helping their cause. Opening the door, she found Tordor standing at the kitchen counter sipping Slayer blood.

"Hey," she said, approaching and eyeing the container in his broad hand. "What does it taste like?"

Swallowing, he licked his lips, narrowing his eyes as he pondered. "Kind of metallic but full-bodied. That probably sounds weird to someone who doesn't require blood."

Feeling her heart pound in her ears, she asked, "Have you ever drunk directly from someone?"

Setting down the container, he cocked a brow. "Not yet. But I could be persuaded."

Heat surged between her legs as she rubbed the vein pulsing at her neck. Holy goddess in the Passage... Visions of him drinking from her as he filled her deepest place swamped her.

"We could try it," he said softly, stepping closer and running the backs of his fingers up her arm. "I only have half-fangs, so it might hurt, but I can lick you, and my saliva should help soothe it." Grasping her hand, he lifted it and kissed her knuckles. "I'd really like to connect with you that way."

Warning signs flashed in her brain as her erratic heartbeat threatened to choke her. "We'll see. We have lots to try now that I've deflowered you." She dramatically pressed the back of her hand to her forehead. "You've been thoroughly ruined, Mr. Half-Vamp."

Snickering, he released her hand. "I think I'll survive." Lifting the jump drive, he shook it. "All the profiles are loaded and bagels are on the counter."

"Well, then, let me eat up so we can meet General Markson. You ready for this, Tor?"

"Ready," he said with a nod.

Thankful he would be by her side, Esme slathered a bagel with cream cheese, hoping to calm the nervous butterflies in her belly with the hearty breakfast. After they were both full and ready, Tordor led her to the Jeep, climbing behind the wheel to drive them to the secret meet-up.

Chapter 21

E sme observed the trees that lined the gravel road as their Jeep traveled over the rocky surface. As the stones crunched beneath the tires, she glanced in the rearview mirror, unable to shake the feeling they were being watched. Tordor had taken several side roads to ensure they weren't being followed, but her father's network of spies was talented. Was it possible the man from the bowling alley was on their trail? Shivering, she rubbed her arms, hoping they were safe from prying eyes.

"You okay?" Tordor asked, reaching over and squeezing her thigh. "We're almost there."

"I just have a weird feeling I need to shake." Wringing her hands, she flung off the strange vibe. "I don't want to be distracted during our meeting."

Tordor drove to what appeared to be the end of the road. Suddenly, the bushes in front of them began to shake as they slowly opened. Esme's eyes widened as she realized the bushes were attached to a gate of some sort.

"Fancy," she said softly as Tordor drove through. "No one's finding General Markson here."

They traveled down the gravel drive, stopping before a high grassy hill with a metal door. The door opened and two soldiers dressed in camouflaged gear marched toward them. They motioned Tordor and Esme to exit the car, and Esme's eyes met Tordor's before she followed their command.

"Arms in the air so I can frisk you, please," one soldier said as the other directed Tordor to do the same. They complied, and Esme's heart beat with the gravity of the moment as the guard searched her before placing her bag on the hood and pilfering through it. Drawing back, he nodded to his counterpart. "She's clean."

"Same here."

Handing Esme her bag, the guard tilted his head toward the bunker, indicating she should follow him. Tordor fell into step beside her, his hand brushing hers in a show of silent support. She wanted nothing more than to twine her fingers with his and gather some of his unwavering optimism. But she was used to forging ahead alone, so she flexed her fingers, cognizant of the tingle that lingered from his brief touch.

The soldiers led them down a dim hallway under the bunker as Esme's eyes adjusted to the dimness. A light shone ahead as they approached a doorway that led to a strategic operations center. The walls were lined with monitors, each showing a different news or video feed. Quickly glancing at them, Esme took in the breadth of knowledge passing through the small bunker. General Markson was monitoring parts of the entire globe from a nondescript location few probably knew.

"Sorry for the dramatics," a deep voice said from the doorway. "This bunker is privately funded by me, and I can't take the chance of the government knowing of its existence."

"Hello, General Markson," Esme said, turning and extending her hand. The general shook it, his eyes kind under his wire-rimmed glasses and short black hair. His skin was warm against hers, and she immediately felt comfortable with him.

"Hello, Esmerelda. It's a pleasure to meet you in person." Facing Tordor, he extended his hand. "And you too, Prince Tordor. Please excuse me if I seem a bit overwhelmed. You're the first immortals I've ever met besides Clayton—as far as I know."

Smiling, Esme lifted a shoulder. "There are many of us hiding in your world, and we hope to eventually lure them from the shadows. It's safer for all species, especially now that the ether is gone."

"Agreed," he said, gesturing for them to sit in the leather chairs that surrounded a small conference table. Esme and Tordor each flanked the general as he lowered into the seat at the head. The two guards silently stood watch near the wall as Esme drew her bag off her shoulder and located the jump drive.

"Every profile is loaded here, and you can begin your due diligence. If the fifteen prospects meet your requirements, they're ready to be interviewed by you and dedicate their lives to the cause."

"Thank you," he said, taking the drive and slowly examining it. "Amazing how something so important can be placed on something so small."

Admiring his appreciation of the significant moment, she nodded. "We're extremely grateful for you, sir. This partnership will stretch many decades and require skillful navigation."

"On that note, I also have some documents for you to vet." Reaching into his pocket, he pulled out a jump drive. "I'm in my late-fifties and only have a few decades left. I've created some profiles of other high-ranking officers I trust. I want you to study them and approach them if something happens to me. As we learned from Clayton's death, we must fortify our team."

"Thank you," she said, taking the drive. "Although it's best to keep our numbers small in the short-term, we need more than the three of us in the loop. Tordor and I also included profiles of several members of our team who aren't candidates for infiltration. Their skills are best used in the village we'll build at Rausch Gap. If something happens to me or Tor, Larkin and Brienne can step in. I have complete faith in them."

"I look forward to assessing their profiles," he said, "and perhaps even meeting them one day. You two understand it's imperative the site you build at Rausch Gap stay off the radar until we're ready to reveal it?"

"Yes," she said, straightening. "Tordor's got some family members with some pretty intense powers. Those combined with the immortal chemist we've recently hired will most likely lead to us creating some sort of invisibility cloak for the site."

"It's possible my Aunt Evie can generate a shield," Tordor said. "Once we're ready, we'll discuss that with her and keep you in the loop."

Inhaling deeply, Markson studied the jump drive as he rotated it in his hand. "I hope both sides will be ready to accept the other one day. I want my grandchildren to live in a safe, peaceful world." Lifting his gaze, his tone was serious. "Humans have a propensity to squander peace quickly after we achieve it."

"Our people have made the same mistakes," Tordor said. "All we can do is lay the groundwork and hope for a bright future."

"He's an optimist," Esme said, playfully rolling her eyes as she jutted her thumb at him. "It would be annoying if it weren't so helpful. I need it to counterbalance my imminent sense of doom."

Chuckling, Markson glanced between them. "Then I'm glad you found each other." Rising, he moved to the counter on the opposite side of the room and retrieved a laptop. Returning to the table, he sat and opened it before inserting the jump drive.

"If you all are willing, I'd like to go through each profile with you before I begin my vetting process."

"Absolutely," Esme said, scooting her chair closer. "Let's start with Larissa. You're going to love her, and I think she'd be perfect for an in-house job with one of your officers..." Esme carried on, detailing each candidate as General Markson pulled up their profiles. They discussed the prospects well into the afternoon until the hour grew late. Finally, Markson closed the laptop and rubbed his eyes.

"I think we've made some progress, and I thank you both. I'm going to have to end it here because my wife made a casserole for dinner and if I'm not home to eat it, she'll relegate me to eating peanut butter and jelly sandwiches for the foreseeable future." Arching a brow, he quipped, "That's the only thing I know how to make."

Laughing, Esme rose, slipping the jump drive he'd given her into the side pocket of her bag. "You're a smart man, General Markson. I look forward to implementing this program with you."

"As do I." Rising, he shook both their hands, lingering when he shook Esme's. "I just want to say how sorry I am about Clayton. He was a good man. I never would've known he was an immortal until he confided in me. His effortless amalgamation with our people proves it can be done."

"Thank you, sir." Tears welled as she stepped back. "He was very special."

After saying their goodbyes, the soldiers escorted Tordor and Esme to the Jeep. They climbed inside, and Esme absently stared out the window as Tordor began to drive. Her thoughts drifted to Clayton, and she prayed to Etherya and all the other gods that the other members of their team would remain safe.

Tordor reached over, gripping her hand in a show of silent strength, proving once again how well he read her moods. Twining her fingers with his, she rested her head on the plushy headrest as her partner drove them to the hotel.

Chapter 22

After grabbing takeout on the way home, Tordor and Esme returned to their hotel room to eat and share a bottle of wine. Now that the business of the day was complete, they settled into conversation as anticipation of the night ahead loomed. Once they were pleasantly full, he reached over and squeezed her hand.

"Am I going to have to persuade you to come to my bed? Because I'll do it."

"I think I'll allow it." Rising, she tugged his hand. "I'm exhausted, but we can have some fun first."

"I want to please you, Esme," he said as they walked to his room. Stopping beside the bed, his cheeks flushed as slight hesitation laced his tone. "If you're open to teaching me."

"I'm open," she said, her heart fluttering at his guileless request. "And thank you for being a man who isn't selfish." She began to tug off her clothes, heat licking every cell in her skin as he slowly removed his. His eyes locked with hers as he undressed, filled with lust and an unsated arousal she couldn't wait to squelch.

Once he was naked, she stepped forward and ran her fingers over his abdomen, loving how his muscles quivered beneath her touch. "I think I'm going to enjoy this lesson very much."

Smiling, he inched closer. "Are you saying you only want me for my body? Because I've got stuff here too." He tapped his temple.

Laughing, she urged him toward the bed. "Okay, Einstein, let's see how good a student you are. Sit with your back against the headboard."

Tordor plumped up the pillows before resting against them. Climbing on the bed, Esme situated between his legs, shimmying her butt against his shaft.

"Hey," he said, gliding his arms around her and kissing her nape. "Keep wiggling into me like that and I won't be capable of thinking at all."

Shooting him a knowing look, she spread her legs and leaned back into his body. Resting her head on his shoulder, she gazed into his forest-green eyes.

"The first thing you should always do is ensure the woman is slick and wet." Tordor glided his palms over her thighs, drawing them farther apart before touching a finger to her folds. Hissing, she arched toward his touch as he drew his index finger up and down her sensitive slit.

"You're definitely wet," he murmured, resting the pad of his finger against her opening before gently nudging inside. "I could smell your arousal the whole time we were eating. It's so fucking sexy, honey."

"What can I say?" she sighed, relaxing into him. "You do it for me. But we can slick me up some more and that will make it easier for me to release."

"How?" he whispered.

Touching her lips to his, she whispered, "Kiss me as you touch me, Tor."

His mouth captured her in a crushing kiss, devouring her lips as his fingers toyed with her most intimate place. That talented tongue roved over every inch of her mouth, causing her to shudder as he consumed her like his last meal. Drowning in the desire of the moment, she felt more wetness rush to her core, ready to ease him inside when the moment arrived.

Breaking the kiss, she spoke against his lips. "Move your fingers higher."

He stared into her eyes, following her command as she reached between her legs. Guiding his fingers, she placed them over her pleasure-filled little bud.

"Right there," she said, removing her hand and allowing him to cover her clit. "Now, you stroke it in small circles to stimulate it."

Her eager student began to circle his fingers, the pressure too light as she shook her head. "Harder," she rasped, biting his lower lip as he groaned. "You won't hurt me."

Increasing the pressure, he circled the tight bud. Heavy breaths rushed through his lips as he watched her, assessing her reaction to his ministrations.

"Make sure to keep it wet," she instructed, grinning when he reached down and gathered her honey on his fingers before resuming the pleasure-filled strokes. "Good job."

His shiver rolled through her, delighting her as he shined under her praise. Esme had never been super dominant in the bedroom, but there was something sexy about holding this massive immortal in the palm of her hand as she taught him how to please her.

"You like being praised," she whispered, running her lips over his jaw.

"By you?" he asked, arching a brow. "Definitely."

Chuckling, she nipped his earlobe before placing her lips on the shell of his ear. "That feels so good. Use your other hand to play with my nipple and I'll definitely come."

A low-toned growl exited his lips as he lifted his hand, cupping her breast before pinching her nipple between his fingers. Realization entered his expression, and he lowered his hand, gathering her wetness before lifting it to her nipple. Esme watched with slitted eyes as he spread her essence over the taut bud before beginning to gently pinch it as he stimulated her clit.

"Oh god, that's good…" she purred, leaning her head back on his shoulder and closing her eyes. "You definitely get an A-plus for effort."

Laughing, he ran his silken tongue along the shell of her ear. "I love making you feel good, sweetheart," he said, the timbre of his voice so low and sensual it sent a fresh rush of arousal between her thighs. "Tell me what else you need."

"That voice…" she moaned, shaking her head against his shoulder. "Give me some dirty talk. I don't care if you suck at it. You can recite the ABCs for all I care. Just say it in that sexy-as-sin voice."

"What should I tell you?" he asked, increasing the pace with his fingers at her core and on her nipple. "That you're the cutest damn thing I've ever seen and I can't believe I finally found you?"

"Too sappy," she teased, undulating into his ministrations. "Dirtier."

She could hear the wheels turning as he tried to gin up the dirty talk.

"Should I tell you how amazing it felt to have you wrapped around me?" he asked, lips brushing her ear as his hands played with her body. "That I've spent all day counting down to this moment?"

"Getting warmer…" she moaned, writhing under his fingers. "Oh…Tor…yessss…right there…"

"My gorgeous little Elf," he whispered, placing soft kisses along her hairline. "Come for me…"

Esme shuddered, taken by his sweet, silken words...pushing into his fingers as they took her to the pinnacle. Her eyelids fluttered as thousands of tiny sparks ignited in every cell of her skin. Suddenly, her body snapped, diving headlong into the orgasm as his warm breath caressed her ear. Moaning his name, she quaked and trembled under his hands, reaching to still them as her body drowned in bliss.

"No more," she cried, her body unable to take any more of the pleasurable onslaught from his eager fingers.

Her tender student held her, absorbing her tremors as she collapsed in his arms. Blissful and sated, she sighed, cuddling into him as his warmth surrounded her.

Returning to earth, Esme felt his cock swell against her lower back, ready and eager to plunge into her warmth. Slowly lifting her lids, she smiled and gave a small nod.

Her lover wasted no time, sliding his hands under the swell of her ass and lifting her. Deft as an artist molding clay, he lifted her atop his thighs, gripping the base of his shaft and searching for her core. Esme's breaths were staggered and heavy as he dragged the tip of his cock through her wetness, dousing it with her essence.

Resting his forehead against hers, Tordor began to push inside. Widening her legs, she attempted to adjust to the position. Her back rubbed against the scratchy hairs on his chest as she straddled him, relaxing her inner muscles so he could nudge inside from behind.

"Holy shit..." he rasped, inching deeper with every small jut of his hips. "You feel incredible."

Her lips sought his, drawing him into an intimate kiss as he claimed her. Bracketing him with her thighs, she worked her hips, drawing him deeper as he groaned into her mouth.

"Esme..." he whispered, beads of sweat dripping from his forehead onto her shoulder, marking her in his scent as he loved her. "I've waited so long for you..."

The tender words almost cracked her heart into a thousand pieces since she knew their time together had an expiration date. One day soon, she would leave her affectionate prince behind to find the woman he was *truly* meant to be with...truly meant to *love*.

But for now, she would enjoy the moment, wrapped in the arms of a man who was so much more than the diplomatic heir she'd expected to find on the battlefield after Bakari's defeat. Never had she anticipated what he would become to her: a lover, a confidant and a genuine soul connected to her on a level she'd never experienced. Tordor was exceptional, and she understood how lucky she was to gain his trust and be his first lover.

"I'm thankful for you too," she whispered, pushing away the sting of tears that threatened to cloud her eyes. "Now use that thick cock to fuck me, Tor. Hard and deep, so I feel you everywhere."

Groaning, he gripped her hips to anchor her as he increased the pace of his thrusts. Emitting a harsh laugh, he shook his forehead against hers. "You're better at dirty talk than me."

Joyful laughter emanated from her throat as she basked in the glory of making love to someone who made her laugh. She'd rarely laughed when making love, and it opened something inside her that was raw and free.

"Damn straight, buddy." Pressing her palms to his thighs, she gripped tight, holding on as he pummeled her tight channel from behind.

"Can you come again?"

"I already came," she cried, leaning her head back on his shoulder. "Don't stop. I love how you feel inside me...*oh my god...*"

Primal, deep grunts vibrated against her back as he fucked her in long, fluid strokes. His muscles tensed beneath her, and Esme knew he was close. Clenching her inner muscles, she squeezed his cock, pushing him to the edge as his fingers dug into her hips.

His head snapped back before his thick frame bucked under her, surging deep inside as he began to come. Holding on for dear life, Esme rode him, reveling in his unintelligible words as he released deep in her core. She wrung the pulsing jets from his cock, sucking him dry as he buried his face in her neck and moaned her name. Grinning with sated desire, she absorbed his trembles, taking a mental snapshot to remember the intimate moment long after she'd exited his life. Determined to stay in the moment, she settled against his rapidly cooling body, inhaling the musky scent of his skin.

Tordor's lips trailed across her neck, then her jaw, finally resting on hers as he gave her a searing kiss. Staring deep into her eyes, he murmured, "You're the best teacher I've ever had. By far. Hands down."

Unable to control her laughter, Esme rocked against him, setting it free as his laughs mingled with hers. Tightening his arms, he sighed with contentment as his shaft began to soften inside her body.

"I like it from behind when I'm on my hands and knees too. We can try that next time."

His body shuddered at her admission.

"Will there be a next time? I really hope so. I've already been plotting some non-creepy ways I can sneak into your tent at Rausch Gap."

Squinting, she asked, "Are there non-creepy ways to sneak into someone's tent?"

Pursing his lips, he pondered. "Probably not. You're going to have to let me in."

"We'll see," she teased, easing from his embrace. "For now, we need to clean up before we ruin the sheets. Come on, lover." Rising on wobbly legs, she extended her hand and led him to the bathroom.

After they'd cleaned up, they stepped back onto the soft carpet beside the bed. Lifting hopeful eyes to hers, he asked softly, "You're going to sleep here, right?"

Esme's chest rose with the ragged breath that indicated she knew it was a bad idea. Sex was one thing, but cuddling was a whole other level of intimacy. One that would only exacerbate their connection, making it that much harder to break.

Still, she nodded and stepped closer. Tordor turned down the covers and eased inside, reaching for her as she stood beside the bed. Fear caused her heart to pound as she slid into his embrace, easing into his side and resting her cheek on his chest.

"Not everything has to be doom and gloom, little Elf," he said, stroking her hair as her eyes drooped. "That's a lesson I'm going to teach you."

"It sounds true when you say it," she said softly, lips brushing the hairs dotting his chest as she spoke. "Even though I know it's not."

"We make our own truths, Esme. You're strong enough to write a new story for your future. I hope I'm in it when you decide to stop running. I really like being in your story, sweetheart."

Sighing at the sweet words, she decided arguing was futile. His optimism was one of the many things she admired about him, so she allowed it, even if it was temporary.

One thing Esme knew above all else was that *all* happiness was temporary.

Still, in the darkened room as his snores began to echo beneath her, she couldn't deny the small flare of hope that kindled deep within her fortified heart.

Chapter 23

E sme awoke to the pleasurable slide of Tordor's thick lips against her nape. Taking advantage of their last morning of privacy, she rolled onto her back, sinking into the soft sheets as Tordor loved her, slow and tender in the fresh light of dawn.

They were quiet as they moved, their bodies communicating everything seamlessly, and she wrapped her legs around his broad waist, hugging him to her as if she'd never let go. His lips formed an adorable pout as she pushed his fingers away, replacing them with hers at her core so they could peak together.

"It's easier this way," she whispered, cupping his jaw with her free hand. "I promise it feels good."

Tordor rolled his hips, pressing deeper inside, and her head fell back on the pillow as she reveled in his guileless desire to please her. Clutching his shoulder as her hand worked between their bodies, they reached the pinnacle before he collapsed atop her quaking frame.

Afterward, they rose, Tordor tugging her toward the bathroom in an outright invitation. Realizing they might not have the opportunity to shower together again, she climbed underneath the spray, allowing him to wash her with the soapy cloth.

Esme returned the favor, cleaning every inch of his body as his cock thickened under her ministrations.

Sparing him a glance, she teased, "I think I've awakened the Kraken."

Chuckling, he ran a hand over her damp hair. "I lived in anticipation for so long. Now that I know what I was missing, I think my body's in some sort of sexual overdrive." Leaning down, he pecked her lips. "Plus, you're naked with me in the shower. It's my ultimate fantasy."

Breathing a laugh, she rinsed her hair one last time before they exited the shower. After drying, Tordor exited the room, returning with her toiletry bag. Setting it on the counter, he said, "Get ready in here with me. We can talk about the next steps at Rausch Gap."

Esme conceded, mostly because she knew they wouldn't get the same level of privacy once they returned to base. Retrieving her toothbrush, she began her regimen as they discussed the next phase of their plan.

"I'm open to interviewing Frederik's brother if he's willing to head up construction at Rausch Gap," Tordor said, rinsing away the toothpaste before dispensing shaving cream on his fingers. As he rubbed it on his face, he continued. "We'll need immortal and hybrid workers for construction, plumbing and all the other jobs needed to create a village from scratch."

Nodding, she ran the comb through her hair, tugging out the knots. "We'll start with asking the team if they know skilled workers. I'd like to assign Larkin and Brienne as co-leaders and begin transferring tasks to them."

Tordor's slight frown was evident under the shaving cream as he dragged the razor over his skin, showing his distaste at her mention of the impermanence of her post. Esme didn't acknowledge it, unwilling to get into an intense discussion before they headed back.

"Larkin and Brienne are perfect leaders if they wish to stay," he said. "We'll also need someone to head up security if those two are going to focus on mayoral duties. They'll essentially be co-mayors if we're using human terms."

"True," she said, opening the drawer and locating the hairdryer. "We'll work on that too. Do you plan to stay at Rausch Gap?"

Narrowing his eyes, he pondered as he continued to shave. "I definitely want to build a home there, but I also want to spend some time traveling the human world to spread the word to other immortals and hybrids." Leaning on the counter, he turned to look at her. "They're our people, Esme, and if I can locate ones who need a safe haven and offer them a place at our compound, I want to do it."

Esme tightened her lips, stifling the quip that immortals and hybrids were *his* people. Although she'd always felt a calling to help them, she would always remain an outsider to protect their safety. It was the way her life was framed due to the circumstances with her father, and she accepted her reality.

"It's a noble cause, and the immortals in this realm have needed a leader for centuries. King of the Human Realm has a nice ring to it," she said with a cheeky grin.

"Queen of the Human Realm sounds even better to me," he said, a challenge in his tone as he arched a brow.

"Well, then, I hope you find a queen one day." Turning on the hairdryer, she yelled, "Sorry, can't hear you. Give me a sec."

Flipping over, she began to dry her hair, unwilling to enter into a frustrating conversation with him. They saw the world through such different lenses—hers with disaster and his with ever-present optimism—and those varying views would never mesh no matter how compatible they were in other ways.

Once her hair was dry and full, she flicked off the hairdryer and fluffed her tresses. Tordor's now freshly shaven face shone under his knowing grin as he approached her, a rather significant bulge beneath the white towel around his waist.

Coming to stand behind her, he cupped her shoulders and stared at her in the reflection. "You're stubborn, little Elf," he said, kissing her hair as his hands roved over her shoulders in a pleasurable caress. Lowering his lips to her ear, he spoke in that deep tone that made her knees quiver. "But I'm stubborn too, and I'm not letting you dictate everything. I got it from my mom, and she's the most hardheaded person I've ever known. Buckle up, honey, because I'm not stupid enough to let you go now that I found you."

Lulled by his words, Esme's breath quickened as she tried to remain impassive.

Sliding his hand to the towel wrapped around her breasts, he tugged it, sending it in a soft rush to the floor. Cocking a sultry brow, he whispered, "Oops."

Unable to control her grin, she leaned back into the wall of his chest. "Yeah, that seemed like an accident."

Reaching for his towel, he chucked it to the floor before pressing his hard length into her lower back. Maintaining her gaze in the mirror, he urged her forward, desire simmering in his olive gaze. Pressing her palms to the cold surface, she widened her legs, bracing for him to claim her.

Bracketing her with his arms, he leaned over her, pressing his front to her back as his shaft searched between her legs. As was always the case when she was near him, her body was already slick, ready to receive him. Sliding his palms over the backs of her hands, he laced their fingers, holding tight as he began to push inside her tight warmth.

"*Mine*," he rasped in her ear, his hips undulating against her as he took her in long, pleasurable strokes. "Say it, Esme."

Arching toward him, she shook her head against his jaw. "I can't, Tor...*ahhhh*...I wish...I wish so many things..."

"I'm going to give them to you, sweetheart," he promised, pushing so deep she felt it stimulate the spot within that held a thousand pleasure-filled nerve endings.

"Oh god...right there...harder!"

Moving his hands to her hips, his fingers dug into her skin as he followed her directive. Small, lust-filled grunts exited his throat as he claimed her, his cock pounding the spot that was sure to send her body into overdrive.

Pressing his face to her neck, he sucked the skin between his lips, and she could feel him burn with the primal need to drink from her. Bracing, she offered herself to him, leaning her head on his shoulder as her vein pulsed beneath his lips.

"One day soon, honey," he rasped, his body now pummeling hers at a rapid pace. "Once I drink from you, I'll never let you go."

Lifting her lids, she focused on the sadness in his eyes, hating that she was the cause of it. If only she weren't so damn practical. If she could afford to live life following the whims of her heart, she'd claim him as her mate and never look back. But life had taught her hard lessons, and it was in the moments when she forgot them that she lost the most.

She wouldn't allow Tordor to become another lesson in her tragic life. Another *casualty*. He was too important. Too *good*.

So she braced herself, giving in to the pleasure as he brought her to the peak with his hard, measured strokes. Dangling off the precipice, she let go, shouting his name as the orgasm racked her body.

Tordor groaned behind her, pressing his face to her nape as he began to violently climax deep within. Taking everything he gave her, she held him, clenching his sensitive skin as he moaned with sated desire. Breaths mingled as they stood against the counter, wrapped in each other as their heartbeats melded.

Lifting his head, Tordor flashed a wily grin in the reflection. "I made you come."

"Holy shit, you sure did," she said, laughter in her tone. "That spot's hard to find, but you're pretty big, so I guess it was only a matter of time."

Pouting, he nipped her ear. "Or it could be because I'm the best lover in the world and you would be insane to ever leave my side."

Laughter bounded from her throat. "Sure, whatever you say."

Concern laced his expression as he studied her. "Are you sore? I should've thought of that. I don't want to hurt you."

"I'm fine," she said as he slipped from her body, noting the slight tenderness between her thighs. "I can handle it, and believe me, it's worth it."

Stepping back, he placed a kiss on her head. "You know, I can lick it and make it better with my saliva." He waggled his brows.

"Well, hot damn. Let's try that when you sneak into my tent once we're back at base. I might let you in."

"Challenge accepted." Winking, he picked up her towel and handed it to her.

Waving it off, she trailed toward the door. "Thanks, but I'm going to get dressed. We need to head back, and I'm starving."

"We can grab some breakfast on the way out. I'll be ready to leave in ten minutes."

"See you in ten."

Striding to her room, Esme dressed and packed her bag, ready to leave the hotel behind and return to her team. They were only at the beginning of a long journey, and she aimed to prepare her team for what lay ahead before she left them behind to accomplish the mission.

Trembly, servant to King Dakath, entered his sire's office chambers anxious to give him the news. "My king, Esmerelda and Tordor have finished their journey to Washington DC and met with the human general. He will now vet the immersion candidates and they're on their way back to Rausch Gap."

Dakath palmed the desk, rising before pacing to the window. Staring out at the dim sky, he rubbed his chin. "I find myself interested in what they're building in the remote human site. Now that my spies have located it, they've supplied decent information, but I wonder if I should see for myself."

Trembly straightened. "Sire, you wish to travel to America? Surely your spies can continue to supply the information you need."

"Yes," he said, noting the annoyance in his voice. "I find my curiosity rampant. My daughter has grown bold in her maturity, and I feel a need to assess. And if she's grown too bold..." Turning, he lifted his chin. "I will need to remind her of my power."

Trembly remained silent, his eyes slightly wide as digested the conversation.

"I will travel to America to see the site at Rausch Gap for myself."

"Of course, my king. Should I make arrangements for you?"

"Yes. I want to travel among the humans to observe them. It's been some time since I left Romania, and witnessing their ignorance and arrogance will reinforce my desire to keep the Elven bloodline pure."

"I'll make the preparations without delay," Trembly said, bowing. Pivoting, he marched from the room and entered his small office, closing the door firmly behind him. Sitting at his desk, he pulled up the secure immortal message board and typed an encrypted message.

Gillam, your brother, the king, has decided to travel to Rausch Gap. His curiosity about Esme's actions is cause for concern. As you know, I only wish the best for my kinsmen and want to remain neutral by providing helpful information. You will not be able to respond to this message. May the ancient god protect your soul.

Your Brother's Royal Servant

Cutting the secure connection, Trembly resumed his duties and began to make travel arrangements for his king.

Chapter 24

T ordor made good time on the trip back to Rausch Gap. As he drove, he contemplated the past few days. Never did he imagine he'd lose his virginity in a hotel room on the outskirts of Washington DC, but hey, life was a roller coaster of unexpected twists and turns, and he wouldn't have it any other way. Not only had he finally made love to the woman of his dreams, but he'd also chipped away at the nearly impenetrable wall surrounding her tender heart.

If he was lucky, he might just tear it down completely and convince her to stay with him. Only time would tell.

As they neared the site, Esme's face lit up in anticipation of seeing the rest of the team. She could deny her connection with them, but her excitement was palpable. Tordor hated the narrative she'd embraced along the way. The one where she'd convinced herself it was too dangerous to form connections. Breaking that narrative had become one of his biggest goals, and he was determined to succeed.

"We should meet with Larkin and Brienne first," he said, the Jeep shaking as he drove over the gravel road and came to a stop before the clearing that housed the tents.

"Definitely. Better make sure they want the job before we declare them co-mayors, right?" She flashed a grin.

Nodding, he parked, stepping out to retrieve his bag and make sure she had everything. In an act that was now instinctual, he placed his hand on the small of her back as they walked to camp.

"Hey, boss!" Larissa said, jogging up and giving Esme a hug. "How did you and our diplomatic prince do? Am I going to be moving to DC?" She chucked her eyebrows.

"General Markson is vetting you now, so don't commit any crimes or rock the boat and you should be fine." Squeezing her upper arm, Esme glanced around the camp. "I see our tents are still up. Thanks for keeping an eye on them."

"Happy to do it," Larissa said with a salute. "We had some rain, but I checked both tents and they're fine."

"Hopefully we'll have more permanent structures here soon and won't have to worry about the rain. Speaking of that, Tor and I need to meet with Larkin and Brienne."

The two soldiers approached, and Esme asked them to accompany her and Tordor to the river. Once they were secluded, they sat on a soft patch of grass as Esme cleared her throat.

"Well, guys, I can't believe it, but we're underway with Phase I of the implementation plan. General Markson will be done vetting the first fifteen recruits soon, and then we'll move to Phase II where we'll recruit thirty more."

"How do you plan to find them?" Brienne asked. "I know the immortal royals have candidates in their realm, but it's also advantageous to find immortal candidates living here. They're already acclimated to human life, so they'll easily blend in."

"That's why I wanted to meet with you both separately," Esme said, leaning back on her hands. "Tor has notions of traveling the human realm and finding immortals who might need his help." Tordor nodded as she continued. "He'll inevitably find good candidates along the way and needs a place to send them to prepare to be vetted."

"Rausch Gap is perfect, but since I'll be traveling a lot, I can't commit to leading," Tordor said. "That's why Esme and I want to ask you two to become co-leaders of the village we'll build here." Smiling, he gestured between them. "If you're willing, that is. I know you had a life in the immortal world, Larkin, and Brienne...well, I'm not quite sure where you lived before you connected with Esme, but if you're willing to put down roots, we'd love to have you."

"I've served your mother for centuries and it's been a great honor," Larkin said, trailing his palm over the grass. "But the immortal world holds...memories for me that I carry in here." Tapping his chest, he formed a sad smile. "I want to keep the good ones but leave the painful ones in the old realm as I build something here. I think that's what my partner would've wanted."

"I didn't realize you lost your mate," Esme said, reaching over and squeezing his wrist. "I'm so sorry, Larkin."

"Thank you. We shared something extremely special for the short time we had together, and I know I can build something here that would make him proud." He paused, seeming to assess their reactions. "And none of you are flinching, so I assume you don't mind that your co-leader is gay."

Esme's eyebrows drew together. "Why would we mind?" she asked, bafflement in her expression. "Hell, love is hard enough to find. I don't disparage anyone who finds it in whatever way it manifests for them."

Larkin looked toward Tordor.

Shrugging, Tordor shook his head. "Doesn't matter one bit to me, Larkin. You're one of the best soldiers I've ever known. I'm honored by your loyalty to my mother and to our cause here."

"My loyalty is to you too, Prince Tordor. I'll do whatever I can to help as you expand your rule here."

Inhaling a deep breath, Tordor drew up his leg, resting his arm on it as he contemplated. "I guess I'm going to be the royal leader in the human realm whether I'm ready or not."

Reaching over, Esme patted his thigh. "You're ready. I think you were kind of born for it, Tor."

Reveling in her praise and confidence in his abilities, he allowed the sentiment to surge through his veins.

"While we're all sharing our feelings, I bat for the same team like this one," Brienne said, gesturing with her thumb at Larkin. "So you're leaving the first settlement in the human world in the hands of two gay soldiers who've never done anything but fight and scrap. I'm not sure if you two are batshit crazy or brilliant, but I'm in."

Esme's throat glistened in the rays of light that filtered through the trees as she tossed her head back and laughed. "Hell yes, guys. You're both going to do great, and our people here are very lucky." Facing Tordor, she wrinkled her nose. "Should we rename the site though? Rausch Gap is a mouthful, right?"

Rubbing his chin, Tordor nodded. "We definitely could think of something more appropriate for our people..."

"How about Eternal?" Larkin asked. "Eternal, Pennsylvania. It signifies our immortality and a place to put down roots."

"I love it," Esme said, eyes glowing. "Guys?"

Tordor and Brienne both nodded, and Esme beamed.

"Eternal, Pennsylvania, here we come!" Spreading her arms, she gestured over the forest.

"We need to start interviewing skilled workers immediately. We're going to need planners, architects, contractors and the whole gamut," Tordor said.

Scowling, Brienne sighed. "This co-leader thing is going to require me to do paperwork, isn't it?"

"I'm afraid so," Tordor said. "But we'll make sure to commission a training center where you can keep your combat skills sharp in between papercuts."

"Bribery will get you everywhere, and I'm happy to oversee the building of the training center so I can make sure it's up to spec."

"Done," Tordor said, admiring her sense of humor. "As Esme said, I'm going to build a home here to stay between travels, and I'm always available for anything you two need."

"Well, then," Esme said, rubbing her thighs, "I think this calls for champagne. Tordor and I stopped along the way and grabbed a few bottles, hoping this would be the outcome." Rising, she planted her fists on her hips. "Who wants to get tipsy and celebrate?"

Lifting to their feet, the four leaders headed back to camp to deliver the good news to the team.

Tordor spent the rest of the day planning with the team, cognizant of Esme's presence even when they weren't together. Every so often, he would glance at her while she stood in the distance discussing future plans with Larissa or one of the other soldiers. Even when she didn't look back, her spine would straighten and her cheeks would flush, and Tordor thanked the goddess she carried the same awareness of his presence.

Once night fell and the camp was quiet, Tordor slipped on his shoes and padded to her tent. Unzipping the fabric, he glanced inside to find her sitting with her laptop open in the dim light of the lantern beside her. Grinning, he stepped inside.

"Whatcha studying there looking all serious?" he asked, zipping the tent behind him.

Arching her brows, she gave him a knowing look. "Are you sneaking into my tent? Should I call security?"

Frowning, he froze as he studied her. "Do you want me to leave?"

Sighing, she extended her hand. "No. I'm just annoyed because you're so damn cute, especially when you pout like that. Come on. Let me show you what I'm looking at."

Elated at her invitation, he stepped toward her, kicking off his shoes before lowering to the soft sleeping bag that lined the bottom of her tent. Sidling up to her, he listened as she pointed to the screen.

"I was doing more research on creepy dude. That led me down a rabbit hole on some of the immortal chat sites. Have you ever heard of Nymphs?"

Pondering, he shook his head. "Outside of the human fantasy novels Heden gave me, I haven't."

Nodding, she pointed to a blurry picture of a woman with lavender eyes. "This is posted under the 'Nymph sighting' thread. There are about one hundred of them altogether. People with purple irises whose pictures were snapped since the human camera was invented."

"And they all live in the human world?"

"Supposedly." Glancing up at him, her face was a mask of confusion. "Your aunt and cousin have purple irises. Do you know where they originated?"

"Nope," he said, stretching his arm over her shoulders and leaning in to study the picture. "Sadie says it's a recessive immortal gene that rarely surfaces. When Adelyn's mom left her at Sadie's clinic, it's what prompted her to call Lila and see if she wanted to adopt her."

"That's sweet," Esme said, relaxing against him as she grinned. "Two people connected by something rare who found each other."

Inching closer, he asked softly, "Are we still talking about Lila and Adelyn?"

Chuckling, she nodded. "Yes. I'm not letting you draw me into a deep discussion, Tor. It's going to devolve into an argument, and I don't want to go there with you. I need to stay in the moment."

"Esme—"

Covering his lips, she shook her head. "I was very clear about the terms here. You're so good at pushing me, but you also need to know when to stop. I don't want the rest of our time together to be spent discussing impossible outcomes."

"Tell me your biggest fear," he said softly, running his thumb over her lower lip. "Tell me why we can't at least try to make this work."

Tears filled her eyes, and his heart threatened to shatter into a thousand pieces. Hating that he was the cause of her distress, he pulled back. "Sorry, we don't have to—"

"Have you ever watched the life of the person you love the most drain from their body? Imagine watching your mother die while you stood helpless and inept."

Tordor stiffened, unable to imagine the terrible scenario of Miranda dying in front of his eyes.

"I don't understand what that has to do with us—"

"I won't let you become a casualty, Tor," she interjected, anger infusing her tone along with the agony of her losses. "Everyone he's killed has meant something to me, but you..." Drifting off, she worked her jaw, searching for words. "You're such a bright star and someone who represents the future of your people. I can't let him hurt you because of me."

"I can take care of myself, Esme."

With a forcible shake of her head, she closed the laptop and set it aside, balancing on her shins as she cupped his face. "I can't lose you too. I won't be the reason your light is extinguished. Nothing is going to change my mind. When you care about someone as much as I care about you, you make sacrifices to ensure that person's safety."

Repositioning to sit on the ground, he stretched out his legs, lifting her to straddle him as she wrapped her legs around his waist. Staring deep into her eyes, he stroked her soft hair.

"You're allowing your fear of losing me to ensure you lose me," he said, a slight teasing in his tone. "What if I'm the person who breaks your streak? What if we figure it out? Dr. Tyson is arriving tomorrow, and Larkin has already started building a lab for him with the materials he requested. Heden has confirmed he can have any state-of-the-art equipment his heart desires. He's going to create potions to circumvent your father's poisons, Esme, and I'm a competent fighter."

Gently gripping her bicep, he gave a few teasing squeezes. "Maybe not as tough as you, but Uncle Latimus taught me a few things."

Laughing, she swiped her arm under her nose. "I have no doubt you're fierce, but I can't erase the memories, Tor. Maybe I'm being shackled by fear. But I'd rather be a coward than see you die."

Exhaling a long breath, he shook his head. "I never thought I'd fall for a pessimist. You're really going to make me work to retain my unyielding optimism."

"Are you falling for me? I thought I was just giving you sex lessons."

"Call it what you want, sweetheart, but we both know I'm tied up in you." He brushed her lips with his. "And I have no desire to untangle myself. Ever."

Her wistful sigh lit a small kernel of hope in the far reaches of his heart. There in the tiny tent, he held her atop his thighs, hoping like hell they could converge their vastly different outlooks.

"So, super-creeper, you snuck into my tent," she said, biting her lip under her reddened nose. "I guess that means you're going to ravish me, hmm?"

As much as he wanted to make love to her, they'd just had a rather serious discussion and her eyes were still swollen from the tears that threatened to fall. Since his need to comfort her outweighed his need to make love to her—slightly—he glanced at the sleeping bag below them.

"Honestly, I'd like to hold you and have you tell me your stories. I don't care if they're sad or happy."

Her lips twitched. "Is it because I look like ten boxers destroyed my face? I'm an ugly crier."

"There's nothing ugly about you," he said, winking.

"Well, my lady parts are kind of sore since we went at it in the hotel room. I'm okay with cuddling, but I want to hear more about *you*. You're so close with your family. I'd love to know what that's like."

"Then I'll tell you," he said, shifting her off his thighs so he could reach for his shirt. Tugging it off, he fumbled for the nearby blanket, covering her with it as she lay down on the sleeping bag. Reaching to turn off the lantern, he crawled underneath the blanket and pulled her close, spooning her as they shared a pillow.

"You got to know my mom and dad pretty well while we were at Uteria. Who else should I tell you about? I could tell you the story of how Uncle Darkrip and Aunt Arderin fell in love. That one's a doozie. They got stuck in a cave and she got pregnant with Callie. Mom thought Dad was going to remove his eyes with a spoon."

Laughing, she shimmied into him. "Couldn't Darkrip disintegrate your dad with a thought?"

"Yeah, but I think he loved Arderin enough to let him gauge his eyes out. Thankfully, Dad let him live."

"Tell me more," she said, yawning. "I always wanted a close family. I'm going to live vicariously through yours."

Holding her in the darkness, he stroked her smooth skin as he told her of the great loves his family had experienced...silently longing to add their story to the long list of happy ever afters.

Chapter 25

The next morning, Esme dressed in the quiet light of dawn. Glancing at Tordor, she decided to let him sleep even though he'd probably be amenable to doing yoga with her. He looked so young as he snored upon her pillow, and she took a moment to wonder where he would be when he'd lived as long as she had.

Would their realms survive? Humans were known for entering great wars and developing disastrous weapons. Immortals had also seen their fair share of war. Would it be possible for the worlds to amalgamate and evolve together? Or was it just a pipe dream on which they were wasting their time?

Stepping into the crisp morning air, Esme hoped for a future without war and bloodshed. Having Tordor as the leader in the human realm would certainly be advantageous for all species. Although he was young, he had an intrinsic sense of duty and was a natural leader.

Trekking through the woods, Esme stopped beside the river and inhaled the fragrant air. Whiffs of evergreen and cedar surrounded her as the water gurgled nearby. Lifting her arms, she began to stretch, forming poses that would ease the tension in her weary body.

The conversation with Tordor last night had been rough, but it was important she maintain clarity with him. Ending their romantic relationship would be hard, but hopefully he would eventually understand her decision stemmed from a deep sense of love.

Smiling, she closed her eyes and pondered the sentiment. *Love.* She hadn't felt it in so long—hadn't allowed herself to—but her handsome half-Vamp certainly didn't make it easy to maintain the barriers she'd built around her heart. Was she falling in love with him?

Arching to the left with her hands above her head, she stretched as one word echoed in her head: *Yes.*

If she weren't so hardened and weary, Esme could see herself building a life with Tordor. One where she took her place beside him as he grew into the magnificent leader he would become in the human world. A life where they strived to help their people and traveled the Earth together. One where they had children with slightly-pointed ears and eyes the color of wet leaves in the summer forest...

Snapping her eyes open, Esme clenched her jaw and began a new series of postures. Daydreams were for people who weren't hunted. She'd do well to stick to her nightmares. At least they represented reality.

Suddenly, her ears perked as a branch snapped to her left. Gasping, she dropped her arms, her hand seizing the gun she'd holstered at her side. Drawing it, she aimed toward the sound, telling her ragged heartbeat to calm down so she could listen.

Another rustle sounded and she cocked the gun, ready to blow off anyone's head who threatened her team. Planting her feet, she called, "Show yourself! I'm armed and I'm not afraid to use it."

A man stepped from the nearby brush, hands held high as his dark eyes assessed her. He wore all-black underneath a stern expression and thick black hair.

"You followed us here from DC," she said, tightening her finger on the trigger. "Why were you spying on us in the bowling alley?"

"I'm not a threat to you, princess," he said, his posture open even if his face was impassive. "I wanted to observe you and Prince Tordor to gain intel."

"Sounds pretty threatening to me."

He began to step forward, and she shot the ground beside his foot. Scowling, he retreated, holding his hands higher as he angrily stared at her.

"I'm armed too, but I don't want this to get ugly."

"What's with the tattoo?" She tapped her neck. "Do you still serve my father?"

"No. I defected centuries ago along with your Uncle Gillam. I serve him now. That is, until you decide to take your rightful place as the true leader of the Elves."

Feeling her mouth fall open, she struggled to close it. "I have no desire to rule anyone."

Emitting a laugh, his lips curved. "With all due respect, that doesn't really matter when you're destined for it. Tordor understands this and is learning to fulfill his destiny in a way that's true to his nature. It's time for you to do the same, princess."

"Stop calling me that!" Stomping the ground, she tried to manage the confusion whirling in her head. "My father disowned me and I'm a hybrid. I have no place amongst purebred Elves."

"Your uncle would disagree, but that's a discussion for another time." His features contorted into something ominous as he spoke the next words. "Your father has grown quite curious and won't be able to stop himself from approaching you. I've come to warn you and make sure you're prepared."

"He's coming here?" she asked, fear lacing her veins. "To Rausch Gap?"

"Yes."

Throat closing with terror at the thought of her team being harmed, she shook her head. "I won't let him hurt them."

"He wishes to hurt you most. Remember that, princess. Also remember that you are his greatest vulnerability. His love for your mother prevents him from harming you. Use that to your advantage."

Still reeling from the possibility that her father might travel to Rausch Gap, she remained silent, attempting to digest the information.

Gingerly stepping back into the brush, he said, "It's not in your nature to shoot me, so I'm going to back away. I'm sorry I startled you—here and at the bowling alley. Know that you have supporters, Princess Esme, and we're ready to follow you whenever you decide to lead. We also embrace Prince Tordor as the leader of immortals in this realm and hope you will consider ruling together. A united front will help defeat your father. He has grown too powerful and lost all vestiges of the goodness he once possessed. It is time for a new era."

Tordor's voice echoed through the forest, calling her name as her head snapped back toward camp. He'd inevitably heard the gunshot, and Esme knew the team would arrive in seconds. Pivoting back to the man in black, she realized he'd disappeared.

Clutching her weapon, she ran to the brush, searching for him in the dim morning light, but it was no use. He'd vanished as sure as the last patch of snow on the first day of spring. Frustrated, she emerged from the brush, encountering a worried Tordor, Larkin and Brienne as they rushed toward her.

"I'm fine, guys," she said, flipping the safety on the gun and replacing it in the holster. "He's gone."

"Who's gone?" Tordor asked, approaching and patting her shoulders, arms and sides as he searched for injuries.

"I'm good," she said, planting her hand on his chest, her tone indicating she needed distance to gather her wits. Her caring half-Vamp understood immediately, backing away but retaining a watchful eye. Concern emanated from his strong frame, and she felt the urge to reassure him.

"It was creepy dude from the bowling alley," she said, scowling as she glanced at the brush. "He said a lot in a very short time before he disappeared, but the gist of it is that he's working with my uncle."

"The one who defected?" Tordor asked.

"Yes. They seem to have a notion that I'm a princess who will take my father's place as the ruler of the Elves."

Tordor's eyebrows lifted. "Well..." he said hesitantly, "you are, Esme."

"Ohhhh, no," she said, holding up her hands. "I told you, I have no wish to lead. And I'm not even a purebred Elf. I honestly have no idea what he was talking about."

Tordor's expression was questioning, as if he was challenging her to accept the things they'd discussed. That she had a bigger purpose. That it was time for her to stop *running*.

"Anyway, he says he's not a threat and he didn't hurt me, so I'll believe it for now. I didn't get his name, but perhaps I can find it if I keep scouring through the immortal message boards." Looking each of them in the eye, she said solemnly, "He warned me that my father is on his way here."

"Fuck," Brienne breathed.

"Yeah, not great news," Esme quipped. Running a hand through her hair, she fanned her lips as she exhaled a frustrated breath. "For now, we need to get Dr. Tyson settled when he arrives today. Then I need to detail the team on everything I know about my father's powers. Hopefully, Dr. Tyson can create some potions to alleviate fatal poisoning if anyone is shot with one of his weapons. The team can also prepare to confront him." Swallowing thickly, she looked to the ground. "Then we can discuss whether I should stay or leave. If I'm gone, perhaps it will decrease the probability my father will show up here."

"No," Tordor said. "You're not leaving, Esme—"

"I'm going to do what's best for the team, Tor," she interjected. "That's always been my objective."

Tordor remained silent, their gazes wary as they studied each other.

"Okay, I'm terrible in awkward situations, so you two stay here and hash it out," Brienne said, pointing between Tordor and Esme. "Come on, Larkin. Let's give them some privacy and make sure everyone at camp is okay."

With a nod, Larkin followed her back to camp.

Cementing her gaze to Tordor's, Esme observed the anger simmering in his eyes.

"Now isn't the time to run, Esme," he said, his tone firm. "We need to stay united."

Emotion welled in her throat as she longed to make him understand her desire to save the team. To save *him*. But she knew it was extremely difficult for a child borne of love, protected and sheltered, to understand the trauma she wished to prevent for those she cherished.

No matter how hard she tried, she and Tordor would never see the world through the same lens.

The thought brought her immeasurable pain since it meant relinquishing the opportunity to create a life with the only man she'd ever considered might be her true mate.

"I'm sorry," she whispered, unable to control the wobbling of her chin. "I don't want to hurt you—"

"Then don't," he said, cupping her cheeks as his soulful plea reflected in his eyes. "You're stronger than this, sweetheart."

"It's not about being strong," she said, shaking her head, knowing he would never understand. "It's about learning from the past—"

"Bullshit!" he hissed, pushing her toward the large tree behind her. As her back hit the bark, she gazed up at him, hating the look of raw anguish on his features. "I care about you too much to allow your fear to win."

"That's not your choice—"

"It is if I'm your mate." Placing his hands on each side of her head, his fingers squeezed the timber. "Are you going to deny you feel it too?"

Her eyes darted between his as she struggled to answer.

Expelling a frustrated breath, he rested his forehead against hers. "Not every love story is tragic, Esme. Sometimes people just slip into love and it's easy and *right*. My parents struggled to find it, and I was prepared for a long, winding path too, but I've found it so easily with you. You're my person, sweetheart. Don't you understand?"

"I've never been anyone's person."

Releasing a frustrated breath, he shook his head. "You're a lone wolf by choice. I get it because I was too, in a way, before I met you. I kept myself from connecting until I met someone I didn't have to force it with. Until I met *you*."

Her lips formed a sad smile. "It's not that easy..."

"It can be," he murmured, brushing his lips against hers. "Let's make it easy, sweetheart." Pressing his lips to hers, he consumed her, channeling his passion into a blazing kiss...

Tordor's body vibrated with frustration and lust as he devoured Esme's lips. Perhaps if they spoke with their bodies instead of their minds, she'd turn off the defense mechanisms and just *feel*. Plunging his tongue into her mouth, he drank her essence, needing her as surely as the air rapidly entering and departing his lungs.

She kissed him back with ardor, wrapping her arms around his neck as she strained toward him. Sliding his hands under the smooth curves of her backside, he lifted her, thrilled when she wrapped her legs around his waist. Balancing against the aged bark of the tree, he sipped and licked her, wishing she would release her fears and lower her walls enough to love him back.

It was true what he'd said about his parents. Tordor had often wondered if he'd have a perilous road to love like they'd had. Instead, his had been rather steady ever since Esme appeared on the battlefield months ago.

Until now, when she was determined to erect roadblocks he found unworthy of what they were on the precipice of building together.

Breaking the kiss, she exclaimed, "Damn it, why are you such a good kisser?"

"Because I was born to kiss you, little Elf," he said, reveling in her shiver as she absorbed his words. "I'm afraid to say anything more because it might make you hightail it out of here before I can get you back to camp."

A throaty laugh exited her lips. "You know me too well. It's disconcerting."

"Maybe it's just the way it's supposed to be. I won't ask you to promise me forever. But let's ditch the talk of running for now, okay? We're in this together, hon—"

"Tor—"

"Please, Esme?"

Sighing, she shook her head. "The pout. Always with the pout. You're lucky it's so cute."

"This pout?" he asked, pointing to his mouth.

Her chuckle surrounded them, shoring up the cracks that had snaked through his heart when she mentioned leaving.

"Yes, *that* pout. Fine, let's stay in the moment." He gently set her on her feet, squeezing her arm as she straightened. "Well, come on. We've got a ton to discuss with the team and we're not getting any younger."

Grasping his hand, his stubborn, gorgeous Elf led them back to camp.

Once the team reconvened, Esme detailed everyone on the encounter with the man who'd sworn allegiance to her uncle. The team was solemn as she discussed the option of leaving, and several of them pleaded for her to stay. It warmed Esme's heart, but she also wanted to make the best decision for everyone involved. She informed them she would stay but inwardly vowed to stay strategic and flexible as the situation progressed.

They also discussed the need to gather more intel from the mysterious man who'd approached Esme by the river.

"We need to track him down and question him," Tordor said as they sat around the banked campfire. "Larkin and Brienne, do you think you can track him?"

"Absolutely," Brienne said with a nod. "I'd like to take today to fortify the camp and give everyone a refresher on shooting and self-defense."

"And I'll need to acclimate Dr. Tyson when he arrives," Larkin said. "I'm willing to head out with you first thing in the morning to track down our mystery man and question him."

"Works for me," Brienne said.

"Excellent," Tordor said, rising. "Let's all make sure we complete a refresher with Brienne today and ensure our firearms work. If you see anything out of the ordinary, report it immediately."

Affirmation collectively sounded from the group as the meeting adjourned.

Dr. Tyson arrived shortly before noon in a rental car that puttered up to the campsite. Stepping out of the vehicle, he gazed at the site behind his wire-rimmed glasses.

"Well, I guess I'm at the right place," he said, trailing over to Larkin and extending his hand. "You weren't kidding about it being in the middle of nowhere."

"Glad you made it safely," Larkin said, shaking his hand. "You remember Brienne. Let me introduce you to the rest of the team."

After the introductions were made, Larkin led Dr. Tyson to a tent they'd set up as a makeshift lab until a permanent one could be built.

"Heden shipped the materials you requested, and Brienne and I set them up for you as best we could," Larkin said, gesturing to the various beakers, test tubes, flasks and other equipment.

"This is a good start," Dr. Tyson said, perusing the equipment. "We have electricity here?"

"You've got a full-service portable power station," Larkin said, pointing to the box in the corner with various outlets and plugs. "When that one dies, we have more."

"Excellent. I'll need to scour the area to see what natural shrubs and herbs are available."

"Let me know when you're ready," Larkin said with a nod. "I'll accompany you so you're protected."

"Thank you," Dr. Tyson said before Larkin led him to another tent.

"This is your personal quarters. Until we build some shelters, you'll be roughing it. Hope that's okay."

"You were clear about the conditions," Dr. Tyson said, peeking into the tent. Straightening, he squared his shoulders. "Thank you for inviting me to the team. I'll do my best to create effective antidotes against Dakath's poisons."

Larkin gave an affirming nod, patting Dr. Tyson's shoulder before urging him to unpack and settle in. As the team completed their training duties, another vehicle pulled up, causing Larkin and Brienne to draw their weapons. A tall, lanky man stepped out of the Jeep, his lips forming a lazy grin as he held up his hands.

"Wow, didn't expect to have a gun pulled on me on day one. I'm usually much smoother."

"Jaxon!" Tordor called, striding forward and extending his hand. "Great to see you."

"Thanks, Prince Tordor," he said, shaking. Leaning in he whispered conspiratorially, "They know I'm one of the good guys, right?"

Laughing, Tordor nodded. "Just Tor is fine, Jaxon, and they definitely do now. Come on, let me introduce you."

After introductions were made, Jaxon retrieved his backpack and pulled out a large clear plastic bag. "I was instructed by Tatiana to retrieve bark from the Methuselah tree in Inyo National Forest in California. It's the oldest tree in the human realm, and she said it has some kick-ass magical properties."

"Fascinating," Dr. Tyson said, stepping forward and taking the bag. His eyes roved over the weathered bark as excitement emanated from his thin frame. "I look forward to studying it and creating some potions."

"Good stuff," Jaxon said, craning his neck to glance over the camp. "Sooooo, uh, do you guys have an extra tent for me? I'm kind of digging hanging in the human realm and would like to stay here so you can bring me up to date on Dakath and the immersion plan with the human general."

"You're welcome to stay as long as you want," Tordor said, cupping his shoulder. "We have a tent for you and could use another soldier trained in combat."

"At your service," he said with a salute. Leaning in so only Tordor could hear, he muttered, "Larissa's pretty cute. Is she taken?"

"Okay, buddy, let's have you settle in before you blaze the seduction path. And she's most likely going to be leaving us to infiltrate the human government as one of the first fifteen candidates."

"Bummer. It was worth a shot."

The team milled about the site getting to know each other as the afternoon sun trailed across the sky.

Once darkness set in, the group sat beside the glowing fire, eating dinner as they stayed alert. Eventually, several headed to their tents as the hour grew late.

"Brienne and I are light sleepers and we'll be armed," Larkin said, rising and giving a nod to Esme. "Sleep well knowing we'll protect you."

"Thank you, Larkin."

When only a few people remained beside the fire, Esme rose and extended her hand to Tordor, who was sitting beside her.

"I'm taking Tordor to my tent so Jaxon can sleep in his," she said, addressing the group. "Anyone got a problem with that?"

They all shook their head as Larissa beamed. "It's about time, if you ask me!"

Rising, Tordor took Esme's hand. Uttering a soft "good night" to the group, he followed her to her tent.

Chapter 26

Once inside, Esme faced her lover, placing her hands on his chest as she struggled with her next move. Her conversation with the man beside the river that morning had replayed in her head all day. The need to approach him and gather more intel burned in every crevice of her soul.

Moreover, she needed to speak to him alone. Not because she didn't trust Tordor or her team. Instead, she knew that approaching the secretive man alone would allow her to gather the best intel in the shortest amount of time.

And if her father was coming, time was of the essence.

Gazing up at Tordor, she anticipated how pissed he would be when he discovered she'd decided to approach the man alone. On a scale of one to ten, she was guessing about one hundred.

Knowing that, she felt an innate desire to love him now...to give him something to remember in the morning when he awoke and found her gone.

Rising to her toes, she drew his lips to hers, kissing him with fervor as he groaned and tugged away their clothes.

Once their heated skin was bare, she drew him to the blanketed floor, urging him to lie on his back as she straddled him. Reaching to cradle her face, his eyes shone with the love she wasn't sure she deserved as her heart pounded in her chest.

"I like this position," he said, forming a sultry smile. "Should I get you wetter first?"

"Oh, my dear half-Vamp," she said, brushing his lips before trailing soft kisses over his jaw and down his neck...moving lower until she stopped at his nipple. Pressing her lips to the soft skin—several shades darker than the rest of his body—she nipped the tiny peak. "I'm going to get wet just by kissing you." Extending her tongue, she licked his nipple as he groaned.

"Why does that feel so good?" he rasped, clutching her hair. "Goddess, I love it when you touch me."

Thrilled with his reaction, she toyed with his nipple before kissing a path to the other one, repeating the tender ministrations. Her massive Slayer-Vampyre writhed beneath her, his reactions so genuine and open as she loved him.

Once the small points of his nipples were wet and turgid, Esme gazed into his eyes as she trailed her lips down the scratchy patch of hair that stretched from his chest to his navel.

"Sweetheart..." he whispered.

"*Shhh...*" she said, placing wet kisses around his hips, aware of his rapidly swelling shaft above the juncture of his thighs. "I hate to tell you this, my sexy Vampyre, but *I'm* going to be the one to suck *you* first."

A ragged groan escaped his lips as his fist tightened in her hair. Reveling in his possessive grasp, she touched her lips to the base of his cock. Eyes glued to his, she drowned in the blazing desire of his green orbs as she extended her tongue...gliding it up his sensitive shaft as he hissed.

"*Ohmygod,*" he rasped, the words jumbled together as he struggled to breathe. "No one's ever kissed me there..." His hips jutted toward her mouth, and she smiled at his loss of control.

"Now, now," she said, giving a *tsk, tsk, tsk,* "you need to be a good boy and wait 'til I'm ready."

"Fuck," he breathed, shaking his head on her pillow. "I'm sorry, sweetheart. It's taking everything I have not to shove myself inside that pretty mouth. How am I supposed to have patience while your lips are so sexy and wet?" Reaching down, he ran a finger over her bottom lip.

"The buildup is better that way," she said, nipping his finger. "You can clutch my hair, but let me stay in control. I promise I'll take care of you."

"Okay," he whispered, sliding his fingers deeper in her hair and holding tight. "I'm probably going to come in thirty seconds if you suck me."

Grinning, she licked her lips, ensuring they were nice and wet before placing them on his burgeoning shaft. "Darling, that's the point," she murmured, enthralled with his tremors as she spoke against his skin.

Her massive immortal quaked and shuddered beneath her as she placed slow, wet kisses over his most sensitive place. Gently gripping his thick length, she lifted it, gazing into his eyes as she ran her lips over the head.

"I love holding you like this," she whispered against his flesh. "Kissing you right here..." Dipping her tongue in the tiny ridge at the tip of his cock, she imbibed his salty taste as his hips bucked beneath her.

"Please stop teasing me, honey," he groaned, his pleading expression her undoing. "I need you."

Opening wide, she covered the mushroom-shaped head with her mouth, sliding over his hard flesh as he moaned beneath her. Closing his eyes, he surged into her wet mouth, striving to go deeper.

"Relax, Tor..." she gently commanded, noticing his jaw clench as she withdrew her mouth. "Let me do the work."

"I'm dead," he muttered, inhaling a sharp breath when she closed around him again and slid over his taut flesh. "Send me to the Passage."

Smiling around his cock, she began to work him in her mouth...gliding back and forth...dragging her tongue along the wet skin as he uttered unintelligible words beneath her. Gazing at her with unfocused eyes, he clenched her hair, anchoring her as he began to slowly move his hips.

"I'm sorry," he rasped, his cheeks flushed as he panted. "I just need to fuck you like this. You're so beautiful, Esme..."

Nodding, she gave him control, letting him jut into her mouth in slow, even strokes. Reaching for his sac, she began to massage the sensitive area as he wailed in ecstasy. His handsome features were a mask of concentration, and she could tell he was holding back.

Popping free, she said, "I don't care how fast you come. I just want you to feel good."

And then, before she knew it, her lover rose, grabbing her by her hips and flipping her to her stomach. Crawling over her, he growled against the shell of her ear. "No way in hell am I coming without you."

Drawing her hips up, he commanded softly, "Get on your hands and knees, the way you told me you like it."

Entranced by his deep voice and throaty command, she followed his directive, balancing on her hands and knees. Looking over her shoulder, she wiggled as she braced, ready to take everything he could give her.

Tordor gripped Esme's hips, feeling his eyes cross with lust as she wiggled her luscious ass, ready to be claimed. Wanting to beat his chest with raw, primal emotion, he squelched the urge and moved closer, encircling the base of his shaft and running it through her slick folds.

"Jesus, honey," he rasped, closing his eyes at the onslaught of pleasure. "You weren't kidding about getting wet while you sucked me."

"I love making you feel good," she moaned, pushing against his cock as he clenched his teeth. One day, he'd learn how to control the urge to come the second he touched her. For now, he would focus on giving her pleasure and trying his best to ensure they reached their peak together.

Nudging the tip of his cock through her tight opening, they groaned in unison as he pressed forward ever so slowly. Sucking in a deep breath, Tordor slid home, pushing farther until he was buried to the hilt. Licking his fingers, he reached around, searching for the tiny nub that would bring his lover ultimate pleasure. Finding it, he began to rub in firm circles as he withdrew before sliding back inside her tight warmth.

Esme groaned below him, her fingers clenching the blanket as she moved her hips to meet his thrusts. Each time he retreated, he gazed at her slick essence upon his cock, overcome with being covered in her sweet honey. Their bodies glistened in the dim light of the electric lantern, and he leaned forward, nudging her hair from her wet nape with his nose.

Licking the soft skin of her neck, instinct took over as he yearned to drink from her. Scraping his fangs against her flushed skin, he moaned her name as his hips worked against her body and his fingers caressed her engorged clit.

"Yes!" she cried, baring her neck to him as her body moved in tandem with his. "Drink from me. *Oh god...Tor!*"

Positioning his lips over her pulsing vein, he licked her one last time, his saliva ensuring she would feel no pain. Pressing the points of his fangs to her skin, he impaled her, his body jerking against hers as blood surged inside his mouth.

Closing his eyes, he drew her life-force into his body. Never had he imagined the ultimate connection he would feel as he claimed his little Elf, possessing her so thoroughly with every plunge of his cock and pull of his lips.

Esme groaned beneath him, her body rocking along to his jagged thrusts, and he wanted to weep with the knowledge he'd finally found her. So many years of wondering if he was unable to form intimate connections. It turned out he was just waiting for her.

A tingling sensation rocked the base of his spine, and he increased the pressure of his fingers, knowing he was seconds from coming. Focusing on bringing her to the peak, his fingers worked with frenzied strokes.

Suddenly, her back arched, a blissful laugh leaping from her throat as she began to convulse around him. Her tight, wet folds squeezed his shaft, all but drawing the first drops of release from him as he began to come. Thick pulses shot inside her quivering core as the little imp milked him, her orgasm choking him in a series of pleasurable spasms.

Collapsing beneath him, she clenched the soft sleeping bag as she melted into a pool of simmering pleasure. Tordor followed, unable to relinquish the claim he had on her tight channel, nor the one on her neck. Covering her with his large body, his cock continued to pulse inside her wet depths as he allowed himself a few lingering pulls of her blood.

Careful not to drink too much of the intoxicating essence, he drew back, his tongue rasping over her neck in smooth strokes to close the wounds. His sated Elf sighed beneath him, eyes closed as he licked her.

"Now who's dead?" she mumbled, a satiated grin under her flushed cheeks. "I'm never moving again."

"Good," he muttered against her sweat-soaked neck. 'If fucking you keeps you near me, I'll do it all day long for eternity."

Shimmying into him, she breathed a laugh. "My lady parts might have something to say about the frequency, but I could probably be convinced. What's a little stretching and soreness in the long run?"

Worried for her, he withdrew, mesmerized by the sight of his release trailing down her inner thighs. The primal satisfaction at marking her surfaced again, and he gazed at how thoroughly he'd claimed her as the evidence of their loving glistened in the dim light.

"You definitely staked your claim," she mumbled, causing him to smile as she all but read his thoughts. "There's a cloth and a bottle of water in my bag if you want to clean us up."

Reaching for them, he wet the cloth and began to trail it over her skin, loving how she quivered as he cleaned her. "I think I get it from my dad. Vampyres are much more primal than Slayers." Dragging the cloth over her skin, he took his time, wanting to cherish her. "But I've never felt this until you, sweetheart. It's just intrinsic."

Rolling over, she lifted eyes filled with sated desire to his. "Come lie with me," she said softly.

Tordor wiped his shaft before tossing the cloth aside. Lowering beside her, he grabbed the blanket and pulled it over their rapidly cooling skin. Resting on his elbow, he planted his head on his fist as he trailed his fingers over her neck.

"Are you okay? Did it hurt?"

"It felt so good," was her soft reply as she ran her smooth leg over his hairy one. "I loved having you drink from me. Did I taste good?"

Squinting one eye, he pretended to contemplate. "Kind of salty in spots, but you were okay."

Swatting his chest, she giggled, and Tordor embraced her playful, open expression. Rarely did he see her so relaxed, and he craved more nights with her where she would let down her walls and let him in completely.

"You tasted so good," he whispered, lowering to kiss her. "My delectable little Elf."

Sighing against his lips, she threaded her fingers through the hair at his nape. "Tor..."

"Yes?"

Her eyes darted back and forth between his. "I've never said it to anyone, you know. Except my mother."

He hadn't been sure, but he suspected she'd rarely spoken those three little words. They required intimacy and trust, and it was something she rarely offered because of her inherent desire to keep others safe.

"I have a pretty big family, so I've said it to them." Rubbing the tip of his nose against hers, he said softly, "But I've never said it to anyone else."

Her throat bobbed in the soft light as fear mingled with the emotion in her eyes. Staring deep into them, he allowed the silence to linger, understanding words were still a bridge too far for her to cross. Since he was an eternal optimist, he wouldn't give up hope, knowing he'd come closer than any other man in her life.

For now, that was enough.

"Thirteen," he said, tracing his finger under her eye.

"Huh?"

"Thirteen golden flecks in your right eye, and fifteen in your left. I promised myself I'd get close enough to count them one day."

Her tiny nostrils flared as tears filled her eyes, covering the sparkling flecks. "You did?"

Nodding, he kissed each of her eyebrows, wanting to ease the tension in the winged curves. "I've promised myself so many things when it comes to you, sweetheart. One day, they're all going to come true."

Palming his cheek, she ran her thumb over his lip, causing him to shiver. "I can't make promises, Tor. I'm so sorry."

"I don't need you to promise something I already know, Esme." When she opened her mouth to argue, he captured her lips in a poignant kiss, unwilling to hear excuses as to why they had no future. The time to admit what they meant to each other was fast approaching, and he needed to tread carefully while still urging her along.

She kissed him back, the movements of her lips and tongue against his so sweet, her taste more magnificent than anything he'd ever known. Settling into her, he draped his leg over her thighs, resting his head on the pillow beside hers as they cuddled.

Exhausted from their lovemaking, their eyes drooped as they studied each other, two lovers intertwined, wondering what the future would hold. The last thing he saw before he succumbed to sleep was his little Elf, love shining in her eyes, as she wished him sweet dreams in the darkness.

Chapter 27

Esme's eyes shot open and she immediately registered Tordor's warm body beside her. Perking her ears, she heard the steady chirp of the crickets and realized it was still pitch-black outside. Armed with resolve, she quietly slipped from beneath the covers and dressed.

After stuffing her laptop in her backpack, she quietly shifted it over her shoulders. Facing the immortal who'd stolen her heart as sure as the most skillful thief, she thanked the gods he was a sound sleeper. As much as she chided him for his snoring, it certainly came in handy at the present moment. Lifting her phone, she typed a text, informing him she was going to track down the mystery man and that Larkin and Brienne should remain at camp until her return.

Sparing him one last glance, she quietly unzipped the tent and headed to one of the Jeeps.

Inserting the key, she started the engine and kept the headlights off until she'd backed away and began the trek down the gravel road.

After driving for twenty minutes, dim sunlight began to crest over the horizon. Esme stopped at a coffee shop in nearby Pine Grove and secured a booth. A chipper server appeared asking if she wanted breakfast.

"Just some coffee, please. I'm going to do some work but let me know if you need the table back."

"We've got plenty of tables," the server said, smacking gum as she smiled. "You passing through? Haven't seen you here before."

"I'm always on the move," Esme said. "But I like Pennsylvania. It's a pretty state."

"Oh, honey, you should see my home town. Ardor Creek is even nicer than Pine Grove, but all the small towns in Pennsylvania have a certain charm."

"I'll have to check it out one day. Thanks, Laura," she said, reading the woman's nametag.

"One coffee coming right up." Sticking her pen behind her ear, she sauntered away.

Esme opened her laptop and got to work. Hours passed as she scoured the immortal message boards for the name of the man who'd surprised her in the woods. She was determined to find him and extricate every piece of information he possessed.

"Bingo," she whispered, straightening as she scrolled. A man named Castian had responded to a post searching for Elves who'd dissented from Dakath. Clicking on the thread, she followed it until the found the username. Castian7945. Opening her web browser, she searched for email addresses with the same handle.

Another immortal board popped up that she was unaware of. Following the threads, she found another post from Castian7945, along with an email address. Opening her browser, she composed a message from her anonymous account, hoping it would connect her with the man she'd encountered yesterday.

Dear Castian,
I was surprised by your visit yesterday but wish to meet to discuss further. Please reply with your contact number.
The Princess

Sitting back, she waited, sipping her coffee as the minutes ticked by. Suddenly, her email dinged and a reply appeared: (505) 756-3498.

Scrambling for her phone, she texted the number.

Esme: I'm at the coffee shop on Main Street in Pine Grove, PA. Would like to meet with you.

The text bubble appeared as anxious butterflies flitted in her belly.

Castian: Meet you there within the hour.

Breathing a sigh of relief, she texted him the confirmation.

And then she began to steel herself for her meeting with the mysterious man in black.

C astian appeared forty-five minutes later, dressed in his signature black as he strode to her booth. Sliding inside, he cocked a dark brow. "Taking a field trip from Rausch Gap, Princess?"

"Call me Esme, and I'm sure you knew I'd find you after dropping the bomb that my father intends to approach the site." Leaning forward, she spoke with gravity. "We don't know each other well yet, but let me assure you, I'm stubborn. Before you walk out that door, I'm going to know everything." She pointed to the entrance.

Sitting back, Castian rested his arm on the back of the booth as Laura appeared to take his order. After ordering a coffee, he twirled Esme's used wooden stirrer through his fingers.

"I have nothing to hide from you, Esme. My intention is to help you."

Esme studied him, sensing no malice in his expression. "You said you worked for my Uncle Gillam. How is he? I haven't seen him in several centuries."

"He lives a life off the grid in Scandinavia, which makes him happy." Leaning forward, he rested his forearms on the table. "He's grown tired of your father's antics and wishes to prevent Elven hybrid deaths. I and many others have pledged allegiance to him. His goal is to have you claim what is rightfully yours so he can rest. Until then, he keeps a watchful eye, and we try to maintain some semblance of peace."

Esme studied him, feeling as if he was leaving out part of the story. "Why isn't he here? If this mission is so important, why didn't he come and tell me himself?"

"I told you," he said, a muscle twitching in his jaw, "he deputized me to take care of things in the field."

Esme stood, slamming her laptop closed and stuffing it in her bag. "I've been around a long time, Castian, and I can discern a lie from a mile away. I'm not going to align with someone I don't trust." Slinging her bag over her shoulder, she began to walk away.

"Wait," he said, gripping her wrist. "I'll tell you the truth. Sit down. You're making a scene."

Glowering, she stood firm.

Sighing, he rubbed his forehead. "Please sit down, princess. I swear, I'll tell you everything."

Giving in to her curiosity, she returned to the table, waiting in silence as Laura dropped off his coffee. Stirring it, his expression was pensive. "Your uncle was poisoned two centuries ago. We have no idea how

Dakath infiltrated his home, but it made its way through Gillam's veins before he was discovered unconscious and near death."

Concern welled as her heartbeat accelerated.

"He was taken to the healer in the rural town he lived in and the poison was leeched out of him. He survived, but he was paralyzed from the waist down."

"Oh my god," she said, shaking her head. "I had no idea. I should've gone to him—"

"He didn't want anyone to know," Castian said, showing his palm. "Least of all you. He was impressed with your desire and ability to help our people and didn't want to interfere with your life."

"Does my father know he's paralyzed?"

Castian's eyes narrowed. "It's possible. His spy network is vast, but we've done a good job keeping Gillam off the radar. They vowed never to speak again when Gillam dissented, and it's possible Dakath thinks he's dead from the poisoning. Regardless, your father is more focused on targeting hybrid Elven children. Gillam is a vestige of a time long passed."

Taking a moment to digest the information, Esme gnawed her lip. "After I deal with my father, I need to visit Uncle Gillam. It's been far too long."

"He wouldn't want to detract from your purpose—"

"I understand," she said, holding up a hand. "But he's my uncle and the man who saved me after my mother was killed. We lost connection when I learned to live on my own, and he was still in my father's council. Although I loved him, I could never fully trust him as long as he was aligned with my father." Glancing down, she traced the table. "But he hurt him too, like he hurts everyone." Sighing, she shook her head. "So much pain."

Running a hand through his dark hair, he studied her. "You could stop him by challenging his throne. Many would support you, Esme."

She breathed a laugh. "Thanks, but I'm all set." Twirling her thumbs atop the table, she gnawed her lip. "You seem like a loyal servant to Gillam. Why don't *you* challenge my father's throne? I have no desire to lead. Perhaps it should go to a purebred Elf like you." She tapped her ear, indicating she could read his heritage by his pointed tips.

"Unfortunately, my soul is too black to ever lead."

Glancing over his clothes, she wondered if that was why he chose to dress so somberly. "What crimes have you committed that are so terrible?"

Sipping his coffee, he eyed her over the cup, debating whether to tell her. Arching a stubborn brow, she waited.

Setting down the cup, he inhaled a deep breath. "I was your father's chief executioner for centuries. I've killed more of our kinsmen than I care to admit."

Esme's eyes widened at his admission.

"When I die, my soul will inevitably reside in the Land of Lost Souls. Until then, I'll do my best to gain retribution. It will never erase my sins, but perhaps it can even the tally, if only a little."

Studying him, she said softly, "It's never too late to repent and start over. That takes courage."

"Thank you." He gave a brief nod.

Returning to the task at hand, she asked, "When does my father plan to enter the US?"

"His spies have been reporting back to him on your progress. Your father is wily and always looking for the best opportunity to strike. It's not about quantity of destruction for him. It's about the severity of the pain it will cause you."

"Truth," she responded, feeling her lips form a frown.

"Then you must know that he'll come after Tordor first."

Emotion choked her as she struggled to breathe. "I never should've given in to my feelings for him. How have I not learned this by now?"

"Esme," Castian said, his tone urging her to meet his gaze. "You deserve love like everyone else. It's about time you showed your father you're willing to fight for it."

"It's pointless to fight someone you know will win."

"What if this time were different?" he asked, his voice filled with determined resolve that caused a small glimmer of hope to well in her chest. "You have a talented team surrounding you. Larkin and Brienne are excellent soldiers. Jaxon was trained by Latimus himself. Dr. Tyson can concoct potions to counteract your father's poison weapons."

Shooting him an acerbic look, she said, "I'm going to pretend I'm not freaked out that you know everything about the clandestine team I've built."

Laughing, he tilted his head. "You have Tordor...and you have *me*."

"You're willing to fight with us?"

"I am," he said without reservation. "Why let Dakath to take the offensive? Let's prepare for a fight and show him we mean business. Dr. Tyson can create special poisons that lace our bullets that Dakath has never seen." Leaning forward, he pounded the table with his fist. "What if *you* brought the fight to *him* for once?"

"I can't start an immortal war on human soil. The immortal royals have been clear about that, and it would be disastrous for the implementation plan."

"Your father is coming whether you like it or not, Esme."

Chewing her lip, Esme debated. "It's such a huge risk. I'm so used to running." Scrubbing her hand over her face, she feared she might drown in indecision. "I need to talk to Tordor and his parents. Until I discuss with them, we're wasting our time."

Rising, he threw a ten-dollar bill on the table and jerked his head. "Then what are you waiting for? Let's head back to Rausch Gap. I'm going to need a ride, by the way. I took a rideshare here."

Huffing a laugh, she rose. "Quite presumptuous, aren't we? Who says I trust you?"

Lifting his sleeve, he held out his wrist. Sentiment flooded her veins as she stared at the mermaid inked on his skin, long hair flowing as she balanced on a rock that jutted from the sea.

"All of Gillam's followers wear this tattoo on our wrist to counteract your father's mark," he said, pointing to his neck.

"My mother would sing to me about mermaids all the time," she said wistfully.

"We bear this mark as a symbol of allegiance to Dyana and the daughter she bore. The princess of the Elves and our future queen."

Shooting him an incredulous look, she said, "I don't know about that, but the tattoo has earned you a ride back to camp." Lifting a finger, her tone grew stern. "If you so much as harm one hair on my team's head, I'll chop both tattoos off and shove them down your throat. Do you hear me?"

"Loud and clear, princess," he said, holding up his hands. "Now, if you're ready, I'll reiterate that time is of the essence."

Pivoting, she strode toward the entrance of the coffee shop. "No reiteration needed. Come on."

Once he folded his body into the passenger seat, she revved the engine and began the trek back to Rausch Gap.

Chapter 28

Tordor sat in Esme's tent reading her text message as his jaw clenched in anger.

Esme: I know you're going to be pissed, and I'm sorry. I've gone to track down the mystery man and get answers. I'm confident I can find him, and it will save time since I have the most knowledge of the situation. I've followed my gut for centuries and can't stop now. Even if you hate me, I'm doing this because I care about you and our team. Xoxo

Inhaling a slow breath, Tordor struggled to manage the frustration that welled within. Part of him wanted to follow her. To track her down and sate the part of him that wished to protect her.

But his practical side knew that would only manage to push her away. Navigating Esme's boundaries was a precarious task, and if he pushed too hard, she'd most likely run.

And running was no longer an option. In his opinion, at least.

The laptop chimed as the video chat popped up, and Tordor balanced it on his legs.

"There's our handsome son," Miranda said, beaming as she sat beside Sathan on their large four-poster bed in the expansive bedroom at Uteria.

"Hey, guys. How's it going?"

"Oh no," Miranda said, her expression clouding with worry. "Esme's not there. What happened? Is everything okay?"

Rubbing the back of his neck, he began to update them on the details of the past few days.

"So, creepy guy isn't a bad guy after all?" Miranda asked.

"I don't think so, but we still need to be cautious," Tordor said. "Esme wasn't here when I woke up this morning. She's gone to track him down."

"By herself?" Miranda asked. "That must be why you look like you want to murder someone."

"It's infuriating, Mom," he said, running a hand over his face. "She's so used to operating alone. Since I'm pretty sure she's my mate, we're definitely going to need to work on that."

"Wow, son," Sathan said, stroking Miranda's shoulder as he pulled her against his side. "That's really special. We're happy for you."

"Your dad fell for me the second he saw me outside Astaria the night we met. Of course, he's obstinate and annoying, so it took me much longer to figure out I loved him back."

Rolling his eyes, Sathan muttered, "How nice it must be to create revisionist history in your head, woman."

Grinning, Tordor watched their interplay, his heart full as they teased each other.

"*Anyway*," Miranda said, blowing a tuft of hair off her forehead, "we're here if you need us, sweetie. True love and relationships are really hard, but I know you're going to figure it out."

"I hope so."

Miranda's eyebrows drew together. "What do we need to do to help you with Dakath's threat? Should I have Latimus send a squadron? Do you want Evie and Darkrip to help?"

"Once I have more information, I'll let you know. Having Evie and Darkrip on standby is definitely a good idea. I don't know if his intention is to hurt Esme, to destroy our team, or to start a war. Esme will have more information once she returns, and I'll stay in contact with you all."

"Even though we don't want a conflict on human soil, we'll do whatever we can to protect you," Sathan said. "We'll prep Evie and Darkrip to be ready for your call."

"Thank you for supporting my efforts here." Lifting his chin, he steeled himself to give them the news. "I plan to build a home here at Eternal. That's the new name we've decided on."

"Love it," Miranda said with a nod.

"It's going to be a home base, but I don't plan on being here a lot. You see, there are these message boards here filled with immortals who need me..." As he told them of his plans, his parents shared a knowing smile.

"We already figured you were staying, son," Sathan said, approval in his tone. "We're extremely proud of you for forging your own path."

"Thanks, Dad. I hate to leave our family in the immortal world, but I have this intense calling to stay and help our people here."

"It's very noble, Tor," Miranda said, beaming with pride. "To stick with the stuffy tradition your father loves so much, we'll have a crowning ceremony when you return home to visit. King of the Human Realm has a nice ring to it."

"I don't need a ceremony, guys—"

"As much as your mother chides me for upholding tradition, I think it's important we declare you king there," Sathan said, scrunching his features at Miranda. "It will establish you as our chosen leader and create a barrier to anyone who wants to claim power. As the immortal presence grows in the human realm, we need order to maintain peace."

"Okay," Tordor said, rubbing the blanket beneath him as he conceded. "I don't need the title, but I see the purpose."

"The best rulers are the ones who don't seek the position," Miranda said. "They do it from a deep-rooted need to help others." She flashed a cheeky grin at Sathan. "We did a good job with this one, blood-sucker. Hope the next one is just as honorable."

Tordor's eyes widened. "Are you trying to tell me something?"

Beaming, she bit her lip and nodded. "You're going to have a sister! Or a brother...but we really want a girl this time."

Overcome with joy, Tordor felt elation zing down his spine. "Wow, guys. I'm so happy for you. I can't wait to meet her. Or him," he finished with a wide grin.

"Your mom is handling the morning sickness like a champ," Sathan said, kissing her forehead, "and we can't wait to have you home again so we can hug you, Tor."

"Once we get the first fifteen recruits implemented in the US government, I promise I'll visit." Glancing at his watch, he said, "On that note, I'm expecting a call from General Markson any minute."

"We love you, sweetie," Miranda said with a wave.

"Love you both so much. I can't wait for us to be together. One day soon, I promise."

After the final goodbyes, Tordor closed the screen and set the laptop aside. Unable to control his grin, he allowed the knowledge that he was going to have a sibling sink in. Feeling his expression fall, he realized how much he wished Esme were there so he could tell her. Somewhere along the way, she'd become the person he wanted to share his good news with. As the irritation at her insistence on doing things alone festered, the phone rang, and he went over logistics with General Markson.

Tordor agreed to secure lodging for the fifteen candidates in a hotel in DC over the next few days. General Markson would meet with them one-on-one at clandestine locations to conduct the interviews so they wouldn't be discovered. Once the interviews were complete and the candidates approved, they would assume their roles in the government.

The unification of the species would truly begin.

Rising, Tordor stepped outside, performing the stretches Esme had taught him. A twig snapped behind his tent, and Tordor stepped around, searching to make sure he wasn't being watched. Joy welled in his chest as Esme appeared, hesitation in her eyes as she inched closer.

"Whatcha doing out here all by yourself?" she asked.

Arching his eyebrows, he studied her. She seemed pensive as she waited for him to speak, probably assuming he was going to yell at her. "Honestly? I was thinking about how good a yoga teacher you were." He squinted one eye. "And how pissed I am at you."

Her throat bobbed as a pained expression crossed her face. "It shouldn't be a surprise that my first instinct is to tackle something on my own, Tor. I've done it my whole life."

Placing his hands on his hips, he stood firm. "It's time for you to make different choices, Esme. To learn to lean on others. To lean on *me*." He jutted his finger into his chest.

Blowing a breath through puffed cheeks, her shoulders deflated. "I don't know if I can." When he began to argue, she showed her palms. "I don't want to fight. Once we address the current threat from my father, I'll let you yell at me all you want. For now, I need to update you on what I learned from Castian."

"Castian?"

"Creepy dude."

"Got it." Rubbing his forehead, he contemplated. "I just spoke to Markson. He'll begin the in-person interviews in two days."

"That's good news." Shuffling the leaves with the toe of her shoe, she said softly, "My father is on his way here, Tor. Castian all but confirmed it."

Giving in to his intense need to touch her, Tordor skated the backs of his fingers over her arm. "Then we'll face him together." Stepping closer, he asked, "But what happens after? Will you stay with me and finish what we started?"

Sucking in a breath, her eyes swam with indecision. "I don't know. You can call me a coward or whatever else you want, but it stems from the place right here that cares about you." She tapped her chest over her heart. "I care about you so much, Tor," she whispered, the trembles of her chin sending cracks down every chasm in his heart.

"Come here," he whispered, drawing her into a firm embrace as he stroked her back. Her arms surrounded him, squeezing him so tight he struggled to breathe.

"I'm sorry. My only goal was to find out everything about my father's threat so I could protect everyone."

Drawing back, he placed his fingers under her chin, tilting her face to his.

"I want to make you promise you'll stop doing this 'lone operator' routine, but honestly, I'm not sure you can help yourself."

Laughing, she cocked a brow. "Wow, you really get me. It's weird."

Cupping her jaw, he edged closer. "But I promise you this, little Elf. We're going to work together to change that routine. Do you know the difference between me and everyone else in your life?"

Heavy breaths escaped her lips as she whispered, "What?"

"I'm not going to let you push me away. The sooner you accept that, the sooner we can build the life we want. *Together.* If you get scared and run, I'll find you. I don't begrudge you for being afraid, but it would be really nice if you could learn to lean on me instead of hightailing it to Timbuktu."

Wrinkling her nose, she teased, "That one's not really on my bucket list, but I get your point."

"Always with the quips. You're lucky you're so cute."

"Am I cute?" she asked, rising to her toes as she threaded her arms around his neck.

"You know you are," he growled. "Now kiss me to remind me why I'm so crazy about you."

Her lips captured his, moving tenderly as he held her close. He felt her regret...her longing...her *love* in each swipe of her tongue against his. Groaning, he drew her deep, inhaling her soft mewls as she pressed her body against his.

Breaking the kiss, he brushed his fingers over her hair. "I'd love to kiss you all day, but I want to talk to Castian and vet him myself."

"Fair enough. I'd like your opinion of him before we brainstorm how to deal with my father. And Tor?"

"Hmm?"

"I really am sorry."

"No more apologies," he said, tugging her toward camp. She fell into step beside him as he grinned. "Just make different choices. I know you can do it, little Elf."

She smiled up at him, the glimmer of hope in her eyes instilling calm where his frustration had recently resided. Tordor could work with hope. Lacing his fingers with hers, they trailed to find Castian.

Chapter 29

Dakath stepped off the plane in DC, watching the humans shuffle around as they stood to retrieve their bags. He could've transported to Rausch Gap, but it never hurt to keep a watchful eye on the species you were determined would remain separate from your own. To study their practices and nuances to learn why some immortals found the beasts so enchanting.

As Dakath had learned long ago, studying your enemy when they were oblivious taught one how to torture them best. And, oh, how he reveled in torture.

"Need help with your bag, sir?" a man asked, causing Dakath to scowl as he reached for the bag in the upper compartment. How dare the human address him as if he were frail and meek? If only the insect knew he could incinerate him with a snap of his fingers.

"No, thank you," Dakath said, slipping the bag over his shoulders. Once in the terminal, he sat and enjoyed a cup of tea, watching the humans buzz through the airport as if they had somewhere important to go. As if their limited lives had meaning. How strange the significance they gave themselves. Such arrogance for a mortal species.

The Elves had lived in simple oblivion once too. It had almost destroyed them. Dakath wouldn't allow an inferior species to co-mingle with his and create the same mistakes. He knew deep in his bones that keeping the Elves pure was the only way not to fall into the chasm of oblivion again.

Dakath would not survive another destruction like the great flood. Therefore, he must prevent it at all costs.

Done with watching the humans, he trailed out of the airport, hailing a cab so he didn't draw attention to himself. Instructing the driver to take him to the nearest park, he exited and waited until the man drove away. Then he transported to the coordinates the spies who'd been watching the ITU's site had sent him.

Materializing, he nodded to the three Elves before him. "She knows I'm coming?" Dakath asked, the men curtly nodding as the leader spoke.

"Castian warned her. As reported, he's aligned with her, sir."

"Since he aligned with my brother, I'm not surprised," Dakath droned. "What do I need to be aware of?"

"They employ the scientist who worked with Bakari. He's preparing potions and has lined their bullets with poisons."

Dakath's lips curved into a sinister smile. "Good. It will allow me to assess their strengths and weaknesses. I wish to see the immortal prince with my own eyes so I can scrutinize him myself. I might not even kill him. Leaving him alive will help me play the long game."

"How so, sir?"

"Once they breed, of course. How magnificent would it be to allow them to procreate and then kill the wretched offspring and the immortal heir in front of her? She might never recover."

"The offspring would be your grandchild, sir," one of the men said, his eyebrows drawing together.

"Hybrids who represent nothing the gods intended when they created our world," he snapped, slicing his hand through the air. "A pestilence I can eradicate."

The men remained silent as Dakath stared into the distance.

"Let's wait until the morning sun is high to approach them. I want to see her face when I appear." Rubbing his chin, his eyes narrowed. "I do love how much my daughter fears and detests me. It's a potent combination."

"Yes, sir. We have a vehicle if you don't want to transport. We've set up camp on the opposite side of the river, two miles from Rausch Gap."

"Excellent." Striding to the car, he handed one of the men his bag and slid into the front seat. "I haven't slept under the stars in ages. The fresh air will do me well."

As his men shuffled into the car, Dakath absently stared out the window, a strange anticipation lacing his veins. He hadn't gazed upon Esmerelda in some time. Would she still look like Dyana?

Unable to suppress his yearning for his long-dead love, he held onto the handle above his head as the car sped down the highway toward Rausch Gap.

Chapter 30

The team spent the day acclimating to Castian's presence while preparing for Dakath's imminent arrival. Jaxon and Larkin worked together to scout the nearby terrain, returning with news of a recently banked fire two miles away.

"It's probably my father's spies," Esme said, staring at the far-off horizon.

"Will your father approach us tonight?" Tordor asked.

"No way," she said, scowling. "He'll approach us in the light of day so he can see my reaction. I'll try to stay cool, but I'm sort of terrified of the bastard, so we'll see how that goes."

"We're all here to protect each other," Brienne said. "To protect *you*, Esme. This time, you won't be alone."

Sentiment clouded her features as she squeezed Brienne's hand. "Thank you. Thank *all* of you for being in the trenches with me. It's quite foreign, but it feels pretty damn good."

Tordor smiled as she acknowledged him with a nod, referencing the euphemism he'd used when they'd sat on the couch in the hotel courtyard after Clayton was killed. It seemed like centuries ago, although it had barely been weeks, and he marveled at everything that had occurred in such a short period of time.

Larkin and Brienne agreed to rotate shifts keeping watch as the rest of the team headed to their tents. Tordor entered Esme's tent, knowing she would appear once she said good night to Castian.

"Well," she said, entering the tent as he removed his pants and shirt, leaving on his boxer briefs. "I guess I'm creeping in on you now." Zipping it behind her, she faced him and grinned.

"Come on, creepy stalker," he said, lowering to the sleeping bag and waving her over. "I have something to tell you."

Kicking off her shoes, she also removed her pants and did that thing women did where they removed their bra and pulled it through the sleeve. Striding toward him in her T-shirt, she sat beside him. "I'm all ears."

He told her about Miranda's pregnancy, loving the genuine reaction that lit her features. "Oh, Tor, that's amazing. Congrats. I'm so happy for you, big brother." She playfully punched his arm.

"It's definitely awesome and makes me think about having my own kids one day," he said, knowing he needed to tread lightly but feeling compelled to broach the subject with her in case she bolted again. He wanted complete honesty between them and would settle for nothing less. "Maybe ones with slightly pointed ears and thirteen flecks in their right eye."

Tender emotion contorted her features as she expelled a wistful breath. "Tor..."

"Okay, twelve flecks. You drive a hard bargain, but I'll concede."

With a poignant smile, she scooted closer. Staring at him with openness and sentiment, she spoke softly. "Tomorrow could be a disaster, Tor. If he hurts anyone..." She reached over and clutched his wrist. "If he hurts *you*, I don't know what the hell I'll do. I can't think beyond tomorrow. I'm sorry."

Disengaging from her grasp, he slid his palm over hers, lacing their fingers. "Okay, sweetheart. I'm proud of you for having the courage to face him. I won't push you...for now." Lifting his finger, his fangs pressed into his lip as he grinned. "But we'd have some cute kids. You know, down the road. Once I figured out how to make you stay with me for more than twenty-four hours."

Tossing her head back, she laughed before scooting closer. "They'd be adorable. That's all I'll say because discussing this any more is going to freak me out."

Conceding for the moment, he tugged her to the blanket, holding her as she told him about her Uncle Gillam, his paralysis and the network of Elves who'd pledged their loyalty to him...and to her.

"You'd make such a good ruler, sweetheart," he said, stroking her soft skin as she nuzzled into him. "I knew it from the first day I met you."

"I don't want to rule," she said, yawning as her body relaxed into his. "I just want to help my people and avoid my father's torture."

"As my mom told me earlier, those who don't wish to rule are always the best leaders because they lead from a genuine place."

"That's true," she said quietly, her lips brushing his chest as she spoke. "Your mom's pretty smart. She's such a beacon of hope for all the immortal women out there who are bogged down by the ancient traditions of our people."

Caressing her soft skin, Tordor smiled.

"So are you, Esme," was his soft reply. "My scrappy, caring little Elf. Whether you want to admit it or not."

Her response was a soft snore, followed by a heavier one as she fell asleep against his chest. Chuckling, Tordor decided he'd tease her once she awoke, although her snoring wasn't nearly as loud as his. Turning down the lantern, he curled into her, breaths mingling as he followed her into slumber.

The team awoke with the sun, each member solemn and thoughtful as they stepped outside their tents to greet the day. Esme knew there would be no yoga this morning. Instead, it would be spent preparing for a confrontation with her father. Praying to all the gods for her team's safety, she entered Dr. Tyson's tent, ready for his instruction.

"The bullets are laced with poison," Dr. Tyson said, holding one between his fingers as he addressed the team. "It's not made from the tree bark since I haven't had time to analyze it fully, but it's a poison I developed for Bakari, and it's effective."

"And you have an antidote?" Brienne asked, arching an eyebrow. "Just in case one of the suckers accidently lodges in one of our bodies?"

"I do," he said, setting the bullet on the table and lifting a syringe full of yellow liquid. "I've prepared ten antidote syringes and can prepare more if needed."

"Excellent," Esme said. "I have no idea how many men he'll have with him. Hopefully, we won't inadvertently start a war."

"Did I hear talk of war?" Evie asked, lifting the flap and breezing into the tent. "Looks like I'm just in time."

"Hey, Aunt Evie," Tordor said, striding over and enveloping her in a warm hug. "Thanks for helping us."

Drawing back, she wrinkled her nose. "Hell, this is way better than governing any day. Since we don't know how many people Dakath is bringing with him, I'm first-line, but I'll send Darkrip a message if we need him too." She tapped her temple.

"Thanks, Evie," Esme said before making eye contact with everyone in their tight-knit circle. "And thank you all for being willing to stand with me. For the first time in my life, I'm not facing him alone. It's…" Clearing her throat, she swallowed the lump of emotion lodged there. "Well, it's pretty fucking awesome. And that's coming from the most independent person on the planet."

"We're honored to be by your side," Tordor said, his tone reassuring as he placed a supportive hand on her back.

Steeling herself, she gave a firm nod and walked to the table to load her gun with the poison bullets. The team did the same, the air heavy with anticipation. Once they were armed and ready, they stepped outside, steeling themselves under the bright rays of the morning sun.

Head held high, Esme marched toward the edge of the site, leading her soldiers as they filed behind her, resolved.

The river gurgled nearby as birds sang songs in the tress above. Narrowing her eyes, Esme spotted the figures in the distance. Three men dressed in black, flanking a tall, slender man with pointed ears. As they approached, the team stood firm, ready to confront the king who'd cultivated immeasurable power over his centuries on Etherya's Earth.

Long strides carried her father toward her until he came to a stop, leaving a few yards separating them. Lifting her chin, she spoke, determined not to let her voice waver.

"Hello, Father," she said, straightening her shoulders.

"Esmerelda," he said with a regal bow of his head.

"I regret to inform you that we are under contract for this land and you and your men are trespassing."

A sinister chuckle left his lips, wrapping around the forest like thick smoke. "You have grown bold in your maturity, daughter. Although it rankles me since you are a hybrid pestilence, it also stirs something in my weary soul." Narrowing his eyes, he rubbed his chest. "Yes, I feel it here. An unwanted sense of…*admiration*. Your mother would be proud."

"Don't talk about my mother," she said through clenched teeth. "You *murdered* her!"

A muscle ticked in his jaw. "I regret how your mother's life ended, Esmerelda. But like all humans, her life had an expiration date. I merely managed to shorten her timeline."

Esme clenched her fists, cognizant of how badly she wanted to punch the bastard in his long, austere nose.

"Your life was supposed to be finite as well," he said, taking a step forward as his men followed behind. The sound of guns cocking behind her indicated her team had pulled their weapons. "You were never supposed to exhibit the immortal gene. It's a travesty I've never been able to remedy."

Tears welled in her eyes as she struggled with how much her father hated her. It was a tough pill to swallow, even for one as strong as she.

"Well, asshole, I'm immortal and I'm here for the long haul. I won't deny your torture is excruciating. Losing Clayton and all the others you've harmed has come close to breaking me so many times."

"Gabriel did an excellent job when he assassinated Clayton," Dakath said, patting the man's shoulder beside him. "I was pleased to hear his blood splattered across your pristine skin. How tragic," he said with a *tsk, tsk, tsk.*

"Yes, another soldier to do your dirty work. How noble," she sneered. "But you didn't break me, Father, and as you can see, I have a formidable team surrounding me."

"Watch your tone," he warned, eyes narrowing with hate. "You forget how powerful I am." His fists began to glow a dark green at his sides.

Fear laced Esme's veins as she gazed at his glowing hands.

"You're not the only one with party tricks," Evie taunted, her hands glowing red.

"Crimeous's daughter," Dakath chided, his lips forming a sinister smile. "Esmerelda has amassed powerful allies indeed."

"I have," Esme said, absorbing the energy of her team as they flanked her. "You came all this way to observe us?" She gestured around. "Here we are. I'm not hiding from you this time because that would only make you more determined. The immortal royals are going to build a base here and it's going to be highly fortified."

She moved her hand toward the gun on her hip. "There. Now your curiosity is sated." Grasping the gun, she drew it from the holster and aimed directly at his head. "Now. Get. Off. My. Site."

Dakath clenched his fiery hands as anger clouded his expression. Heavy silence pulsed in the dense woods as seconds ticked by. Lifting his hands, he formed a malevolent sneer.

"Don't do it, Father!" Esme called, the words drifting as a loud boom echoed in her ears.

Sucking in a sharp breath, her eyes grew wide as Dakath emitted a menacing growl...and deployed two spheres of scorching energy directly at her.

Chapter 31

Tordor jumped into action as soon as he saw the ominous fireballs. Lurching toward Esme, he knocked her down, both of them emitting an "*oomph!*" as they crumpled to the ground. Palming her face, he struggled to catch his breath as he asked, "Are you okay?"

"Yes," she said, nodding as gunfire rang out around them. Rising, he dragged her to her feet and stepped in front of her, shielding her from her father and his men.

"I'm supposed to be protecting *you*," she said, clutching the back of his shirt and drawing him back. "You're more of a target than me since he knows wounding you will hurt me."

Tamping down the need to carry her off the grass and hide her in a secluded area until the skirmish was over, Tordor urged her to follow him. They ran behind the protective wall Evie, Larkin, Brienne and the other soldiers created as they fired at Dakath.

Sizzling fireballs of energy continued to fly through the forest—from Evie and Dakath—as Dakath's men rained bullets on their team.

"Fall back and take shelter behind the trees!" Larkin called, circling his hand in the air. The soldiers dispersed, running to find shelter as they fired back. Esme ran behind a large oak tree and Tordor followed, both of them panting as they craned their necks to see if Dakath's men were advancing.

Brienne unloaded a fateful shot between Gabriel's eyes, and the man gasped and fell to the ground, his body seizing and shaking before he expelled his last breath.

"One fucker down, three to go!" Brienne called.

They continued to fight, bullets and fireballs whizzing through the air before Larissa emitted a loud wail. "Fuck! The bastard hit me." Clutching her shoulder, she tried to stop the bleeding.

"Retreat to Dr. Tyson's tent so he can examine the wound!" Esme called.

"I want to stay and fight!"

"You're no good to us dead," Brienne said, jerking her head. "Get out of here. That's an order."

With a frustrated *harrumph*, Larissa ran toward Dr. Tyson's tent, cagily dodging bullets so she wouldn't be struck again.

"Cease fire!" Dakath said, raising his hand.

Tordor observed the glowing light that surrounded his fist recede as the spray of bullets stopped. Striding toward Gabriel, Dakath kneeled, touching the man's neck to search for a pulse. Clenching his jaw, he shook his head and rose. "Gabriel was one of my best men. I don't want to lose more."

"You're going to lose every fucking one of them and your own life too if you don't retreat," Evie said, her hands still glowing as she stood tall.

Dakath's jaw clenched as he contemplated. "I have made a rare error in judgment. I should've brought more men. I underestimated your allies, Esmerelda. Well done."

"You may hate me, Father, but I have no desire to hurt you," Esme said, slowly easing from behind the tree. Tordor tried to pull her back, but she shot him a look that said, "Let me handle this." Terrified, he gripped the tree bark, feeling the pounding of his heart all the way to his fingertips.

"I just want you to leave me alone so I can help other immortals," she said, her voice raspy with emotion as she slid behind Evie.

"That may be your goal now, but you are an imminent threat to my throne."

"I don't want your throne," she said, exasperation in her tone. "I just want peace."

"Liar!" he cried, lifting his hand and touching his fingertips to his thumb. Suddenly, Esme zoomed across the grass, Dakath drawing her toward him with an invisible tether before clutching her neck. Tordor hoisted from behind the tree, sprinting toward her as Evie stood in his path.

"No, Tor!" Evie cried, gripping his forearm.

"Stop, or I'll crush her windpipe!" Dakath commanded.

The need to protect Esme warred with his fear Dakath would hurt her. Tordor stood with his feet planted on the ground as the team pointed their guns at the man holding his mate in a death grip.

"Why don't you just kill me?" Esme pleaded as Tordor's heart shattered into a thousand pieces at the agony lacing her tone.

"I would if I could, Esmerelda," he gritted, spittle flying from between his teeth as he inched closer, his nose almost touching hers. "I've wanted to so many times over the centuries."

"Then do it! I know you feel pleasure from torturing me, but killing me would be the ultimate prize, wouldn't it?"

"I can't kill you, you infernal wretch!"

Gasping as his hand tightened around her neck, she gripped at his fingers, trying to pull them away. "Why?"

"Because I promised her, you fool!" he screamed. "And I couldn't live with the knowledge I broke the last vow I made her!"

Esme's eyes widened as her body went lax under his grip.

Dakath stared into her soul, hate causing his nostrils to flare as the full weight of his admission bore down on them.

Esme's lips worked back and forth, and she struggled to breathe as realization dawned. "That's what she whispered to you...before she died." A pain-filled moan escaped her throat. "She made you promise not to kill me."

"Yes," he rasped, harshly tossing her to the ground. Esme's fingers clutched the damp earth as she sucked in gulps of air. "I'm a twisted soul but feel nothing more twisted than to honor my last promise to your mother."

Unable to stop himself, Tordor rushed toward Esme, crouching beside her and pulling her into his arms. "I've got you. Breathe, sweetheart. I'm here."

Dakath's eyes formed angry slits as he observed Tordor comfort her. "But I never promised not to *hurt* you, Esmerelda. And I believe I know exactly how to do that." Lifting his hand, he formed a sphere of energy.

"No!" Esme called, scrambling to block Tordor's body. Terrified for her, he tugged her behind him, the task difficult since she fought him with wailing hands and legs. "No, Tor!"

Holding her behind him with strong arms, he balanced on his knees as Dakath glared, ready to strike. The sounds of triggers cocking filled his ears the moment before he was engulfed in a fiery ball of energy. The buzzing light surrounded his entire body, rendering him inept as he fell to the ground.

Dakath wailed as one of Evie's red fireballs pummeled his chest. "This is only the beginning!" he screamed, falling back as he clutched his chest. "Build your site and make it thrive. Once you're comfortable in your cocoon, I will return to destroy you!" Tilting his head back, he closed his eyes and disappeared.

Bullets rang out as Dakath's two remaining men retreated, running through the forest to the river as they skillfully evaded the shots.

Lying on the damp ground, Tordor observed the leaves sway on the tree branches above his head, moving in slow motion as his body began to shut down.

"Tor!" Esme called, her voice faraway as she leaned over him. Wet tears dripped on his face, trailing over skin that covered a body now immobile and useless.

"Oh my god," she cried, patting him with her hands. "He's dying. Help! Evie!"

"I'm here," Evie said, wrapping Tordor in her arms as his teeth began to chatter. "Where's Dr. Tyson?"

"Let me assess," Dr. Tyson said, lowering to his knees and touching Tordor's neck. "He's burning up. His body appears to be absorbing the energy, most likely because his self-healing abilities are trying to break it down. But if the Slayer DNA in his cells absorbs too much, they're going to incinerate."

Tordor struggled to breathe, wishing to speak but rendered inept and unable to talk.

"I'm not a medical doctor, but my advice would be to get him to Uteria. The immortal physicians might be able to concoct a serum from your and Sathan's blood, Evie. If they can inject him with it quickly, it might mingle with his self-healing blood and allow him to heal."

"Okay," Evie said, clutching him close. "I'm going to transport him to the clinic at Uteria." Focusing on Esme with the same olive-green eyes as Tordor, she said, "I'll send Darkrip to come and transport you."

"Thank you," Esme said, barely able to see Tordor's face through her tears. Caressing his cheek, she whispered, "I'll be there soon. Promise."

His eyes grew heavy as he tried to nod, each cell in his body burning as the energy encapsulated it, manipulating the cell structure.

Her words drifted off as Tordor closed his eyes. They fluttered several times before he felt the world drift away as Evie began to dematerialize.

Suddenly, he felt himself being transported through space and time. Slowly losing consciousness, he sent a prayer to Etherye, asking her to let him live. Goddess, he had so much to live for. How could he leave Esme when he'd just found her? There was so much more he needed to say...so much more life they needed to live...*together.*

Swimming through the darkness, he lost the battle with unconsciousness.

Chapter 32

E sme immediately set up a conference call with General Markson to introduce him to Brienne and Larkin. As she was setting up the laptop in her tent, Darkrip poked his head through.

"Esme," he said, holding the tent flap above his head. "Evie sent me to transport you to Uteria."

"Thank you," she said, rising and pointing to the laptop. "I just need to take care of a few things here so I can give Tordor my full attention."

"Absolutely," he said with a nod. "I'll be ready when you are."

Ten minutes later, Esme sat between Larkin and Brienne as they video chatted with General Markson.

"I want to keep you briefed on everything, General, but I also want to assure you, we are dedicated to the implementation. Larkin and Brienne can be trusted with any questions moving forward and I'm always available by cell."

"I look forward to working with you both," Markson said, his brown eyes kind but businesslike. "As a soldier, I understand that conflicts happen. I see the worry in your expression, Esme, but I won't let the skirmish deter me. We've come too far now."

"I agree. We will continue to monitor the threat from my father. If you concentrate on placing the immortals, we'll make sure they're surveilled by the immortal army's best. Our priority is keeping everyone safe—both human and immortal."

"I have no doubt. Larkin and Brienne, I'll be in touch soon."

After ending the call, Esme spent a few minutes with Dr. Tyson so he could detail her on the samples he'd gathered from the battle.

"I was able to harness some energy traces from some of the leaves Dakath's energy spheres incinerated," he said, showing her a petri dish with ashes. "It will help me create potions to counteract his powers."

"Well done," Esme said, thanking the goddess that *something* good had come from the skirmish. "Keep me posted. Building you a state-of-the-art lab is our first priority once the sale is complete."

He gave her a nod of thanks and returned to his work, hunching over the desk as he studied his notes.

Finally, Esme strode to Larissa's tent, poking her head inside to find her massaging her arm underneath the bullet wound.

"How are you feeling, Larissa?" she asked, concerned as she sat beside her.

"I'm okay," she said, shaking her head. "I just need to let it heal. Dr. Tyson said it was a clean shot, thank the goddess." Pursing her lips, she studied Esme. "I also think it might be a sign from the universe or something. As excited as I was to be one of the candidates for the immersion program, showing up with a gunshot wound isn't ideal."

"Probably not."

"So I'm going to stay here if that's all right with you. I'm sure the immortal royals have another candidate who can take my place." Flashing a cheeky grin, she shrugged. "Plus, I really love it here. This hunk of dirt has become my home, and I want to help build it."

"I'm on board with that," Esme said, enfolding her in a gentle hug before rising. "Take care of everyone. I have to go."

"Will do, boss." Sympathy laced her expression. "Tell Tordor we're all rooting for him."

Esme stepped from her tent and approached Darkrip. "Ready."

The Slayer-Deamon nodded and surrounded her with his arms. Closing her eyes, Esme rested her head on his shoulder, anticipating the moment when she would be able to hold Tordor again.

Darkrip transported them to Nolan and Sadie's clinic located on the lower level of Uteria's castle. Releasing her, Darkrip's eyes were solemn. "Miranda was in there when I left." He gestured with his head toward the doorway. "If you need anything, she has my number."

"Thank you," Esme whispered before he backed away and disappeared.

Esme eased into the room, noticing Miranda sitting beside Tordor, her hand over her mouth as she stroked his arm with her other hand. Her pain was palpable, and Esme wanted to retch at the fact that *she* was the cause of it.

Her father had hurt Tordor because Esme cared for him. The knowledge was crushing.

Inhaling a sharp breath, Miranda's head snapped as she sensed Esme's presence. Standing, she formed a warbled smile. "Hey, Esme. He'll be so happy you're here. Come on." She waved her over.

"I..." Esme's nostrils flared as she slowly approached. "I'm so sorry, Miranda. This is all my fault..."

"What?" Miranda asked, her dark eyebrows drawing together as she slid her arm over Esme's shoulders. "That's not even close to true, sweetie."

"It is," she said, her eyes roving over the multitude of tubes and IVs pulsing air and medicine through Tordor's body. "I knew this would happen."

"Hey," Miranda said, facing her and cupping her shoulders. "I don't want to hear any of that from you, young lady. And since my son is head over heels for you, I'm going to talk to you like the mother-in-law I'm sure he'll make me one day soon."

Swiping her nose, Esme laughed. "I'd be honored to be your daughter-in-law, Miranda, but I don't deserve it. Not even close."

"Okay," she said, slicing her hand through the air. "We're going to cut this little pity party because my son needs you, and that's all that matters right now. But when he's healed, we're going to have a nice long chat about why you think you don't deserve love."

"I'm not sure there's enough time in eternity to have that conversation," Esme sighed.

"Well, we'll make time." Urging her toward the chair, Miranda gently pushed her to sit. "I've been sitting here for a while and need a break. Nolan has him in an induced coma. He made some fancy concoction of Sathan and Evie's blood, and we're hoping it will help."

"I thought he'd heal quickly since he has Sathan's self-healing blood."

"Sathan is the most purebred Vampyre, so Tordor's Vampyre half ensures quick self-healing for normal injuries. But his Slayer half is vulnerable to immortal powers or poisons—"

"Like my father's," Esme interjected softly.

"Yes."

Sighing, Esme ran her hand through her hair. "How can I help him?"

"Just talk to him," Miranda said, rubbing her shoulder. "I know it will help."

Nodding, she grasped Tordor's hand as Miranda squeezed her arm and left the room.

Lifting his broad hand to her face, she rubbed her cheek over the back of it, reveling in the feel of his skin. Closing her eyes, her stomach churned with raw emotion.

"I'm so sorry, Tor," she whispered, pressing her lips to his hand as she spoke. "I should've left the camp. Should've left the team." Lifting her lids, she stared at his handsome face, his expression peaceful as his lungs rose and fell from the breathing tube.

"Please be okay," she said, palming his cheek and gently caressing his lukewarm skin. "I need to know you're okay. Then I can do what I was meant to do all along and leave you to find someone who won't get you killed."

Images of every person her father had murdered flashed through her brain. Her mother. Clayton. Valentina. So many others...

Pressing her face to his palm, she cried tears of agony at the knowledge she'd come to help him heal in order to leave him.

It was the only way she could ensure her father wouldn't hurt him again.

<h1 style="text-align:center">Chapter 33</h1>

T ordor's status remained unchanged in the days that followed. Miranda offered for Esme to stay in Tordor's room, which also resided on the lower level, and sleeping in the room he'd inhabited brought her a small semblance of peace.

At night, before she fell into her nightmares, she would cuddle the pillow close, inhaling his scent as she prayed to Etherya for him to wake up. In her bargaining prayers, she promised she would leave as soon as he healed. She just wanted to see him smile one more time—to gaze upon those brilliant green eyes filled with limitless affection—and then she would go back to a life of solitude to keep him safe.

Every day, she sat by his side, rotating with Miranda, Sathan and his other family members when she needed fresh air. The walks around the compound were soothing, and she remembered Tordor telling her he liked to run through the lush forests. Sometimes, she would hike through the thick trees and brush, trailing her hand along the bark, wondering if he'd jogged the same path. Wishing she'd asked him more about his past...and knowing she'd lost the opportunity when her father harmed him.

Every night, when she returned to his bed, she would slip into her nightmares. Visions of her father murdering Dyana transformed into visions of him hurting Tordor...and sometimes, of him hurting children with deep green eyes and slightly pointed ears. *Their* children. The ones she could never have although they already seemed so real in her dreams.

Several days after Tordor's injury, she sat by his bed, smiling at the kind Doctor Nolan when he appeared.

"How's our patient doing today?" he asked in his crisp British accent.

"Same as usual, Nolan," Esme said, feeling defeated. "Even though you removed the breathing tube yesterday and he's no longer in the medically induced coma, he's not waking up."

Striding over, Nolan used his stethoscope to listen to Tordor's heartbeat before lifting a small light from his pocket. Lifting Tordor's eyelid, he shined the light in one eye, then the other, looking for a response.

"His pupils are dilating, so his autonomic systems are functional." His lips formed an empathetic smile. "Immortal energies and powers aren't always explainable with medicinal or holistic treatments. Dr. Tyson has created a potion from the tree bark Tatiana recommended, and Evie is on her way to retrieve it. Hopefully, that will help."

Esme gnawed her lip, clutching onto the small kernel of hope in her gut.

That afternoon, she headed out on her usual walk through the woods. As she entered the forest, Miranda's voice chimed, "Hey, I figured you could use a companion today."

Esme's heart slammed in her chest. She didn't want to be nervous around Miranda, but the guilt at Tordor's injury was crushing. Even though she'd been kind without expressing a morsel of blame, Esme felt it anyway.

"Oh, I...well, I usually walk by myself to clear my head."

Miranda arched a brow. "You seem to think you have a choice in this. Didn't my son tell you how stubborn I am?"

Laughing, she nodded.

"Then come on," Miranda said, trudging ahead as Esme fell into step beside her. "Tor wasn't kidding when he said you were a lone wolf. Have you ever allowed yourself to lean on anyone, Esme?"

Her lips fluttered as she expelled a deep breath. "The moment I begin to lean on people, they die."

Stepping over a log, Miranda grimaced. "Heavy. And a bit dramatic. My husband would say you've won a prize if I'm calling you dramatic."

Glancing at her, Esme formed a genuine smile for the first time in days. "Tor also told me how funny you are. He said Sathan's the serious one and you crack the jokes. I'm a quipper myself. Your son teases me for it all the time."

"Hiding behind humor—or drama," she said, lifting a finger, "is easy in the short-term, but it doesn't allow you to share your innermost feelings and fears with others." Halting, she planted her fists on her hips as Esme turned to face her. "And if I know Tor, I'm betting he wiggled under those thick walls you've built."

Esme kicked a leaf with her toe. "He did, although I tried to keep him out. Even though I knew he would become a target, I let him in. It was so fucking reckless."

"Esme," Miranda said, inching closer and taking her hand. "I hate to tell you this, but you can't control everything that happens. Even if you close yourself off and live on the side of a mountain for eternity, people are going to get hurt. Life is messy, and we all end up with scars."

"But I can prevent him from being targeted," Esme said, swiping away an errant tear. "As soon as I know he's okay, I'm letting him go. I can't control everything, but I can get as far away from him as possible, and that will keep him safe."

Miranda tilted her head, her full lips forming a wide grin as she studied her.

"You're...smiling?"

Huffing a laugh, Miranda's teeth flashed in the sunlight. "Oh, yeah. You're insane if you think he's going to let you go. My stubbornness is in his blood. You must know this."

"He can't find me if I hide. I'm pretty good at it."

"What a life," Miranda said, her eyes narrowing. "Hiding away from the man you love. Sounds exhausting and extremely sad."

"What else am I supposed to do?" Esme asked, exasperated as she lifted her hands. "Do you want him to get hurt again? Because that will absolutely happen if we're together." Stepping forward, she asked angrily, "Do you want your grandchildren to be targets?"

"You're asking the wrong question, Esme." Miranda placed her palm over her heart. "I just want him to be happy. If that means he's with you, even it increases the possibility of danger, I still want it for him. You'll understand once you have your own kids. Your desire for them to experience happiness supersedes anything else."

Moving her hand to Esme's chin, she tilted her head to stare into her eyes. "And since your mother's not here, I'm going to be extremely presumptuous and speak for her. *She* would want you to be happy, Esme. It would break her heart to see you hide away from your mate. Now, you can tell me to pound sand, but I know deep in my heart it's true."

"It goes against everything I've believed for centuries," Esme whispered. "I only know one way to keep people safe."

"Then, my dear, it's time you learn another way."

Esme's chin quivered as she formed a broken smile. "You make it sound so easy."

"Choices are easy. Pushing away the fear to make them is the hard part."

Craving some space to process, Esme took a step back and inhaled a large breath. "I can see why you're such a good ruler...and where Tor got it from. You're very wise, Miranda."

"Um, can you tell that to my husband, please?" She batted her eyelashes. "The infernal man takes all the credit for my brilliance." She playfully swiped her hair off her shoulder.

Thankful for the levity, Esme chuckled. "I'll be sure to tell him."

They stood silent, surrounded by the chirping birds, as Esme digested the conversation.

Checking her watch, Miranda pointed toward the castle. "We should probably head back. Nolan should be ready to inject Dr. Tyson's potion soon."

"Okay." Falling into step beside her, Esme glanced over. "Thank you, Miranda. I'll think about everything you said. I appreciate...well, I appreciate you accepting me. These are strange circumstances to say the least. I'm probably going to win the award for most awkward introduction of a son's girlfriend."

Tossing her head back, Miranda devolved into laughter. "Honey, you fit right in with our crazy family. The stories I could tell you..."

"Tor told me some. I thought I had a fucked-up father, but Evie's dad was pretty terrible."

"The worst. My dad wasn't a picnic either, although he's Father of the Century compared to Dakath and Crimeous."

They hiked back to the castle, both pulling up a chair beside Tordor and continuing to talk as they kept him company. He breathed steadily beside them, unconscious as their connection slowly grew.

When Nolan arrived and injected Dr. Tyson's potion, Esme clutched Miranda's hand, hoping like hell the serum would work. And then she allowed Miranda to lead her to the kitchen, where they refueled on Glarys's tasty leftovers.

The next morning, Esme rose and showered in the adjoining bathroom. Once dressed, she headed to the infirmary. As she approached, her ears perked at the sounds of revelry coming from the room. Picking up the pace, she jogged through the doorway to find Tordor sitting up in bed, Miranda holding him in a smothering hug as Sathan cupped his shoulder.

Joy surged within as a cry leaped from her lips. Heads swiveled toward her before Miranda waved her over.

"You're awake," Esme said, rushing over on shaking legs. "Oh my god, Tor! You're awake." Miranda and Sathan stepped back, allowing her to rush in and throw her arms around him. "Thank the goddess."

His arms surrounded her, weak but firm, before he broke into a terrible coughing fit.

"Let's give him some space," Nolan said, his tone gentle as he urged Esme away. Patting Tordor on the back, he tried to soothe his hacking coughs.

"He's going to be okay, but the energy zapped the cilia in his lungs. They need to regrow before he can breathe without coughing.'

Crossing her arms, Esme clutched her heart as it pounded from seeing him in such pain. His struggle to breathe was evident, and she stood frozen, wishing like hell he'd never come into contact with her father.

"He's awake?" Callie asked from the door, breezing in with Adelyn and Rinada behind her. They whizzed past Esme, each rushing the bed before Nolan ushered them away.

"He needs air, everyone," Nolan said. "I know you all want to hug him, but he's going to struggle to breathe for a few days."

"I'm...fine..." Tordor wheezed, coughing into his fist before taking a few labored breaths. "Want to hug you guys..."

His cousins closed in, each enveloping him in a hug as Miranda and Sathan stood nearby. Observing them, Esme took a moment to soak in the small glimpse of a true family. It was something she'd never experienced, and as his cousins and parents fought to hug him while chattering away, Esme knew this was the time to leave.

If she allowed herself to be alone with him, he would most likely plead for her to stay. He'd look at her with those gorgeous eyes and convince her she was his future.

But Esme knew the truth: he would only have a future f she let him go.

She'd wanted to remain by his side until he healed, needing to know he was okay. Now that she had the confirmation, she had to be strong enough to let him go.

Silently backing out of the room, she was able to escape without anyone noticing. Scurrying to Tordor's room, she quickly packed her bag. Tossing it over her shoulder, she jogged up the stairs and out of the castle into the bright, warm day.

Coward. The word echoed in her mind as she ran to the main square and down the train platform stairs. After purchasing a ticket, she rode the train for hours to the last stop south of Restia.

Then she walked across the battlefield where the final conflict with Bakari had occurred. Striding past the place where she'd first met Tordor, she took a moment to stop and inhale the fresh air. It was where she'd embarked on the first—and most likely the only—time she'd ever fallen in love. Reveling in her feelings for Tordor, she reminded herself that leaving him was the best way to honor their love.

Setting him free would ensure he had the future he deserved. He could only do that if he were *alive*.

Immeasurable pain coursed through her as she accepted her decision. Then she ran to where the ether once stood and opened the invisible gate with the code only she and her team knew. Closing it behind her, she ran toward her own future. One without her mate, but one where he would remain unharmed.

In the lonely days ahead, Esme would cherish that knowledge and make peace with the awful choice she'd felt compelled to make.

Chapter 34

Tordor swam through the murky waters of unconsciousness for a small eternity. Each day, he would wade through the blackness, striving to reach the surface so he could breathe.

Each day, he remained unable to break through.

It was torture since he knew Esme was on the other side, most likely blaming herself for his injuries. Sometimes, he would hear her in his coma-induced dreams pleading for him to wake up. Her sweet voice soothed him, and he ached to return to her. To assure her that although her worst fear had come to fruition, he still loved her and would choose her for eternity.

Miranda and Sathan's voices also called to him, as well as the rest of his family. Goddess, he was so lucky to have them. He yearned to envelop Esme into his fold. To build a future where she received the same love and devotion he'd always known.

To show her that happiness didn't have to be a struggle.

And then, as if propelled by some unseen force, Tordor suddenly broke free of the gloomy darkness. His lids snapped open and his parents were there, drawing him into their arms as he struggled to breathe. He hugged them with the scant strength he possessed before searching to find his mate.

His little Elf rushed over, relief mingling with joy on her gorgeous features as she clutched him tight. Tordor wanted to tell her so many things. That he would be okay. That it wasn't her fault. *That he loved her.*

Unfortunately, his damaged lungs had other ideas, and he could barely breathe, much less speak.

His cousins blazed into the room and he was enveloped in another round of hugs before Nolan urged them to let him rest. Although he ached for Esme to curl against him in the bed, he fell back into slumber before he could ask her.

Hours later, he awoke to find Miranda sitting beside the bed, a resigned expression on her face.

"What's wrong?" he rasped, coughing into his fist as she rubbed his arm.

"Don't talk. Nolan said your lungs need time to heal." Squeezing his hand, she shook her head. "Since you have your father's practical streak, there's no need to draw this out because you're going to find out eventually."

Tordor's eyebrows narrowed.

Sighing, she ran a hand through her dark hair. "She's gone, sweetheart. She's made up her mind that she's a danger to you and thinks this is the best way to protect you." Arching a brow, she tilted her head. "Man, you really had to go and find a stubborn one like your ol' mom, huh?"

Frustration hummed in his veins as he processed her words.

"The good news? Nolan says you're going to heal and that will allow you to track her down. I won't even pretend you're not going to look for her as soon as you're back to one hundred percent."

Tordor nodded, his lips curving.

"Your Dad and I will help you. We'll start with walks around the compound once you can breathe better, and Nolan said you should be able to start jogging again in a week or so. Slowly, though, okay?" She lifted a finger. "You're no good to me or Esme or our people if you don't give yourself time to heal. That will give Esme time to think too...and time to miss you. She needs that."

Accepting her wisdom, Tordor vowed to spend every day regaining his strength.

And then he would track down his little Elf and convince her they belonged together.

A week later, Tordor had healed enough to take his first jog around the compound. Finally able to breathe the fresh air, he trailed through the meadows and riverbanks he loved so much at Uteria. He'd spent his childhood building forts there and playing with his cousins, and being home reinvigorated him. When he returned to the castle afterward, he was met with two beaming parents in the sitting room of Uteria's castle.

"You look better, son," Sathan said, patting his shoulder. "How was your jog?"

"Fantastic," he said, sitting in the chair beside their place on the couch. "I didn't realize how much I missed Uteria."

"This will always be your home, and we hope you visit often," Sathan said, draping his arm around Miranda.

"I can't wait to meet my baby sister...or brother," he said, grinning. "I'll definitely be visiting a lot."

"And we hope you'll bring Esme too, once you find her," Miranda teased. "I really like her, Tor. We kind of bonded while you were healing. She wants so badly to make the right choices, and she's always had to make them alone. It's very admirable, but it must be very lonely."

"Not anymore," Tordor said. "I'm determined to show her love doesn't have to end in disaster. You two taught me well, and it's time I put that lesson to good use."

"Sathan," Miranda said, her chin wobbling as she stared up at Sathan, "our baby's getting married."

"Thanks for your faith in me, but I still have to convince her," he said, shaking his head.

"The strong ones always need a push," Sathan said, rubbing Miranda's arm. "I had to order you mom to marry me, but she eventually came around."

"*Pfft*. As if I would take orders from *you*—" Squealing, Miranda devolved into giggles as he tickled her side.

Once the revelry died down, Tordor grinned. "You guys were such a great example. I want to build what you have."

Miranda's expression softened as she reached over and patted his leg. "Our story is ours, Tor. You have to make your own. I know it's going to be magnificent and worthy of our amazing little prince."

"Again, not *little*, but you get her drift, son."

"Shut it," Miranda droned, covering Sathan's lips.

"Nolan said I should be back to normal in a few more days. When I'm ready, I'll head to the human realm," Tordor said, rising. "Once I find her, I'll return, and we can have the coronation."

Miranda stood and squeezed his hand. "Do you know where to find her?"

"I know where to find her," he said confidently.

"Go get her, son," Sathan said, tugging them both into his arms. "And tell her we're happy to welcome her to the family."

Ready to claim his future, Tordor spent the next few days healing and wrapping up things at Uteria. Then he returned to the human world, excited to hold Esme again...and knowing this time, he would never let her go.

Chapter 35

Ulun Danu Bratan Temple, Bali

Esme sat in the soft grass overlooking the tall, pointed temple that seemed to float above the water. The backs of her forearms rested on her legs, and her spine was straight. Closing her eyes, she inhaled the morning air, symbolic of a new day and the future that still remained unclear.

After she left Uteria, she called Brienne to check on the progress of the immersion. Brienne assured her that everything was running smoothly and she and Larkin had it under control. Breathing a sigh of relief, Esme absorbed the news.

Feeling lost, she debated what course to take next. Although she wanted to visit her Uncle Gillam, she was smothered in heartbreak and knew she needed to process it before moving on. Armed with that knowledge, she headed to Bali and to the beautiful temple she'd always dreamed of visiting.

The temple grounds opened early, and she booked a hotel close by, wanting to arrive each morning before the tourists. It allowed her to sit in solitude and meditate on the heart-wrenching decision she'd made while trying to find some peace.

Lifting her lids, she glanced over the lake, appreciating the beauty of the floating temple, the softly singing birds and the multicolored flowers that lined the grounds. Focusing on her breathing, her eyes drifted shut again as she focused on the swirling emotions within.

Her body jolted when she felt his presence—the invisible tether of energy that stretched between them buzzing and palpable. Not daring to move, she remained frozen, her eyes still closed as the grass shifted beside her.

The energy from his strong body was intense, blanketing her left side in warmth and heat, and Esme pressed her lips together above her wobbling chin.

She'd convinced herself he wouldn't try to find her. That he would understand her choice. But deep within, in the tiny crevice of her soul that craved him, she knew it was a lie. That tiny part of her had desperately wanted him to find her.

And now, he had.

He was Tor after all. Her loving, determined prince and the man she missed so vehemently she had to actively restrain herself from climbing into his arms and begging him to forgive her.

They sat in silence for a while, Tordor barely moving as he meditated with her. His breaths moved in tandem with hers. In...out...in...out...

Finally, as the yellow rays of morning sun began to tickle her cheeks, he spoke to her in that deep voice, sending shivers down every crevice of her frame.

"You made it to Ulun Danu Bratan Temple," he said, his words seeming to echo over the lake as he still faced the rising sun. "It's breathtaking. I can see why it was on your bucket list."

Gazing over the water, she swallowed thickly, the task difficult since her throat seemed to be rapidly closing with each passing minute. "It's brought me some peace, but I know it's only temporary. Every moment of peace I have will be temporary as long as he's alive."

Seconds ticked by as he seemed to ponder. She felt the heat of his gaze on her skin as he spoke. "Then let me experience temporary with you, sweetheart. Even if it doesn't last, we'll have done our best to seize happiness."

Feeling her nostrils flare, she fought the tears that burned her eyes. Overwhelmed with the need to touch him, she reached over and grazed the skin of his arm. "You look healthy," she whispered, forming a shaky smile. "I'm so glad you're okay, Tor."

Slowly sliding his hands under her arms, he lifted her, setting her atop his thighs before running his palms over her shoulders. "I'm okay." Pressing a soft kiss to her lips, he whispered, "I missed you."

"Goddess, I missed you too." Gently caressing his face, she absorbed every freckle and dimple in his handsome features. "How much do you hate me right now?"

His eyes darted between hers, filled with warmth and affection as he grinned. "I could never hate you, little Elf. But it would make me happy if you would stop running and hiding from me." His thumb caressed her jaw in slow, mesmerizing strokes. "If you would just accept that I'm never letting you go."

"Even after you almost died?"

"Even after that."

Sighing, she shook her head. "You're going to be King of the Human Realm, Tor. It's such a high-profile position, and my father is going to focus on ruining it if you're with me."

"Let him try. I'm not scared of him, Esme." He leaned in closer, his tone tender but resolved. "And it's time you stopped being scared of him too. You're so strong, sweetheart. Lean on that strength and lean on me. It's time for you to live a full, happy life."

Staring into his eyes, she debated, wondering if she had the strength to choose a new path. Clutching his shoulders, her fingers dug into his thick muscles as if she were drawing his strength through her fingertips. He remained silent, letting her ruminate in his radiant energy as she absorbed it.

"Is it fair for me to ask you to be with me, knowing it's so dangerous?"

"You're not asking. I'm offering."

Steady breaths moved through her lungs as she contemplated.

Tordor formed a poignant smile. "Esme," he said, threading his fingers through the hair at her nape. "When I started falling for you, it meant so much that you would always be my first."

"I'm honored to be your first," she whispered.

"Not just my first lover, but my first *love*." Gazing deep into her eyes, he said, "I love you, sweetheart."

"Tor..."

"But soon thereafter, I realized I didn't just want the memory. I want the present and the future too. I want you in every part of my life."

"Damn..." she breathed, shaking her head. "What am I supposed to do with that? It's literally the most romantic thing I've ever heard."

"I believe the appropriate response is 'I love you too, Tor, and can't wait to build my future with you.'"

A laugh leaped from her throat. "Is that so?"

"Yes. Come on. I know you can do it."

Her eyes darted back and forth between his, enamored with the mirth and emotion...and *love* that swam in the green depths. Inhaling a deep breath, she slowly released it.

"Tor..."

"Mm-hmm...?"

Joyful laughter welled in her belly, escaping as she breathed the words. "I love you. So much that I'm prepared to let you go so you can have the future you were born for."

"I don't care what obstacles we face," he said as his fingers slightly tightened in her hair, "as long as we face them together."

"I can't believe you want to sign up for my shitshow," she said, trailing her fingers over his cheek. "It's so unfair to you."

"I want every messy, haunted, tortured part of your soul, sweetheart," he teased. "Everything you'll give me. As my queen and eventually as the mother of my children."

"Even if they're targets? Because that's what you'd be choosing—"

"I've already chosen," he interjected. "The question is: will you choose me back?"

Esme swallowed thickly, trepidation warring with love deep within.

"Don't choose with fear, Esme. Choose here." He tapped his finger over her heart.

Whooshing out a breath, she went lax in his arms. "Damn it. I think I chose you the first moment I saw you on that battlefield. You're every- thing I never knew I wanted and that I probably don't deserve."

"You deserve to be happy, hon. We both do."

Warm tears ran down her cheeks as he swiped them away. Drawing her close, he captured her lips, sliding his tongue over hers as she kissed him back. Lost in his taste and touch after what seemed like a small eternity apart, she wiggled into his hard length, wrapping her legs tighter around his waist as they breathed each other in.

"Goddess," he rasped, sucking her tongue between those full, sexy lips, "I missed you. Please don't ever meditate without me again."

Devolving into laughter, she shook her head. "Never. You've signed up for a life of limitless yoga and meditation with this tortured Elf, buddy."

Flashing that adorable grin, he whispered, "Can't wait. Might as well get started." Gripping her waist, he turned her to face the lake before resting his chin on her shoulder.

Wiggling her backside between his strong thighs, she gripped his fore- arms when he encircled her waist. Her strong half-Vamp held her as they stared at the temple before them, shrouded in the light from the rising sun.

"So beautiful," she rasped, overwhelmed by his scent and the beat of his heart against her back.

"It is," he murmured, trailing kisses along her neck. "I can't wait to share more sunrises with you, Esme."

Closing her eyes, she settled into her mate, basking in the gentle warmth of his embrace and the cadence of his breaths beside her ear. After so many centuries of heartache and loss, she'd finally gained the courage to allow him to choose her, and by some miracle, she was ready to choose him back.

Esme would always worry for their safety, knowing her father wouldn't rest in his relentless pursuit to exterminate every Elven hybrid from the planet. But where she'd once been ready to relent, she was now ready to fight—for her people, and the man she loved, and the children they would bring into the world.

For them, she would do her small part to make Etherya's Earth a safe and peaceful place with the help of her immortal mate, who had finally proven Esme wasn't destined to live an eternity of solitude after all.

Rather than being a mistake or being born into a life that was never supposed to exist, Esme now understood she was born to be Tordor's mate. The best way to honor him was to embrace that destiny for the magnificent gift it was.

Ready to claim her future, she settled into the first sunrise of their shared eternity.

Epilogue

D akath stood at the window of his castle, overlooking the thatch-roofed houses below. His people had lived in them for centuries, and thanks to their remote location in the mountains of Romania, they'd mostly avoided human interaction. Sure, Dakath had employed human technology when needed. It only made sense to take advantage of the new realm by learning from the inferior species. But for the most part, he wanted their slice of Earth to remain pure. To recreate the Elven kingdom in all its glory so the ancient god would never harm them again.

"Sire?" Trembly called, striding into the room. "You wanted to see me?"

Narrowing his eyes, Dakath focused on the Elves milling about the village, all of them thriving under his rule, not even cognizant of everything he did to help them remain the pristine species that had been created after the dawn of time.

"The people love me, do they not, Trembly?"

"Well, yes, my king," he said, confused. "They revere you."

Facing him, Dakath clutched his hands behind his back as he paced. "I fear many don't remember the devastation of the flood. How it ripped apart families and almost destroyed our people."

"The newer generations might not grasp the devastation completely, but the elder Elves understand."

Halting, Dakath squared his shoulders. "I have done my best to ensure we don't anger the ancient god. I have ruled with a firm hand and tried to establish a new life for our people here. We cannot retain the Elven heritage if it is diluted with human blood."

"I understand, sire."

"Then you also understand that we have now gained new enemies. The immortals have dreams of comingling and cohabitating with humans. They support immortal-human hybrids and will soon wed their heir to a human-Elven hybrid."

"I believe they think the ether was destroyed so we could all inhabit one realm."

With a frustrated huff, Dakath swiped a candlestick from the nearby table, the metal crashing and clanking on the floor as he seethed. "Fools! We will not lower ourselves to human standards. The Elves are the oldest species on the planet, and I will *not* let us die out by diluting the bloodline until we are just memories in old fairy tales told by mortals."

Lifting his hands, Trembly asked, "What would you have me do, sire?"

Glancing toward the window, he pondered. "Do you think they would fight for me? Since they revere and fear me."

"Most of your subjects are farmers and laborers, my king, but if you ordered it, they would have no choice. They are terrified of your powers and would not defy you."

Lifting his gaze to Trembly's, his lips formed a cruel sneer. "Good. We must move forward in our effort to protect the Elves and our heritage at all costs."

"Yes, sire."

"Trembly, I want you to observe the subjects and report back to me with who is strongest and most cunning."

"Absolutely," he said with a nod.

"Once I have your report, we'll begin the next phase of my plan."

Trembly's throat bobbed. "What phase?"

Dakath's thin lips formed a malicious smile. "I'm going to build an army. One that will rival Latimus's and employ more technology than the humans."

Trembly's eyes grew wide. "You mean to fight them?"

"When the time is right, yes," he said with a nod. "I need years to build something formidable, but I am an extremely patient Elf and have time to spare."

Trembly remained silent, digesting his king's words.

"Now go. Do as I request. We will still continue to poison human-Elven hybrids and surveil Esmerelda's efforts, but our army will take precedence. If all goes well, I can return us to glory as the only species on the planet."

Backing away, Trembly bowed. "Yes, sire." With one last cautious glance, he exited the room.

Returning to the window, Dakath rapped his long nails against the sill, an absent habit he'd never break. Watching his people scurry in their daily duties, he held no reservations about his plan. He'd offered his subjects a comfortable life for eons. Now, their penance was due.

Dakath, King of the Elves, was going to build an army.

And then he would vanquish those who disparaged and disrespected the eldest group of immortals on the planet.

Yes, one day in the future, Dakath would prevail, and the ancient god would be proud. Elves would never live in fear of death or destruction again.

The final chapter of Etherya's Earth would begin.

The immortal compound of Astaria
Three months later

Tordor stood under the bright sun as throngs of immortals stretched over the park in Astaria's town square. Miranda stood by his side, absently rubbing her slightly distended belly as Sathan addressed the crowd.

"My people," he called in his deep, booming voice. "Decades ago, Queen Miranda and I promised you peace. We have done our best to protect you and help our people thrive. Our son, Prince Tordor, is a symbol of our unity and future."

Tordor glanced at Miranda, who wrinkled her nose, silently acknowledging Sathan's austere performance. Since Vampyres held sacred traditions in high esteem and were slightly stuffier than Slayers, they'd decided to hold the coronation at Astaria. It would be recorded in the Vampyre archives, which Sathan had resurrected after the War of the Species ended.

"My son," Sathan said, taking the crown from the pillow held by Kenden and holding it high in the air. "You have taken on the duty of sovereign in the human realm, and we know you will rule with grace and honor." Placing the crown on Tordor's head, Sathan's features glowed with pride as he smiled. "I now pronounce you King of the Human Realm. May your rule be filled with peace and prosperity."

The crowd cheered, some chanting his name, but Tordor only had eyes for one. Esme stood in the front row, nestled between his family, and he winked at her as she crossed one leg behind the other and gave a mock curtsy. Rolling his eyes, he scrunched his features before she blew him a kiss, acknowledging their teasing.

He'd wanted her to be by his side at the coronation, but she'd insisted he be crowned solo. She felt it cemented his rule and would help pave their way with immortals in the human world. Once they were married, they would have a separate ceremony to officially crown her as Queen of the Human Realm.

Esme had agreed to marry him within the year, assuring him they had time. She felt they owed the kingdom a grand wedding since he was the heir, and he was excited to stand before his people and profess his love for her. It gave them time to adjust to living together, which seemed to comfort his little Elf. She'd lived in solitude for centuries, and building a life with someone took time and patience. Thankfully, Tordor was instilled with both.

Once the ceremony was over, Tordor headed into the crowd, mingling with the subjects as the celebration began. Wine flowed and music boomed as the immortals partied long into the night.

After the sun had long set, Tordor led Esme to his room at Astaria, closing the door behind him and sitting on the bed. "Holy crap," he said, scrubbing his face, "I'm beat."

Striding toward him, she crawled atop his thighs, straddling him as she eyed the crown. "Is it weird that I want to bang you in nothing but the crown? Who knew I had a royal fetish?"

Tossing back his head, Tordor let out a joyous laugh before pulling the thick band of gold off his head. "Sorry, but this thing is heavy. I think you'll just have to settle for banging me naked."

Pouting, she shimmied into his crotch. "Oh, fine. You know, I thought a virgin would be more adventurous."

Shooting her an acerbic glare, he lifted her, setting her on the soft carpet before placing a wet kiss on her lips. "Oh, I'll be adventurous, sweetheart. Let's get ready for bed so I can prove it."

They headed to the bathroom, and mischief simmered in her honey-flecked eyes as she stared at him in the mirror.

"You're dying to tell me something," he said, eyes narrowing as he set aside his toothbrush and crossed his arms.

Running her brush under the faucet, she tapped it on the sink before setting it down and facing him. "More like *show* you something."

"Okaaaay..."

She broke into a wide grin. "It's going to blow your mind."

Cocking a brow, he gestured for her to continue.

"Remember how I told you I've been having different dreams lately?"

"Ones where you're on a journey of some sort."

"Right." Blowing a tuft of hair off her forehead, she continued. "I wasn't sure what I was searching for, but last night, I reached my destination."

"Where was it?"

Her eyebrows drew together. "I think it was the Methuselah tree in California. I've never been there, but it seemed to...speak to me. I felt compelled to touch the bark. When I reached for it, my palm began to feel warm. And then..."

Lowering her gaze, she turned up her palm. Narrowing her eyes, she concentrated as Tordor observed her palm turn a bright shade of red. Then he inhaled a sharp breath as a small orb of green energy materialized atop her palm.

"Holy shit," he breathed.

She stuck her tongue between her teeth, concentrating with all her might before the orb disappeared. Slowly lifting her eyes to his, her breathing was labored. "I think I inherited my father's powers," she whispered, wonder in her tone.

"How...? When?" he asked, stunned.

"I don't know. I've never been able to do that before but one of his energy spheres grazed me in the battle. Maybe it..."—she shrugged—"unlocked something inside my cells. Regardless, I think if I find someone to teach me, I can develop it into something I can control."

"Well..." he said, still overcome by the small display, "your mate happens to have several family members who are experts at wielding powers." He pointed at his chest. "I bet Callie would love to help you. And Evie and Darkrip would too."

"Thank the goddess you have magic family members. Any other guy would be really freaked out right now."

Laughing, he closed in and took her hand. Bringing her palm to his lips, he kissed the warm skin. "I'm a bit shocked, but it makes sense you'd inherit his powers."

"I didn't think I could since I'm half-human."

"Your Elven genes are expressed, so perhaps they're overriding your human ones," he said. "I mean, you're immortal, which definitely isn't a human trait."

"True," she murmured, studying her hand. "It's just so...strange. But also hella cool, right?"

Taken by her astonished expression, he nodded. "And it's another defense against your father, so it makes sense to develop it. Just don't use it near my...*important* parts," he teased, glancing down at his crotch. "I need those."

Breathing a laugh, she arched a brow. "Oh, I need them too. Believe me."

As the realization of her newfound capacities settled in, they removed their clothes and slipped into bed. Relaxing between the soft sheets, Tordor drew her against his body as she wrapped herself around him.

"What a day," she sighed, stretching against his side. "I discovered I possess super-weird awesome powers, and you finally claimed your destiny. I'm so proud of you, Tor."

"A significant day for sure. And the next ceremony will be our wedding."

"Can't wait. I've invested in earplugs so I'll survive sleeping next to you."

Chuckling, he turned on his side, drawing her leg over his thigh as his swollen shaft searched between her legs. "Oh, I'll make it up to you, sweetheart."

She threaded her fingers in the hair at his nape. "I'm counting on it."

Gazing deep into her eyes, he found her wet core and began to ease inside. Esme stared into his soul with half-lidded eyes, her breaths shallow and ragged as he claimed her.

Undulating in firm, smooth strokes, he loved her, wishing there were more than words to express the unadulterated bliss he felt whenever she was near. Never had anyone consumed his soul more than his little Elf.

"I love you," she whispered, holding him in the sweetest vise.

"*Esme...*" He surged deep within, trying like hell to reach the place she'd shown him...so thankful for her acceptance as he learned to be the lover she deserved.

"Oh, yeah...that's it. *Goddess*, that feels good."

Thrilled with her praise, Tordor lowered his mouth to the vein at her neck. She writhed on the bed below him, fingers clenching his hair as she pushed into his firm strokes.

"*Mine*," he growled against her skin as licked her neck, bathing it in his saliva.

"*Yours.*"

They moved in tandem, their bodies falling into a steady rhythm as his fangs breached her neck. Crying his name, Esme exploded beneath him, her fingernails digging into his shoulders as she shuddered. Tordor followed her as heat burned in every pore. Allowing the release to break free, he held her tight, emptying everything into her gorgeous, quivering frame.

Sated breaths echoed against the walls as their muscles melted. Relaxing into her, Tordor licked her sweaty skin, overcome by her taste and smell.

She trailed her fingernails over his scalp, causing him to moan at the intense pleasure. They lazed, sated and sanguine, until Tordor cleaned them up before crawling into bed and spooning her. Wrapping his arms around her, he pulled her close, ready to sleep until he inevitably began to snore and she fled to the other side of the bed. Smiling against her neck at the thought of waking up to her unavoidable teasing, Tordor kissed her soft skin and closed his eyes.

Tomorrow would begin a new phase. One where he would embark on ruling and helping immortals in the human realm, and where Esme would begin to develop her burgeoning powers as she ruled by his side. Still shocked by the revelation, he inwardly acknowledged how remarkable she was.

Perhaps she was supposed to discover her powers once they were together all along. Their love made them stronger than they ever were apart, and the threat from Dakath still remained.

Although she wasn't ready to discuss it, Tordor believed she was destined to claim Dakath's throne. The Elves deserved a kind and wise leader, and the time would come when she would no longer accept his unyielding rule.

For now, they would embark on their future day by day, learning to rule with grace and compassion. *Together.*

Sliding into his dreams, the diplomatic heir joined his mate in slumber, vowing to protect her from any nightmares until the sun rose upon Etherya's Earth.

A delyn, daughter of Latimus and Lila, stood in the shadowed hallway outside the massive banquet room at Astaria. Palm pressed to the ornate wallpaper, she leaned closer, listening to the discussion her father and uncle were having in the now deserted ballroom. They'd had a magnificent fete to celebrate Tordor's coronation, but now, the party had died down and most immortals had returned to their homes for some much-needed rest.

"Do you think it's possible, Latimus?" Sathan's deep voice asked as he stood across from his brother with his arms crossed over his chest. "A new species we've never heard of?"

"At this point, I'll believe anything," was her father's acerbic reply. "We didn't know about the Elves, so if the Nymphs are real, they're probably out there somewhere."

Rubbing his chin, Sathan pondered. "It would explain Lila and Adelyn's eye color. But where are the rest of the Nymphs hiding? Or do you think they've all died out?"

"I don't know. After Jaxon's report detailing his conversation with Tatiana, I scoured Alrec's old reports from his centuries at his post at the foothills of the Strok Mountains. He recorded instances of banked fires surrounded by food waste comprised of bark and leaves. He attributed it to Deamons passing through on missions for Crimeous." Leaning forward, Latimus's voice lowered. "But the thing is, Sathan, Deamons are carnivores. Any food waste left behind should've been comprised of animal carcasses and bones."

Sathan inhaled a deep breath. "Unless the remnants weren't left behind by Deamons at all."

Latimus remained silent as the information set in.

Drawing back, Adelyn pressed her fingers to her lips. For her entire life, she'd always wondered about her heritage. Although she loved Lila and Latimus with her entire heart, she'd always struggled as an adopted member of such a close-knit family that revered their royal bloodlines. Her parents and family had always included her—that was never an issue—but she still felt the yearning to know who she was deep in her core.

Where did her lavender irises come from? She only shared them with one other person on Etherya's Earth, and that was her dear mother.

Adelyn's Slayer birth mother had given her up in a closed adoption, choosing to remain anonymous. Sadie had noted in the records that the Slayer woman refused to name the father of her baby. The space on Adelyn's makeshift birth certificate had remained blank, and that certificate had eventually been replaced with a new one, naming Latimus and Lila as her parents.

"What are you doing out here by yourself?" a voice chimed, and Adelyn gritted her teeth before turning.

"Hello, Desmond," she said, trying to tamp down the annoyance in her voice. "I was just checking to see if my father was still in the ballroom. He's discussing business with Uncle Sathan, so I'm going to head to the room they've prepared for me in the castle to get some sleep."

"I would be happy to walk you to your room, darling," he said, extending his arm.

Clenching her jaw at the unwanted endearment, she shook her head. Goddess, he irritated her last nerve. He was an aristocrat who'd spent the better part of a year trying to woo her, but thankfully, she'd evaded his reach. Her mother had always taught her to be kind, and she didn't wish him any ill will, but she found him exceedingly...*boring*.

Gazing at his outstretched arm, she wondered if she was just taking her frustration out on him. In truth, she'd been on edge lately, ever since she'd gone through her immortal change and grown into adulthood. As the eternity of her life spread before her, Adelyn struggled with the knowledge she didn't feel quite whole. There were questions lingering before her, and she didn't feel capable of building a future until they were answered.

One was about the origin of her purple eyes.

The other was a burning need to understand her birth father's heritage. She'd always assumed he was a Slayer like her mother, but perhaps he was actually one of the mysterious Nymphs Latimus and Sathan were discussing in their hushed tones in the ballroom.

Until Adelyn knew the answer, she knew she'd never be able to seize her future and build the life she was meant to live. After all, how could one build a life if they didn't know the very components that comprised their makeup; that made them who they were deep inside?

"Darling?" Desmond said, urging her to take his arm.

"Thank you, Desmond, but I promised Glarys I'd stop by the kitchen and say good night. I wish you safe travels home." Rushing from the hallway, she left him slightly open-mouthed as his aristocratic nature undoubtedly reeled from her abrupt exit.

Striding down the stairs, she entered the ground-floor hallway. As she passed by Tordor's room, she grinned at the laughter that echoed from behind the closed door. In the past few years, Tordor and Callie had both found love, and she was extremely happy for her cousins.

Entering her room, she closed the door and sat on the plush bed. Would she be lucky enough to find her soul mate one day? Clenching her fist, she acknowledged one deep-seated truth: there was no point in looking for love until she understood herself.

Lying back on the bed, she twisted a lock of her thick brown hair between her fingers as she mulled. Recalling her father and Sathan's conversation, her thoughts drifted to the faraway land at the base of the Strok Mountains. Her brother Jack had taken her camping many times over the years, and she also enjoyed hiking. If she wanted to, she could hike the lands where Alrec had recorded the remnants of the bark and leaves left behind. Perhaps if she dared to look, she just might find the people who left them there.

Would they have purple irises like her? Could one of them even be...her birth father?

Feeling her eyes drift, Adelyn felt the small seed of curiosity bloom in her belly...blossoming as she pondered whether she had the fortitude to follow her intuition and journey to foothills of the Strok Mountains.

Perhaps it was time for Adelyn to finally seize her future and write her own story upon Etherya's Earth...

Before You Go

Well, dear readers, our awesome heir found his true love. I hope you enjoyed Tordor and Esme's story as much as I loved writing it. And don't worry—I'm not going to make you wait as long for the next book. In fact, I have a sneak peak of **Etherya's Earth, Book 8** for you below!

Thank you for reading my books and supporting indie authors.

An Excerpt from Etherya's Earth, Book 8

Adelyn trudged through the muddy forest, sludge caking her shoes as thunder clapped above. Gritting her teeth, she pulled the hood of her coat tighter over her thick brown hair, knowing the rain would knot the curly tresses into a frizzy mess.

"That's going to be fun to comb when it's dry," she muttered, clenching the strap of her backpack as she continued toward the river. "Whose idea was it to camp alone in the woods? Oh, right. Yours, Addie. Nice job."

Since talking to herself was a waste of energy, she pressed her lips together as she approached the river. She'd memorized the ancient map her father had given her, but locating the bridge in poor weather conditions was difficult. Squinting, joy rushed through her veins as she spotted the wooden overpass. Water nearly crested it as the swollen river rushed with white squalls from the howling wind.

The map had indicated there were caves only a few miles across, so it was imperative she cross and carry on. Once inside a cave, she could dry off, make a fire and eat. All she'd seen on her travels that day were wet trees, and sadly, those offered little shelter.

Approaching the bridge, she touched the toe of her boot to the drenched wood. She lightly tapped, alarmed when the bridge swayed slightly beneath her. Gulping, she looked over her shoulder, wondering if she should retreat. Even if she remained wet under a blanket of trees, wasn't it better than falling in the river and drowning?

Contemplating, she closed her eyes, drawing on her inner strength.

"You're the daughter of the greatest soldier on the fucking planet, Addie. Push through. Cross the bridge so you can get out of the rain."

Lifting her lids, she squared her shoulders and began to walk across.

The wood creaked and moaned beneath her, each new sound an ominous warning. Determined not to be deterred, she pressed forward, heart pounding as she neared the other side. When she was only two feet from shore, a swell of water surged over the bough of the bridge, causing it to sway. Planting her feet, Adelyn tried to balance since there were no handrails.

Glancing down, she saw the wood crack and splinter beneath her boots, and she lurched into action, jetting to shore and falling on the wet grass with an "*oomph!*" Looking over her shoulder, her mouth fell open as the bridge collapsed into the river, the shattered wood disappearing as the current carried it downstream.

"Holy shit," she rasped, standing and wiping her legs. They were covered in mud, and she sighed, wishing she'd packed more than one change of clothes. Cursing whatever gods were responsible for the weather in the wretched forest, she gazed at the trees ahead.

Facing Northwest toward where the caves appeared on the map, she continued. Each step claimed more energy, and she realized she was coming down from the adrenaline high of rushing off the bridge. Exhaustion set in as she counted each step in her head, hoping she didn't collapse before she made it to the caves.

Something twinkled through the dim gray air, and she whipped her head, eyes narrowing as she studied it. Was it...a fire? If so, it was a hell of a lot closer than the caves. Deciding to call an audible, she pivoted and walked toward the fire, knowing that if it burned, whoever started it must have shelter.

As she neared the glowing embers, she realized they shone from a fireplace inside a small cabin. She hadn't considered that any immortal lived in this part of the forest so far off the grid. But hell, she'd been wrong before and certainly would be again.

Striding toward the cabin, she gingerly approached, stopping to pull the mini eight-shooter her father had given her for her eighteenth birthday from her bag.

"Better safe than sorry, Addie. But keep it hidden just in case."

Checking that the safety was on, she tucked it in her waistband beneath her coat and carried on.

When she reached the porch, she slowly climbed the two wooden stairs before coming to a thick door. Forming a fist, she knocked—softly as first, but she soon began pounding when no one answered. Frustrated, she reached for the handle, expecting it to be locked. Turing it, she inhaled sharply when it slid open.

Stepping inside, she called, "Hello?"

Silence greeted her, along with the warm fire she'd spotted. Pleasure shot through her as the heat brushed her skin. Removing her pack, she set it on the floor and slid off her coat. Rushing toward the fire, she opened her palms, soaking in the heat as she sighed.

"*Ohmygod*...thank you, Etherya." Rubbing her hands together, she closed her eyes, mired in bliss at finally exiting the cold rain.

Suddenly, a loud *thunk* rang in her ears, and she gasped turning to find a huge beast of a man standing in the doorway. His face was covered with a thick, shaggy beard under an outdoor cap. Narrow midnight-blue eyes shot daggers through her as he grunted. Fear coiled in Adelyn's chest as she noticed the wood at his feet, which must've caused the banging noise when he dropped it on the wooden floor.

"What in the hell are you doing in my home?" he asked, his voice deep and gravelly, as if his windpipe were comprised of rocks.

Lifting her chin, she placed her hand over the hidden eight-shooter at her belt. Gathering her courage, she spoke with confidence although her knees were shaking with fear. "I am Adelyn, daughter of Commander Latimus and Kingdom Secretary Diplomat Lila, and I was trapped in the storm. I saw your fire and needed shelter."

Thick nostrils flared as he gazed at her, his stare so pointed she felt like a bug on the wrong side of a magnifying glass. The beast grunted again, the sound ominous in the small room, before taking wide steps toward her. Straightening her spine, she pulled the eight-shooter from her belt.

"I'm armed!" she cried as the man kept advancing. He approached until only inches separated them. Cocking one of his hairy eyebrows, he pushed his broad pec into the barrel of her weapon, a challenge in his eyes.

Struggling to breathe, Adelyn stood firm, unable to shoot a man in cold blood.

With a frustrated growl, he lowered and picked her up, slinging her over his shoulder as she yelped. Pounding his back with her fists as he carried her across the room, she tried like hell to maim him, but it was no use.

When he reached the door, he roughly plopped her on her feet. Adelyn's boots hit the wet wood of the porch as she straightened and pushed her unruly hair from her head. "How dare you! My father will have you arrested for thi—"

"I don't give a damn who your father is."

Sputtering at his rudeness, she stomped her foot. "I demand to know your name, you...you brute!"

A harsh laugh escaped his throat. Leaning closer, the rasp of his voice surrounded her, causing the hairs on her arms to stand. "I am Leonidas, son of Kilani and Alrec." He gripped the door and backed farther into the cabin. "And *you* are trespassing."

Shooting her one last hateful glare, the infuriating man slammed the door in Adelyn's face.

Acknowledgments

Thanks to April Berry for giving me a reason to finish this book. This series is now officially seasoned, but as long as you and my mom read them, I'll continue to write them! Ha! I appreciate your unwavering support and friendship. Can't wait for margaritas and guacamole soon!

Thanks to Kat Kinney for being the sole reason I ever log onto Twitter anymore. LOL. She's also a great friend, damn fine author and overall amazing person.

Thanks to M.E. Aster and Ri Paige for reading my books and being awesomely cool humans.

Thanks to all the new ARC readers who took a chance on my books this year. Misty, Stella Steph, Robin, Rosemarie, Korra and so many more. I appreciate you!

And thanks to my OG ARC readers too! Lauren and her amazing blog, Julie (hope you loved Miranda & Sathan's scenes), Merissa, Vanda, Kristin and every one of you who take the time to read (or listen) and review. You all keep me going when I want to burrow into the couch, eat potato chips and watch Real Housewives instead of writing.

As always, thanks to Megan, Bryony, Anthony and Sarah for being part of my team and for making my books shine!

About the Author

USA Today bestselling author Rebecca Hefner grew up in Western NC and now calls the Hudson River of NYC home. In her youth, she would sneak into her mother's bedroom and read the romance novels stashed on the bookshelf, cementing her love of HEAs. A huge Buffy and Star Wars fan, she loves an epic fantasy and a surprise twist (Luke, he IS your father).

Before becoming an author, Rebecca had a successful twelve-year medical device sales career. After launching her own indie publishing company, she is now a full-time author who loves writing strong, complex characters who find their HEAs.

Rebecca can usually be found making dorky and/or embarrassing posts on TikTok and Instagram. Please join her so you can laugh along with her!